Walter Besant

St. Katherine's by the Tower

A Novel: Vol.III.

Walter Besant

St. Katherine's by the Tower
A Novel: Vol.III.

ISBN/EAN: 9783337031749

Printed in Europe, USA, Canada, Australia, Japan

Cover: Foto ©Andreas Hilbeck / pixelio.de

More available books at **www.hansebooks.com**

ST KATHERINE'S BY THE TOWER

A NOVEL

BY

WALTER BESANT

AUTHOR OF

'ORTS AND CONDITIONS OF MEN' 'ARMOREL OF LYONESSE' ETC.

IN THREE VOLUMES

VOL. III.

WITH TWELVE ILLUSTRATIONS BY CHARLES GREEN

London

CHATTO & WINDUS, PICCADILLY

1891

PRINTED BY
SPOTTISWOODE AND CO., NEW-STREET SQUARE
LONDON

CONTENTS

OF

THE THIRD VOLUME

PART II. (continued).

CHAPTER		PAGE
XVII.	THE TRIAL	1
XVIII.	THE CONDEMNED CELL	37
XIX.	SATURDAY	55
XX.	THE KING'S CLEMENCY . . .	74
XXI.	RICHARD ARCHER'S GOOD FORTUNE . .	92
XXII.	A SUDDEN CHANGE . . .	107
XXIII.	GEORGE GIVES WAY . . .	125
XXIV.	LORD ALDEBURGH	141
XXV.	SISTER KATHERINE FINDS OUT .	166
XXVI.	PARAMATTA	179
XXVII.	LETTERS FROM HOME . .	198
XXVIII.	THE DEVIL'S LUCK	215
XXIX.	THE VENGEANCE OF THE LORD .	243
XXX.	EVIL HEART AND EVIL EYE	255
XXXI.	CONCLUSION	279

ILLUSTRATIONS IN VOL. III

'WHEN HE HAD FINISHED, HE MADE A LOW
BOW, HOLDING THE VIOLIN IN ONE HAND
AND THE BOW IN ANOTHER' *Frontispiece*

'HE WAS PLAYING AT THE TABLE WITH
GREAT SUCCESS' . *To face p.* 266

ST. KATHERINE'S BY THE TOWER

CHAPTER XVII

THE TRIAL

Now we had not long to wait. Our case, once completed by the prosecution, was immediately set down for trial. We were informed that it would probably be called on Saturday, October 26. As for our defence we had severally and separately stated for Mr. Quellet's information everything that we could possibly remember bearing at all upon the charge. That is to say, I, for my part, wrote out and gave to my attorney such an account of my connection with the club as you have already read in these pages. I described how the members were principally Republican in

B

theory only; how the violent measures advocated on the last evening that ever the club met were proposed by another member (not myself), and reprobated by the Chairman.

Well, I set down many things (I believe I might have spared the trouble), partly because our clever attorney certainly paid no attention to them, partly because the conclusion of the case was resolved upon from the beginning. As for George, he prepared no defence, refused legal assistance, and continued in cheerfulness, unassumed and real, but the rest of us grew restless, and fell into moods of silence, walking about like caged creatures (which, indeed, we were).

On Monday morning George brought a piece of news upstairs from the yard. Our friendly merchant, who was in for forgery, had been sent up for trial.

'It is certain,' he said, 'that the case will go against him. The amount which he obtained by his forgery is very large. There is no hope for him except from the King's clemency, and yet the poor man went off laughing and dancing, taking leave of the prison as

of a place he should never again see, because
he was going to be triumphantly acquitted.
Well, he will come back presently a wiser
man.'

I gave no further thought to the case of
this worthy and virtuous person, whose sentiments were so opposite to his conduct, because my own case now occupied all my
thoughts.

At eight o'clock on the morning of Saturday, October 26, we were all four taken from
the ward and brought to the gate at which we
entered—that which I have called the Gate of
Honour Lost. Here we were handed over to
the custody of the Sheriffs' Serjeants-at-Mace,
eight of them, attended by sixteen Yeomen, all
dressed in blue cloth gowns, and carrying
truncheons. Guarded by these officers we
marched out into the Old Bailey and so down
the street to the Session House. George
marched at the head of us with cheerful and
shining countenance; the rest of us, I fear,
with pale cheeks and trembling lips, though
we endeavoured to assume a confident carriage
and appearance. That man, truly, who can

stand up in a Court of Justice and answer un-
abashed to a capital charge must have the
insensibility of brutishness, or he must be, for
the time, as George was, deprived of his full
reason.   For some moments after we were
placed in the Dock I could see nothing clearly ;
a mist was before my eyes.   I could hear
nothing distinctly ; a ringing was in my ears.
Presently I recovered, and became aware that
the Judges were in their seats, and that the
clerk of the Court was standing up to read the
Indictment.

I already knew the contents of that windy
document, and felt no inclination to listen to
it again.   I therefore allowed myself to look
about the Court.

The Session House of the Old Bailey which,
I suppose, very few people are curious enough
to visit, is a square Hall of good size, lit by
three windows in a row ; through the windows
one sees nothing but the wall of Newgate
Prison.   Along one side is a low gallery for
the accommodation of those who wish to
attend the trials.   I am told that many people
do nothing else but sit and watch the course

of Justice from this gallery. On the side
facing the windows is the Dock, or enclosed
place for the use of the prisoners. On the
opposite side is the Bench which runs from
one side quite to the other. Here are seats
for the Lord Mayor, the Aldermen, the
Sheriffs, the Ordinary, the Justices of the
Peace, and visitors of quality, who are permitted to sit here by the Judges. There
are also desks for the use of the Judges. The
sword of Justice hangs on the wall behind the
chair of the Presiding Judge.

Below the Bench and on the Judges' right
is a square box or pew, in which the witnesses
take oath and give their evidence. On the
other side, at the left of the Judges and under
the gallery, is another box, much larger and
square, divided into two pews for the accommodation of the jury. By this arrangement
the jury sit with their faces in shade, while the
full light of day falls upon the witness and upon
the prisoners. Further, by this arrangement,
the Judges command the whole Court—jury,
witnesses, and prisoners. The middle of the
room is taken up by a large table covered with

a green cloth, on which are laid out a quantity
of law books for reference by Judge or
counsel.   Places are also provided for counsel ;
for solicitors or attorneys, for witnesses waiting
their turn, for reporters, and others.   This
morning I observed that the place was quite
full.   Barristers in wig and gown were
crowded in the body of the hall.   The Lord
Mayor, the Sheriffs, and some of the Aldermen, were in their robes and chains, sitting
beside the Judges.   There were also some
ladies (I heard afterwards, very great ladies)
curious to witness a trial for High Treason.
All gazed curiously at the prisoners—the four
young men charged with attempting a Revolution in imitation of that successfully accom-
plished across the Channel.   Three yeomen
stood before the Dock, one at each side, and
the rest behind.

The Judges who were assembled to try the
case showed by their numbers and their rank
the importance attached to the trial.   Lord
Chief Justice Eyre presided ; with him were
Lord Chief Baron Macdonald, Mr. Baron
Hotham, Mr. Justice Butler, and Mr. Justice

Grose. The majesty of the law was, indeed, made manifest to the most stupid person in the array of these learned and illustrious Judges, and in the awful gravity of their faces.

The indictment having been read, the plea of Not Guilty was entered in our behalf. Then Mr. Attorney-General, who conducted the prosecution for the Crown, rose and informed the Court that three of the prisoners were represented by counsel, while the fourth refused any legal assistance. The counsel for the three prisoners wished each case to be tried separately. He had no objection to this course save on the ground of delay, and should begin with the case against the prisoner Nevill Comines, Secretary to the seditious Society spoken of in the indictment.

Upon this my counsel, Mr. Felix Vaughan by name, a gentleman as learned, I dare say, as he was fluent, rose, and after informing the Court that he appeared for the prisoner Nevill Comines, asked that the Court should adjourn until Tuesday, the 29th, to which course the Court consented.

This done there was nothing but to be marched back again by our friends in the blue gowns and to wait, with as much patience as we could muster, each for his own turn ; but the weary hours crept and dragged.

Tuesday morning dawned at length, and I was once more taken to the Session House, this time to stand my trial in earnest.

The same Bench of Judges sat ; the Court was crowded. The Counsel for the prosecution consisted of the Attorney-General, the Solicitor-General, Mr. Serjeant Adair, and five juniors ; while I had but one barrister, Mr. Felix Vaughan aforesaid, and he was a junior.

If I dwell upon the proceedings of this trial, it is not, believe me, in order to procure for myself the appearance of great importance, but, because in its particulars it closely resembled the trial of George which followed, so that in describing one I am describing both.

At first it seemed as if we should never be able to get a jury, because my Counsel challenged one after the other, either in the name of the prisoner, without assigning any reason, or because they were not freeholders of the

county of Middlesex. At last, however, twelve
men were found and duly sworn, and took
their places.

This done, the Clerk of the Arraigns, one
Thomas Shellen by name, rose and spoke as
follows :

'Nevill Comines, hold up your hand.'

'Gentlemen of the Jury, the prisoner,
Nevill Comines, stands indicted, together with
others——' Here he read over again the long
indictment which I omit. 'Upon this indictment,' the Clerk went on, 'the prisoner,
Nevill Comines to wit, hath been arraigned,
and upon this arraignment hath pleaded not
guilty, and for his trial hath put himself upon
God and the country ; which country you
are. Your charge is to inquire whether he be
guilty of the high treason whereof he stands
indicted, or not guilty. If you find him guilty
you are to inquire what goods and chattels,
lands or tenements, he had at the time of the
high treason committed, or at any time since.
If you find him not guilty, you are to inquire
whether he fled for it ; if you find that he did
fly for it, you shall inquire of his goods and

chattels as if you had found him guilty.   If you find him not guilty, and that he did not fly for it, say so, and no more, and hear your evidence.'

The case was opened by the Junior Counsel in a very short speech.

When he sat down, the Attorney-General rose, with a pile of papers before him, and after arranging his gown so that it should not interfere with his gestures, he began a speech worthy of a much greater case.   I blush, even now, to think that a person so humble as myself should have been the subject of this great oration by one of the most illustrious lawyers of the time.   Why, I was but the Secretary of the Society of Snugs, and he gave me a speech which occupied eight hours in the delivery. He began at nine; he went on with a short interval until nearly five, when the Court rose for dinner.   He had then, however, concluded.

Eight hours !   Could Catiline himself expect more?

He began with great solemnity to inform the jury that the indictment, stated generally

and stripped of its legal phrases, charged the
prisoner with compassing the King's death (a
most terrible crime, indeed, and one of which
I was entirely innocent). He then spent at
least an hour in setting forth the heinousness
of the crime, the various ways in which it
would be attempted, and the opinions of great
lawyers upon it, and especially those of my
Lord Hale, of whose memory he spoke with
the greatest respect. Now when he had laid
down the law and some of the facts, that is to
say, the existence of our poor little Society,
he connected the crime of compassing the
King's death with the members of the club as
follows (I copy from the speech as it has been
printed):

'Gentlemen, I think that the evidence
that I shall lay before you will most abun-
dantly satisfy you that the Associations, of
which the prisoner, through his Society, was
a member, designed to alter the whole form
of the sovereign power of this country; that
it was to form, or to devise, the means of
forming a representative government; to vest
in a body, founded upon universal suffrage

and the alleged inalienable, and, as they are called, imprescriptible rights of man, all the legislative and executive government of the country ; that a conspiracy to this end would be an overt act of high treason cannot, I presume, be disputed. It deposes the King in the distinction of the regal office in the Constitution of the State.

'Gentlemen, I go further. If it had been intended to have retained the name and office of the King in the country, and to have retained it in the person of the present King, creating, however, by the authority of the intended Convention, a new Legislature to act with him, provided they would allow him to act with such new Legislature, and then calling upon him to act against the express obligations of his Coronation Oath, if he could forget it, still would it have been a conspiracy to depose him from his Royal authority as now established ; if he refused to act, he must necessarily be deposed from that authority ; if he did accept, he was not the King of England as he is established by law the King of England. But he could not

accept, he could not so govern, he is sworn
not to so govern; he must refuse, he must
resist, and in consequence of his resisting, his
life must be in danger.'

This argument proved effective. Considering it after the lapse of so many years,
and the dying out of heat and passion, I
think it forced the point. But that matters
nothing now; I have no intention of giving
you the whole of this great speech. You
have seen how the compassing of the King's
death was arrived at. I will try, however,
to show the drift of the address. He proceeded next to speak of the clubs or societies
established in various parts of the country,
artfully comparing them with the famous
Jacobin Club of Paris, from which such vast
evils had proceeded to the kingdom of France.
He then proceeded to describe the Constitutional Society, the London Corresponding
Society, and the Society for Constitutional
Information: he read documents which
proved their opinions and their activity: he
dilated at great length on the mischiefs which
would follow the general adoption of those

opinions—the destruction of the ancient
Kingdom of the Two Islands; the ruin of
trade; the general bankruptcy (this went
home to the jury, who were all tradesmen)
of persons carrying on business of any kind;
the overthrow of religion—not the abolition
of the Established Church alone, but the
complete suppression of every form of holy
religion (some of the jury were Noncon-
formists, perhaps); the wars, both intestine
and external, into which the country would
fall; the neglect of agriculture; the destruction of commerce, great and small; the fall
of all our institutions; the starvation of the
people. What a picture did he draw of
Great Britain, should the people resolve to
rule themselves!

He read extracts from Paine's ' Rights of
Man,' a book praised by the Society for its
constitutional information. Also from Joel
Barlow's ' Advice to the Privileged Orders,'
which had been equally honoured, and,
indeed, had received the special thanks of
the Society. These extracts he connected
with a running commentary, insomuch that

the faces of the jury grew harder, and it was
apparent that they would show no mercy
to those who should be convicted of holding
such opinions.

In a word, the Attorney-General first laid
down certain principles, definitions, and
opinions of great lawyers. Next he described
certain well-known political societies of the
day and their opinions. He then drew a
moving and eloquent picture of the disasters
which would follow the adoption of these
views. He proceeded to connect with the
greatest skill the poor little Society of Snugs
with the great Corresponding Society, and
made out that we were a great and important
body—perhaps the central and most representative body—although occupying a position so obscure and apparently humble.

He then read from our minute books a
great number of passages, all showing the
dangerous character of the Society. It is
quite true that we had offered congratulations
to the Friends of the Constitution, generally
called the Jacobins, in Paris; that we had
passed resolutions of thanks to Tom Paine

and Joel Barlow; that we advocated a better representation of the people. I dare say there were many other resolutions which could easily be twisted about so as to show sedition, or treason, or anything you please. At the same time we were, I maintain, a harmless body of obscure people who loved to talk, and would have done no harm.

Lastly, he made a great deal of the riot, which he called a rebellious and illegal gathering together of the King's enemies. It was advocated, as was shown by the minutes, in the club itself on Saturday; it took place, headed by a member of the club, on the Sunday. The minutes which he should read would prove so much. (Alas! my unfortunate minutes! Why, why had I not followed the advice of the Marquis?)

Enough of the Attorney-General.

It was, as I have said, five o'clock when he sat down, after a most eloquent appeal to the jury. The Court rose for dinner.

At seven o'clock the case was resumed, and the first witness was called.

This was the landlord of the King's Head tavern, where the club met. He deposed that the Snugs were a society originally founded some fifteen years before by certain quiet and respectable tradesmen of the neighbourhood; that it had met every Saturday evening during that long period; that he himself was not, and never had been, present at the meetings; that to his certain knowledge all the original members of the club had either retired or were dead; that the club was founded for convivial purposes only; that he had never been informed of any change in the character of the club, but he had observed that of late the members had ceased to sing and drink less, but talked the louder. As to what they talked about he knew nothing, and had never inquired; he was wholly ignorant, and had never suspected that he was harbouring a seditious and treasonable association. The officers of the club, he said, were one George Williams, Chairman, of whose occupation and residence he was ignorant; and Nevill Comines, the prisoner at the bar, whose father was High Bailiff of

C

St. Katherine's Hospital. Shown a certain
box, he recognised it for the box in which
the papers and property of the club were
kept.

On cross-examination he said that he had
known many respectable tradesmen members
of the club; that he had heard voices raised
in conversation or argument, and might,
perhaps, have heard something of what was
said; that he had never heard any treasonable talk whatever; and that he was himself
a loyal subject of King George. The door
was kept locked, but that was also the custom
with Freemasons, the Lumber Troop, the
Gormagogs, and other societies who commonly
carry on their proceedings in lodges (or rooms)
tyled or closed.

The next witness was a runner, who
deposed to taking away from the tavern the
box lying on the table, with the papers and
books of the Society; these he identified.
Another witness, one of my superiors in the
Admiralty, deposed to my handwriting in the
book of minutes. Cross-examined: Gave the
prisoner an excellent character for intelligence
and zeal at his desk.

I think it was at this point that my counsel, Mr. Vaughan, called attention to the lateness of the hour, though, for his own part, he was ready to go on till any hour. It was in the interests of the jury that he ventured to ask his learned friends if they intended to finish their evidence that night.

His learned friends said that it was impossible; their evidence was not half concluded. Then, after more of that wrangling without which no business can be conducted, the Court consented that the jury should be accommodated by the Sheriff with beds for the night, and adjourned the case (it being then half-past twelve) until eight o'clock in the morning.

They took me back to the ward, where the others were quickly awakened and eager to know how the case went on. When I had finished telling all I remembered it was close upon four in the morning. That night, however, I had no sleep; yet I was no longer terrified. The utmost majesty of the law, after you have watched it for a whole day, presents its points of human imperfection.

Even though a man wear the wig and the robes of a Judge, he presently shows himself to be a man. I say that I was no longer so much awed by the appearance of the Court as beaten down and overwhelmed by the vehemence of the Attorney-General. So great a criminal; designs so monstrous; conspiracies so wide-spreading, caused his speech to be like a raging torrent. I had never believed myself to be so great a sinner. Nay, I had never felt myself a rebel or a traitor at all. Therefore, excited, anxious, and stricken with amazement, I lay awake until the time came to go back to the Court, where I stood as the clock struck eight, unrefreshed by the night, and anxious only to have it over, and to know the worst.

They began calling the rest of their evidence. Why set down what each man proved? Why stop to tell of the constant wrangling between the counsel—of the little points of contradiction when some witness blundered? Dates, distances, clocks, watches, handwriting—everything gave my counsel an opportunity. I know not what he was paid,

but he earned his money. They proved the
riot, and they read the minutes which spoke
of the violence proposed and carried.

Then they called Richard Archer.

This villain, as he was about to prove
himself, stepped from the body of the Court,
where I had not seen him, and entered the
witness-box. He glanced at me as he took
his place. He met my indignant eyes with a
scowl such as I had never seen upon the face
of any human being—a scowl of malignity
and hatred. Perhaps it was only the natural
expression of his own shame. For why should
he hate me? What harm had I ever done to
him? None, to my knowledge.

He took the Book and his oath, and then
turned to the counsel for examination. He
was perfectly self-possessed, calm, and easy—
one would have said that he was accustomed to
the presence of Judges. He even looked handsome, his black hair brushed back from his
white face, and tied with a silk ribbon, neat.
His brown cloth coat was neither above nor
below his station. His manner was respectful;
he answered the exact questions put to him;

and his language was that of one who has
received a superior education, and knows how
to express himself with correctness if not with
eloquence. With such ease and confidence
did this man betray his friends and comrades.
Oh, front of brass!

He deposed, therefore, that he was by
calling a schoolmaster, and that he taught
the school of St. Katherine's Hospital, being
servant of that honourable Society, and
residing in a house provided for him within
the Precinct. He was also organist to the
church, and played for the services on
Sundays and High Days. Further, that he
had joined the club called, foolishly, the
Sublime Society of Snugs, in the belief that
he should be honoured with the society of
sober and respectable men—chiefly substantial tradesmen and shopkeepers—who, over
a cheerful glass and a song, would converse
upon such matters as occupy public attention
from day to day, and that within the proper
boundaries of loyalty and decorum, such as
fitted his own station in life and his calling.

I observed, at this point, that the jury-

men of the trading classes, who do not regard
as of much account a mere schoolmaster,
were greatly impressed by the modesty with
which this man spoke and carried himself.
He actually understood that a schoolmaster is
honoured by the company of a draper or
grocer. A very worthy young man this.
Even the Lord Chief Justice nodded his head
in approbation of his excellent sentiments,
and the Attorney-General, with a wave of his
hand, wafted them with encouragement into
the jury-box.

'In gradual course,' he went on, 'a change
came over this originally harmless assembly.
The men of substance left it; new members
came in, chiefly of the mechanical class; he
hoped, at first, that they were respectable and
sober-minded men, not unfit to associate with
himself, though not of the class and position
of their predecessors. Three or four, however, belonged to the better sort; of those one,
Nevill Comines, was the son of the High Bailiff
of St. Katherine's, and held an appointment in
His Majesty's Admiralty; another was a student
of the Temple; a third had been a student at

Oxford University, but was expelled for atheism. There was also one George Williams, who was the Chairman and a very dangerous person. The conversation now became highly seditious in character; the most radical changes were freely discussed and approved; the murder of the French King was freely advocated before that lamentable event took place; the club entered into correspondence with the Constitutional and Corresponding Societies; passed resolutions conceived in a revolutionary spirit, and called out for the overthrow of the Constitution and the reform of Government in every branch. As for himself, he said that he was pained and grieved at first, but remained silent, hoping that the club would return to its original spirit. When this proved impossible, he still remained with the intention of preventing mischief.

'Now, Richard Archer,' said the Attorney-General, 'I ask you to carry your memory back to the Saturday evening, the day before the riot took place. Do you remember anything?'

' I do remember that evening.'

' What can you tell the Court about that evening ? '

'There was a meeting at the club as usual. And there were delivered one or two most violent speeches, that is to say, speeches advocating violence.'

' Do you remember who spoke ? '

' There were several. The most violent speech was that of the prisoner.'

' Do you remember what he said ? '

It is incredible to relate what followed. This man—this villain of the deepest dye— actually quoted passages from his own speech on that evening, and gave them as mine. He put his own exhortations to violence into my mouth—mine! Why, I had said nothing. I voted in the minority with the moderate men. But the minutes contained an account of what had passed *without names*. Was there ever a more detestable monster?

He was perfectly safe ; the prisoner could not open his mouth ; no one else was in Court who could speak to what had been done. As

for the other members of the club, they were
scattered and disguised, every man happy in
not being pursued, none so ill-advised as to
venture their necks within reach of the Old
Bailey.

My advocate then took him in hand. He
made him reveal the whole of his past life.
At first I thought it would damage his
evidence when he told how he was formerly a
barefooted boy who had no father, and whose
mother took in needlework. But this, I soon
saw, was ridiculous, because there is no disgrace in making your way upwards. My
counsel seemed to make a point when he
pressed the witness as to remaining in the
club after its sentiments had become dis-
tasteful to him. He made him confess that
he had never protested against the
opinions of the members. Questioned
on the subject of betraying friends and
comrades, he grew for the first time con-
fused, but quickly recovered, and said that
his duty to the King was above the claims of
private friendship. Asked how much he was
going to receive as a reward for his treachery,

he said that he had received nothing, and was not aware that anything would be done for him. Asked whether on that Saturday evening he had not himself introduced one of the prisoners, he confessed that he had done so in the hope, he said, of keeping him out of more mischief. 'But,' said my counsel, 'there can no greater mischief happen to any man than to be hanged, drawn, and quartered, for a rebel!' Asked if he had not himself exhorted the club to violence, this perjured villain flatly denied that he had spoken at all that night. 'Not even to protest against disloyalty?' asked the counsel. 'Not even that,' replied Richard Archer.

So he stepped down from the box, his evidence done, meeting my look once more with a malignant grin. I have never, before or since, felt (as then I did) a consuming desire to kill a man. Could I have killed him on the spot, I would have done so. This I now confess with shame. He who kills a man in intention breaks the commandment as much as he who actually slays another, so that I was a murderer as well as a traitor. When he sat down, I understood very well the effect of his evidence :

(1) The jury were now fully persuaded that I was a violent and dangerous revolutionary.

(2) They were also persuaded that I, with my friends, had been constantly crying out for open rebellion.

(3) That it was after my exhortation that the riot, which they magnified into the march or progress of a rebellious army into the heart of London was carried out.

At the beginning of the trial, if I caught the eyes of the man Quellet, he would nod and smile, as much as to say that our time was coming. He now kept his back turned to me, and he smiled and nodded no more. This I understood to mean that his former assurances were futile, and the case was lost.

Other evidence there was, but of a formal kind.

My counsel addressed the Court in defence. He spoke first of the youth and previous good character of the prisoner.

Next, in admitting that the prisoner held
views much to be regretted and fatal to good
government if they were to be carried into
effect, he contended that a great many other
people in this country, carried away by zeal
and by dreams of universal liberty and peace,
had similar views, but that the Government
had not thought proper to arrest these people,
whom all the gaols in the country could not
accommodate.

'Gentlemen,' he said, 'the prisoner is
young: he has been carried away by excess
of generosity to excess of folly. He thought
that the moment a Republic was proclaimed
all ills would cease, all crimes would vanish,
every man would love his neighbour, none
should cheat or overreach—and, in fact, the
kingdom of Heaven itself would begin its
long-wished-for reign upon the earth. But,
gentlemen of the jury,' he went on, 'it was a
generous, if mistaken dream, and we must not
condemn a young man for dwelling on a delu-
sion which, when he grows older, he will
perceive to be impossible. The Attorney-
General has read extracts from the minutes of

the club to which the young man belonged.
These minutes were no doubt reprehensible,
but they should be considered as standing by
themselves, not as part of the conspiracy or
agitations carried on by the Corresponding
Societies. They are mere theories advanced
by men who argue. Have we not all heard,
when young men get together, views and
opinions advanced in the heat of argument
which in cold blood would be quickly rejected?
It was the misfortune of this Society that its
members kept minutes at all. Had it not
been for this unlucky accident, the young man
now at the Bar before you would be walking
free and unmolested. Well, they unfortunately kept minutes. Mr. Attorney-General,
with all the eloquence for which he is
famous, with all that grasp of law for which
he is so illustrious, has turned these minutes
of an obscure and insignificant club of young
enthusiasts and harmless mechanics into the
mischievous conspiracies of a great Revolutionary Centre.'

These words I remember very well,
because I thought them more likely than

anything that had been said before to influence the jury.

Mr. Vaughan followed up this line of argument for some time, saying it over and over again, repeating it in different words, going back to it, a method which then seemed to me tedious, but which I now understand to be the very best way of driving a thing into the collective minds of a British jury, which is apt to be prejudiced and certain to be stupid. He dilated on the members of the club. Who were they? Watchmakers, silk-weavers, shoemakers, with two or three young gentlemen among them. Out of the whole club, none but these four young gentlemen had been arrested. Where was the President or Chairman? No one knew. That was suspicious, for the President was surely more deeply dipped in sedition than any one else. Where were the other members? Their names were all in the hands of the Government. Why were they not produced to support the evidence of the Crown? Out of the whole list but one was forthcoming—this schoolmaster! This sneaking reptile, who continued in the club long after, according to his own account, he ceased to be in harmony with its sentiments, solely to reap reward by denouncing men who regarded him as their friend and brother. None but this wretched schoolmaster, who would doubtless, if this ancient and venerable Society of St. Katherine's preserved its character for loyalty, receive another kind of reward. Well, he said (this man) that the violent speech of the last night was made by the prisoner. They had no other evidence of the fact. No other evidence at all—not the minutes, because they mentioned no names ; not any other members of the club——

I forbear going on with the speech. Suffice it to say that, if eloquence and reasoning could have saved me, Mr. Felix Vaughan would have done so. But I looked in vain on the faces of the jury for any softening. Hard and unforgiving faces they were. When my counsel sat down they were as hard and as unforgiving as at the beginning of his speech. Long before this candles had been brought—a pair of candles for the desk of every Judge, candles for the table in the Court, candles in the sconces on the walls. I looked at the row of faces on the Bench ; the Judges, severe and stern ; the Mayor and Aldermen, fat and rubicund, but stern ; the Justices of the Peace, men of property and position, scowling at the revolutionary who would deprive them of their all. Even the ladies of whom there were half a dozen, looked as cruel as the women of Carthage. They would have liked to see the man who wanted (so they were taught) to rob them of their fine houses and their wealth dragged and drawn asunder by wild horses. There was no pity in those faces ; the candles showed them hard and cruel as the faces of the jurymen. Whenever I looked about the Court, whether on the Bench, or among the jury, or among the counsel in the Court, I saw written, plain and clear—Condemnation.

It was ten o'clock at night when the Attorney-General rose to reply. He knew very well that the effect of his opening speech was still fresh in the minds of the jury ; he therefore said little. He reminded the jury that he had proved all he had undertaken to prove. He said that no real defence had been set up at all. As for pretending that the club was a convivial club, the very pretence made things worse, because it showed the members carrying on these treasonable practices under cover of good-fellowship. And, as for youth, what man in his senses would acquit a grown man, two-and-twenty years old, of a crime on the ground of youth? Therefore he called upon them for a verdict as loyal men, lovers of King and Constitution, and desirous above all that order and tranquillity should in this country allow every man to carry on his business undisturbed by murderers from France, or by their friends and sympathisers in these islands. So, after a short speech of uncommon strength and vigour, the Attorney-General sat down.

The Judge summed up, also briefly. He pointed out the law, as he had done to the Grand Jury. He told the jury that they had nothing to do with the apparent harmlessness of the club, or with the youth of the prisoner, or with anything at all but the plain law. As well pretend that a young pickpocket must escape a whipping because he had an innocent-looking face, or because the watch which he stole had nothing but a tortoise-shell case. They were, then, to find guilty or not guilty according to the law of the land. And the law was what he himself had laid down for their guidance.

The jury returned a verdict without leaving the box.

' Guilty, my lord,' said the foreman.

Then a sudden horror seized my soul. The Court swam before my eyes; I should have fallen but for the arm of the turnkey who stood beside me. I recovered immediately. The Judge was asking me, with a hard voice and hard eyes, if I had aught to say.

I tried to tell him that indeed I had nothing to say, but my voice stuck. I could say nothing. I shook my head. I was conscious that the people in the Court were murmuring their satisfaction at a verdict so speedy and so just.

The Judge waited a moment for me.

Then he put on the black cap.

At that moment the Ordinary of Newgate appeared behind the Judge's chair, habited in his robes.

The Judge, in an awful silence of the Court, pronounced the sentence—the awful sentence upon traitors, which they no longer carry out in its entirety. No, I cannot repeat it.

He concluded, 'And may the Lord have mercy upon your soul.'

The Chaplain replied, 'Amen.'

When the Judge began his sentence the Serjeant-at-Mace standing on my left seized me by the right-hand thumb and held it, I knew not why. When the Judge came to the last words, he slipped a noose of twine, or thin string, over my thumb and drew it tight. 'Twas the outward sign or token of he rope that was soon to be pulled tight about my neck.

CHAPTER XVIII

THE CONDEMNED CELL

THE left-hand serjeant tapped me on the other shoulder. I turned to leave the Court. The fine ladies were chatting and laughing loudly; the Sheriff was walking out after the Judges; the counsel, the attorneys, the witnesses, and the jury were all tramping noisily out of the place—the show was over. Only Richard Archer—perhaps I was mistaken—lingered behind; the last face I saw was his, with a horrid grin of malignant joy. Well, he had compassed my destruction. What good would it do him?

In moments of great trouble, when the mind is overwhelmed, it is impossible to think of anything; there is no sequence or reason left; the brain has lost its power of control;

there is no power of election or repression
left; there is no will; the thoughts fly about
the brain like thistle-down; they dance like
motes in the sunbeam; they appear and
disappear like goblins.   When our procession
came out of the Session House into the Old
Bailey, first I noticed that the stars were
shining brightly overhead; I wondered why
they took the trouble to illuminate this
gloomy place.   While I was thinking this, I
became aware that my irons were making
quite a new music; their monotonous jingle-
jangle had become a glad and triumphant
song, as if they rejoiced over the verdict—
fetters and the gallows have always been
sworn brothers—certainly they never before
sounded so pleasantly; at first, I remembered,
I used to hate the sound of them.   Now,
however—oh! wonderful!   Would it appear
incongruous if I began to dance to this sweet
music?   Would they increase the sentence—
yet, how could they increase it?   If I were
to sing as we went along?   I even thought
that Sylvia, who was always fond of a new
tune, would like to hear this; I pictured her

dancing with me along the flags between these prison walls, as we used to dance about the apple trees in the orchard.

'This,' said my conductor, waking me out of my dream, ' is the Condemned Cell.'

He had a lanthorn in his hand, with which he threw a little light about the place. I saw that it was quite a small room; there was a barrack-bedstead, that is, a sloping plank—two, in fact, side by side.

'Take this,' he said, pointing to one. 'To-morrow you may have a cell to yourself. This bed is hardly cold yet from Dick Pennyweight, hanged o' Monday. Your turn will come next Monday, unless you get a reprieve. There's the water-jug.'

So saying, he left me at the bedside and went away, locking the door after him and leaving me in the dark.

The sight of the bed filled me with a longing for sleep and rest. I was hungry and thirsty, but I was tired to death. I threw myself down on the bed, dressed as I was, and in a moment fell fast asleep. Strange, that not even the thought that I was lying in this dreadful place could keep me awake one minute.

'Twas then about eleven o'clock. I slept in this condemned cell until seven next morning; then I was awakened by a dismal groaning in the cell. Outside it was daylight, but the small window high up in the wall admitted but a dim twilight. I could see, however, on the bed beside me the figure of a man, crouched like a child, his head on his knees, groaning and crying. Then I remembered where I was, and why. In the condemned cell! Heavens! There was another wretch with me in the cell—another poor creature doomed to die.

'Who are you?' I cried, springing to my feet. 'Who is this other miserable creature?'

'I am an unfortunate merchant in the City; I am Prime Warden of my Company, and churchwarden of my parish church.'

'What!' I cried, 'you are Mr. Thorpe? You are found guilty of forgery? You, who went off to Court like a bridegroom to his wedding?'

'Alas! it is the same,' he replied. 'I am now a disgraced man. I cannot tell how I shall ever recover the shame of the trial; for the rest of my days I shall be pointed out on 'Change. I shall be the man who was tried for forgery and found guilty.'

'Sir! this is the condemned cell; we are both to be hanged! What nonsense is this about 'Change?'

'No, young man'—he sat up in his bed, with dignity—'you are mistaken; I shall not be hanged. You will, of course; but I shall not. Richly you deserve it. You will be hanged, drawn, and quartered, as becomes a traitor to his country. Your friends will be served in like manner. Ha! 'twill be a noble lesson, and a warning to all traitors. What! Laws would be of no use if villains like you escaped. But as for me, 'tis not with me a question of hanging. No, no, that would be preposterous; 'tis the verdict—the verdict—that it is which sticks. Why, I looked for nothing less than an honourable acquittal! I was certain of it. I looked to leave the Court and return to my friends and my

business without a stain upon my character.'
(And yet this man had forged a Bank draft
for 1,500*l.*!) 'I thought we should have had
a great banquet in my honour at my
Company's hall! See the cruel turn of
Fortune! I am found guilty. Was there
ever jury more prejudiced, more obstinate,
more stupid? And for the form of it—only
the form of it—the Judge, who showed by
his face, so hard and stern it was, his opinion
of the jury, was compelled to put on the
black cap and pronounce a sentence'—(he
caught his breath)—'a sentence of the kind
reserved for criminals—for the form of it.'

'Sir,' I said, 'I know not what the form
of the sentence may have been in your case,
but the manner of its exe—I mean its
carrying out—will probably be the same as
my own.'

'Ha!' he gasped. 'Thus it is—this
young man understands nothing. Learn,
sir, that when a man has friends so powerful
as mine, he is not subjected to this infamous
punishment. My friends are nothing short
of the whole great, rich, powerful City of

London. Hang me? The Government cannot do it, sir. They dare not do it. The
greatest city in the world says to the King :
"Your Majesty will be pleased to exercise
clemency in this case. This gentleman, most
unfortunate at his trial—a most worthy,
upright, God-fearing gentleman, will receive
at your Majesty's hands, a pardon full and
free." Nothing short of a pardon full, free,
and immediate, will satisfy the City in this
case. No, no, it is not the sentence that
troubles me. It is the verdict; the malignity of the prosecution ; the perjury of the
witnesses ; the imbecility of counsel ; the
misdirection of the Judge, though I think the
poor man meant well ; the stupidity of the
jury ; all combined to bring about the verdict,
and the formal—the formal—sentence. Next
week I shall be out again. But I fear it will
be some time before my friends will be able
to reverse the verdict.'

Here the warder unlocked the door.

'I shall now dress and go abroad,' said
the unfortunate forger, ' to take the air in the
Press Yard. I should recommend you to

stay here and meditate. A Bible and Prayer Book are in the cell. Remember, young man, thou hast but a few hours to live.'

It was now light enough, the door being open, for me to see what kind of place I was in. First of all, it was a small cell, not more than nine feet by six, but vaulted, and about ten feet high ; in the upper part of the vault was a small window with a double grating ; the stone walls were lined with planks studded with broad-headed nails. A doleful room ; a dismal, horrible place, haunted with the groans and tears of despair, and the sighs of those who fear that their punishment will only begin with their hanging. The most callous criminals grow pale and tremble when they are thrust into these darksome cells.

There are fifteen of these doleful abodes, five on each story. In general, each prisoner has his own cell; but when, as sometimes happens, there are more than fifteen waiting execution, there must be more than one in a cell. Therefore, I found myself with the unfortunate forger.

Though there are sometimes so many

criminals lying in the condemned cells, by the King's mercy they are not all executed. Respites, as everybody knows, are common and easily obtained, under one pretext or the other, so that a man may lie for weeks, months, and even (as has happened) for years, in this dismal place and yet in the end be taken out and hanged. Hope, as is natural, springs up anew with every respite, so that in the end the unhappy wretch does not believe that he must die, and loses all his terrors, and forgets his repentance until it is too late.

When I went forth into the Press Yard—the long and narrow court with high walls in which we had to take air and exercise—I found some of my companions in misery already out of their cells. They were walking up and down the court; my friend, the merchant, with the dignity due to his position; they were sitting in the day-room assigned to us. The friends of the prisoners were already admitted; they brought with them food, beer, cards, tobacco; some, if they were of the better sort, even spirits, if they could be smuggled. We had the yard for fresh air, and the day-room, on the ground floor, for rain and cold weather.

By this time the drinking and the riot of the day had already begun. I say riot because, although the place was a haven of peace compared with the Master Felons' side, it was shocking to see men condemned to die within a few days or weeks drinking and smoking with the utmost indifference and recklessness, gambling and jesting with careless ribaldry. Every morning there came to the Press Yard a certain worthy and pious soul (not a clergyman of the Church of England) who offered his services for prayer with the condemned: by all but a few he was derided and refused. Yet he came daily. This morning I observed that he spoke earnestly to the merchant, in a low voice.

'Sir,' said he, 'I thank you heartily; in the church you will always find me performing my duties. But for prayer in a condemned cell—there, indeed, sir, you must hold me excused. My respite will arrive in an hour or two; my pardon shortly afterwards. There are, however, others—this young gentleman, for instance, to whom your services may be useful.' He indicated myself and resumed his walk, his hands clasped behind his back, his head erect ; it would have been the walk of a great City merchant on 'Change, but for the irons which caused his feet to drag, and clinked as he moved them.

I presently discovered that there is little friendship among these companions in misery. They look at each other for the most part askance, unless they happen to be highway-men, whose calling is regarded by all male-factors with envy or with pride. Shoplifters, forgers, burglars, sheep and horse-stealers, coiners, and the like regard each other with contempt ; and the crime of High Treason I quickly found was abhorred by all. You would have thought, to see their brazen faces and to hear their talk, that they cared nothing for their awful fate. Yet, when I conversed apart with one of them, and marked his haggard, anxious, and roving eyes, his twitching cheeks, his sudden pauses and breaks and silence—nay, the very eagerness with which he drank, it became apparent that the bitterness of death was upon them—they looked forward with fearful hearts. And at night they had to endure the cell—perhaps alone ; perhaps—sometimes more terrible—with a companion : always being startled out of their sleep from time to time when the gaolers go their rounds.

The condemned cells are, in fact, like the rest of the wards in one respect. The men can receive their friends ; they may feast on what they please, or on what they can get ; they may drink ; but little joy comes to them with their drink, only insensibility at the best, or a drunken braggart courage.

All the men, except the merchant, were rough and common fellows, with whom one could not converse. I walked about; I returned to the cell, and sat on the bed.

A strange eagerness fell upon me, I wanted the thing to be over and done with. I wondered how one would feel dangling and turning round and round, like a leg of mutton. As for other things, my parents and my sister, the safety of my soul, I could not as yet think of them at all.

About three o'clock in the afternoon another prisoner was brought to this gloomy place. This was George himself, his trial already over. Yet mine had lasted two long days. He marched along briskly, lifting his legs as lightly as if there were no chains upon them, his face shining, a smile upon his lips.

'Well, lad,' he said, cheerfully, ' here I am at last, to keep thee company.'

'You, too, George? Yet what else could I expect?'

'To be sure, who but I? The trial is over. I pleaded guilty, because when a man is so near his end he cannot afford to tell lies. " Guilty," I said. Well, I thought there would have been no more ado, but the Judge would have sent me off at once. Not so, five long hours did they spend over their evidence and their charges and deliberations. Never mind.'

He shook himself like a dog out of the water.

'That's over at last. A brave show they made with their robes and chains : the Lord Mayor himself is a sight to remember. Nevill my lad, that fellow, Archer, is a villain—a perjured villain.   I suppose he thought to save his own neck, but he is a liar.   He told the Court that the speech at the club about the rising—I believe that was full of lies—was made by you.

'"My Lord," I said to the Judge, "this man is a liar."

'Whereupon the Judge bade me hold my tongue.

'"My Lord," I said, "with submission, the worst you can do to me is to hang me, which I believe you intend, wherefore I am not afraid.   This man," I repeated, "is a liar and a villain."

'"Hold your tongue, sirrah," said his Lordship, sharply.

'"In good time, my Lord," said I.   "This fine speech was not spoken by Nevill Comines, whom you have sentenced to death, but by the witness himself.   He it was who exhorted us to rebellion ; took me to the club, and made me promise to lead the rebels.   A perjured villain !   That is all, my Lord."

'Well, the Judge grew very red in the

face. I suppose he is not used to be spoken to
—prisoners are mostly afraid of a man who
can order them to be flogged and what not
—and he opened his mouth twice to speak.
Then he composed himself, and said gently
that, being the prisoner, I could not give
evidence ; that if I chose to make a defence, I
could do so, but I had already pleaded guilty ;
that I could, however, cross-examine the witness, if by so doing I could mitigate the extent of my guilt. But I had no more to say,
and so they went on, and here I am. We
must make the best of things, lad, though we
shall miss the comfortable room on the State
side. Enough said ; no lamenting, Nevill,'
for the tears were in my eyes at the sight of
this poor fellow. Who could have thought
that, for no sins of his own (of which we
knew), so many evils should have fallen, and
that so suddenly, upon him ? All because his
mistress loved him no longer—there was no
other cause—and for this he must be taken
out and hanged.

' Last night, Nevill,' he went on, ' the news
came that thou wast sentenced. Well, they

will not hang thee. Why? I know not
why; but I am certain that the only one to
suffer for that Sunday's work will be myself.'

'Not hang me? But I am in the condemned cell! My doom is pronounced.'

'Yet they will not hang thee; that I know
full well.'

My heart leaped up; I had not thought
of this chance. What if I should escape the
gallows after all? Man is a selfish creature.
I forgot the fate of George—I forgot everything except the chance that I might yet
escape the gallows.

'How do you know, George?'

'I know——' he hesitated, uncertain, 'I
know because I have been assured. Since I
have entirely submitted to the will of the
Lord; since I know that He hath ordered the
manner of my death for the good of my poor
mistress and sweetheart, I know—perhaps the
Lord hath put these things into my mind—
that none shall die except myself. They have
sentenced thee, lad, through the perjury of
the villain Archer, whose ribs I would

assuredly break with a cudgel were I free.
They will perhaps sentence the other fellows,
our two messmates—that I know not, but they,
too, will escape. No—they will not hang one
of you. And as for me——' He stretched
out his hands and raised his eyes, and his face
became all glorious as one who hath a
heavenly vision, yet we were standing together
in a corner of the Press Yard, and around us
were the vilest and most profligate wretches,
men and women, in the whole of this great
City. 'Oh, that I could die by the cruellest
and most lingering death if only I could restore
Sylvia to health thereby! I see her poor thin
cheeks filling out when I am gone ; she regains
her roses; her eyes are bright again; her
mouth smiles; she dances as she goes; her
heart is light. She has clean forgotten me.
That is as it should be. I shall be dead ; I
shall have died to save my girl. What better
lot, Nevill, what better lot ?'

On Friday evening, about nine o'clock,
when we were already locked up—so that I
knew not until the morning—they brought to

the condemned cells the other two. So that now our party was complete.

All night long I lay awake on my hard bed praying with all my heart and all my soul for an escape—any escape—from the fatal tree. I remembered the words of the old woman : ' He shall not have power to destroy.' Who could be the master of all this mischief, unless it was perhaps the villain, Richard Archer?

The next morning was Saturday—on Monday those condemned, unless a respite came, would be taken forth and hanged.

CHAPTER XIX

SATURDAY

'Now,' said the merchant, in the morning.
'The Governor will send for me as soon as
he is dressed. "Sir," he will say, "I have
great pleasure in telling you that the King
hath been pleased to grant a respite." That
is the first step towards the pardon which will
follow. By the word pardon is meant, in such
a case as mine, not so much the forgiveness of
a crime which was never committed, but the
consequences of a mad and mischievous verdict.
Young man, I would that I could feel an
assurance that your conscience was as clear
as mine. Then you would be enabled to
contemplate your awful fate with resignation,
if not with hope.'

I was by this time buoyed up with the
hope (founded on nothing but George's as-

surance) that the gallows was not to be my
awful fate. Yet the good man spoke so
earnestly that one could not resent his advice.
It was like unto cold water poured down the
back. It recalled the actual truth. This was
the more impressed upon me when I met the
other two, the Templar and the Oxonian, who
had been put to the Bar together, their offence
being exactly the same, in succession to
George, and after a trial of eight hours were
found guilty. The Judge, in their case, dwelt
heavily on the danger of the times, and the
necessity for making an example.

'You are young,' he said, 'but the
youngest can set fire to the house; you are
not too young to know the wickedness of
such an act; you are well educated, which
makes your case the worse. Expect not,
therefore, any clemency. You have con-
spired to bring over to this country the
crimes which now disgrace the ancient kingdom of France; you would destroy the
Throne, the Church, and the Aristocracy; you
would render it impossible for honest men to
pursue their business; you would fill the·

streets with murder and massacre. You
have been prevented in good time; you will
have the satisfaction of feeling, with your
latest breath, that the principles of order, law,
and true liberty are still as strong in the
heart of the Briton as when these things were
fought for and won.'

'Expect no clemency?' Why, then, what
did George mean? Rather, what a fool
was I to rely upon George, whose mind was
weakened by his troubles, so that he could
not see aright! There was nothing, therefore, before us but preparation. And here, I
confess, I had an excellent example set me by
our two companions. One of them (the student of law) set himself earnestly to work
upon the condition of his soul, availing himself daily of the help rendered by that good
and pious man whom I have already mentioned, reading and meditating every day in
the gloom of the cell, whither no one followed him. The other (whom I have called
the Poet) had unhappily abandoned his
religion; chiefly, I believe, because he could
not answer certain questions—as if the whole

scheme of the universe stood open to the
gaze of a lad of twenty-one—but he retained
some faith in the Universal Father, to whom
he composed a hymn during these days, most
beautiful and moving. The horror which
one naturally feels for one who has lost his
religion was, in his case, changed into pity
that a man whose heart was by nature singu-
larly so pious should have to die while that
piety was gone a-wandering out of the right
path. He looked forward to death without
fear. 'We live at the most,' he said, 'for
seventy years ; then we die and are forgotten.
We came from whence we know not ; we go
whither we know not. After we are dead
nothing signifies to us. If there is another
life, which we cannot affirm or deny, it is not
on this earth, but elsewhere, and the loss of a
few years here will not be felt or remembered
there. If there is, on the other hand, no life
to come, then we shall feel nothing and know
nothing, any more than we did in the ages
before we were born, ere ever the world was
made.' 'Twas a strange young man, tall and
thin, of soft speech, yet eager—of brightness

that was sometimes fiery, and of affections always ready. Well, the history in hand will presently tell what became of him.

We spent the morning in this gloomy conversation, surrounded by the poor wretches who were to suffer, like ourselves. One can think of death with resignation : it is the common lot ; there is a hope beyond the grave ; to the penitent forgiveness is promised, to those who are forgiven there are also promised joys of which we cannot even dream ; we are born to a more glorious inheritance than we can even imagine. Yet even to him who dies of a disease which leaves him time for meditation, the prospect of separation causes tears. To me, while I forced myself to think of the life to come, the thought of the shameful gallows would intrude. Then my heart would stop, my pulse cease, and a deathly chill would fall upon me; then I would sit, eyes staring, mouth open, until the horror of it passed away. When I say that I felt this, so also did my companions, except George, who remained in his cheerfulness. Yet, as I knew, his was not

the insensibility of the wretches who drank
and sang with their fellows at my elbow, but
the confidence of one who is at peace with
his Saviour and with himself.

Understand that this was Saturday. If
no respite came, we should suffer on the
Monday morning. After the severe words of
the Judge there seemed no hope. And—a
thing which I had forgotten—who was to ask
for this respite? For we were all four abandoned—cast off by our friends. The meanest,
lowest, poorest rogue in the Press Yard was
richer than ourselves : none so poor but he
had some friends who would plead for him.
We had none.

The striking of the bells—that of St. Sepulchre and that of St. Paul's—became the
knell of a parting soul : the cell was a tomb
—darksome, terrible : the sight of those who
laughed and roystered made the prospect
more intolerable : the high walls found voices
to mock at one : at moments, one seemed to
go mad.

'Courage, lad'—George laid his hand
upon my shoulder—'they shall not hang

thee. Remember, I *know* that none shall die,
except myself. This knowledge has been
placed in my heart, I verily believe, for thy
comfort. Shall Sylvia—shall that girl for
whose sake all this trouble has been raised—
shall she have to weep and mourn because
her only brother has been hanged ? Never !
That will not be permitted. What did thy
eyes gaze upon just now, that made thy teeth
to chatter ?'

'George, I saw a gibbet, and a dangling
body turning round and round, quivering
upon the rope in dying agonies !'

''Twas my gibbet and my body. What
are any agonies to me, seeing that they bring
back joy and health to Sylvia ? My gibbet—
my rope—my body——'

And even while he spoke there came the
respite, as if to show the truth of his prophecy. We were not quite abandoned by
our friends. There was one who, as soon as
he heard the sentence, began to work on our
behalf.

It was the afternoon : the clock had just
struck three : the day was cloudy, and the

twilight was already falling upon this deep
and narrow hole. I saw the Governor himself appear at the other end of the yard, and
with him one who was hidden by the throng.
At sight of the Governor all sprang up with pale
faces and trembling lips, and eyes of longing.
For he brought a respite for some one.

The poor merchant, the companion of my
cell, ran to meet him as fast as his irons
would permit, crying, 'My respite! My
respite! It has come!'

'Sir,' said the Governor, 'no respite has
come for you. Prepare for the worst.'

He fell back, laughing—he actually
laughed. 'It will be here before the night,'
he said. 'The pretence has been carried on
long enough—quite long enough. But I am
not concerned.'

I watched him. He suddenly ceased to
laugh; his cheeks became white, his eyes stared
ghastly. I knew that, like me, he had caught
sight of that gibbet and that swinging body.
Then I saw who accompanied the Governor.

We were not abandoned, I say. We had
one friend still, and he was here. There was

a respite, and it was for us; and the man
who brought it was none other than my old
friend and patron, the Reverend Prebendary
Lorrymore, at sight of whom I was fain to
cover my face with shame.

'Sir,' he said to the Governor, 'suffer me
to have speech with these young gentlemen.
Take me, Nevill, out of this place, which
causes one to understand the tortures of the
damned. Is there no retired spot away from
their sight and hearing?'

I led him with hanging head to the cell.

He sat down on the bedstead.

'Here,' he said, 'is an awful twilight as of
the tomb. Here we can converse as in the
presence of Death and the Great Judge of all.
Nevill, unhappy boy, think not that this thy
fate leaves us callous. Nay——' But here he
stopped, while the tears ran down his cheeks.
I fell on my knees before him. 'Nay,' he
recovered himself, ''twas not to weep with
thee, nor to reproach thee, poor boy. Thy
reading led thee into the false reasoning
which comes of a little knowledge and a lack
of wisdom. Thy generous heart caused thee

to believe doctrines which are easy to proclaim
and hard to be disproved. I blame thee not
for Republican opinions, but for thy secrecy.
Yet will I not reproach thee. Know, then,
Nevill, that the sentence will not be carried
into effect for a week longer yet. There is so
much respite obtained. I had much trouble
to procure this favour because the Judges are
severe, the temper of the better sort is exas-
perated, and the danger from such as have
been thy friends is very great; but there is a
respite.'

He then went on to an exhortation or
discourse on the duty of one in my position,
which I forbear to set down, though I remember it every word.

This done I ventured to ask him concerning
my parents. That my father was still unforgiving, I expected, and that my mother
went all day long in tears surprised me not,
though it added to the remorse of my heart.
Sylvia was unconscious of all, and remained
in the same condition.

At this point, therefore, I thought it well
to inform my patron of the strange reasons

which had led George into the business. I
told him all that I knew; how he conceived
the idea that nothing but his own death
would bring relief to Sylvia; how he would
not kill himself, but sought death in one shape
after the other; how, finally, at the suggestion
of the man Archer, he was brought to the
club and made to lead the mob in the
miserable little riot which they called an
insurrection. This narrative touched him
deeply. I asked him, further, to tell the
Lieutenant and Sister Katherine everything,
in hope that thus their hearts might be
softened.

He was greatly moved. He ordered me
to bring George to the cell where he sat; he
conversed with him alone for half an hour,
while I stood outside the door. Then he called
me again.

'This business,' he said, 'grows more
strange. It seems all—in every point—to
have grown out of that fit which seized
Sylvia. For, first, George was thrown into a
kind of madness—the madness and melancholy
of love—thus he fell a victim to suggestions

and illusions of the Evil One; finally, he became a ready prey to this man—this villain —the serpent whom we have nourished in our bosoms (but he shall stay there no longer), and was put up by him to lead what was hoped would prove a signal for general insurrection. Poor lad! Well, I bade him prepare for death, and he smiled; he says he is already as one dead; he is obeying the Lord's will; Sylvia will recover and forget him; he is happy. Poor lad! Poor lad!'

He presently rose with a few final words of forgiveness and blessing. Before he departed he also spoke to our two companions words of admonition, which they received in good part. So he went away and hope revived. The cell ceased to be a tomb; and the striking of the clock ceased to be a knell for the parting soul. We were safe for a week longer.

The next day being Sunday, we were all taken to the chapel for morning service, except those who refused to go on the pretext that they belonged to some other form of faith, but in reality because the condemned

pew is a most dreadful place. Every Sunday
we had attended the chapel, so that the sight
of the men about to be hanged had grown
familiar. But this was the first time that we
sat in that pew.

Those who know not the chapel or the
prison may be told that it is a large room of
convenient proportions. The pulpit is affixed
to the wall. A large space is railed off at
either end, one for women and the other for
men. The prisoners can attend or not as
they please ; those who do, behave for the
most part with some show of decency, though
sometimes there is a brawl. A small gallery
near the pulpit gives seats to the Sheriff and
others who come to hear the sermon preached
to the condemned ; and these themselves sit
in a large square pew in the middle of the
chapel.

Nine men and two women occupied the
pew on this Sunday—namely, the merchant,
our party of four, four or five rogues, male
and female, and one, a murderer, who was
brought out from the cell where, as soon as
a murderer is sentenced, he is kept on bread

and water, and watched day and night lest he should destroy himself. The middle of the pew is taken up by a black coffin, to remind the worshippers, if they needed other reminder, of the fate awaiting them. The chapel was this day filled with visitors who came to look upon convicts out of the common—a City merchant of good reputation to be hanged for forgery; four young gentlemen to suffer for high treason; these were occupants of the pew not often to be seen. Well, I hope that our bearing and appearance satisfied them. The City merchant looked about the chapel smiling on the visitors; the pretence was to be kept up to the last. He carried a large Prayer Book, and he led the responses, though one of the warders acted as clerk, in a loud and clear voice. When the sermon began, he turned his eyes to his companions in the pew, and, at the more striking periods, he gravely nodded his head, or emphasised with his forefinger, as if to press the point home to them. The wretched murderer seemed beyond all feeling or consciousness; he lay huddled in the corner, and never moved during the whole service. The rogues—who were condemned for smaller crimes—listened in apparent attention; the coffin riveted their eyes; from time to time they passed their hands over their cold, wet foreheads. Poor wretches! If the Church allowed the custom, I would long ago have caused prayers to be said for the souls of those whose flight, upwards or elsewhere, I so nearly shared!

The service came to an end. When it was over, and we rose to go, our friend the merchant, who had borne himself so bravely, as I had noticed before in the Press Yard, turned suddenly white, and gazed with staring eyes before him. Then he reeled, and fell forward, lying along the coffin.

They carried him out and gave him water to drink. Presently he recovered.

'My respite,' he said, when he was brought back to the Press Yard, ' is strangely delayed. I cannot understand the cause of this delay. Any other man would feel uneasy.

But I am not—no—not in the least. It will come to-night—or, perhaps, the first thing to-morrow.'

His daughter came to see him—the poor girl whom I had already seen—in the prison. Alas!—the poor girl! Her eyes were streaming; she could hardly stand upright; she fell upon her father's breast, weeping and crying aloud, so that it tore the heart only to see and hear her.

He laughed; he bade her be of good cheer; he assured her that he should be out of prison in a few days; all would yet go well; she must not believe what was said; with a great deal more. So that she went away at last, persuaded perhaps that her father would yet escape. Alas! poor girl! How would she find herself mistaken in the morning! He slept all night without waking. I thought he was free from care. I have since learned that this long sleep was probably the effect of the heavy load of care upon his mind. Yet I am certain he persuaded himself of his own safety. He should escape the gallows, he thought.

All night long, for my part, I was kept awake by the sound of hammers; they were erecting the scaffold outside the prison. Monday's batch were to be hanged here, according to the new and humane custom.

At two in the morning I heard the ringing of a harsh hand-bell. It was followed by a hoarse voice, bawling so loudly that those who were awake in the condemned cell could hear the words in the dead stillness of the night:

> All you that in the condemned hole do lie,
> Prepare you, for to-morrow you shall die.
> Watch all and pray; the hour is drawing near
> That you before the Almighty shall appear.
> Examine well yourselves, in time repent
> Lest you may to eternal flames be sent.
> And when St. Sepulchre's to-morrow tolls,
> The Lord have mercy on your souls.

My companion in the cell heard not these words; he was sleeping soundly. The door was thrown open while it was yet dark, and the gaolers roused him up.

When he heard that he was to be hanged in two hours he laughed. 'I thought,' he said, 'that the respite would have come on Saturday; as it did not, I perceived that the form was to be kept up. Well, my men, I will dress and attend you. The Governor, however, has the respite in his pocket.'

They offered him what he chose for breakfast; they sat in the cell while he dressed. At half-past seven they told him it was time.

' Ay, ay,' he said. ' Well, we are ready, we are ready; a tedious form, but rules must be observed. Well, I suppose I shall return in a few minutes, unless the full pardon has been already made out.'

So he walked away cheerfully; I went out of the cell after him. The five rogues who were to suffer with him were being led away with hanging heads; the murderer, half dead with fear, was supported on his way; the merchant walked after them, holding up his head, and carrying his hat under his arm as if he was going on 'Change.

Then the bell of St. Sepulchre's began to toll the knell of the dying.

When the unfortunate man arrived in the room where they knock off the fetters and pinion the men, and understood at last that there was no respite for him, but that he must surely die, he fell down, seized with a swoon of the most deadly kind.

They carried him out and supported him to the end, and even the hangman could not tell when he tied the rope whether the unfortunate gentleman was conscious or not. I hope that he remained unconscious after he was turned off.

CHAPTER XX

THE KING'S CLEMENCY

WE spent five days more in this stinking
place, where I verily believe some of us
would have died had our stay been prolonged.
We were still under sentence of death ; and
a respite is so commonly granted on such
trivial pretexts, if only to allow more time
for preparation, that it counts but little, and
should not (as it always does) raise hopes of
pardon or commutation. Our only friend,
the Prebendary, came often, and never failed
(though he was working assiduously in our
interests) to admonish us on the shortness of
the time that remained, and to exhort us to
repentance. Sometimes, in the dead of the
night, when I lie awake, this terrible week
returns to me with all its attendant horrors.

I see the rogues who are to die on Monday
morning rolling drunk about the yard, their
chains clinking, their mouths full of blas-
phemies, bawling ribald songs, supported by
other rogues and drabs like unto them, not
yet condemned to die. I see in a corner
some poor trembling wretch, not so lost to
shame as these, reduced by poverty to crime,
waiting in misery for the day of doom : with
him some woman—wife, or daughter, or
sister—on whose face it is written that death
—any death—would be better than this
shameful fate. I think of what followed for
that poor girl, daughter of the forger : a life
ruined, cast down, and disgraced. Where
doth she now live ? Where doth she hide
her poor head ? I see the tall and burly
figure of George himself in good case, in
spite of his long sojourn in the gaol, cheerful
and contented—even happy, because he
thinks that he knows the will of the Lord,
and is obeying it. Now he who does his duty
cannot be far wrong. As I recall this scene,
so full of shame and pity, I feel again the
heaviness of the sentence, and expect again

to hear my own knell rung and my own funeral service read.

Enough of it.

On Thursday morning, my patron having given us no hint of what was likely, the Governor ordered us to be conducted from the Press Yard to his own house.

'Is it another respite?' I asked the warder.

'Prisoners in the Press Yard are never taken out for a simple respite, they only leave it to be hanged, or for chapel, or to hear a change in the sentence. But I know nothing. Bless you, the Government don't send messages to the warders. If it's good news, gentlemen, a guinea is the least I can expect.'

'A guinea from each,' said he of the Temple. 'Push on, man, I feel these cursed chains already slipping from my ankles. To escape from this abode of all the devils I would be content to become like that other eminent traitor, Lambert Simnel, a scullion in the Royal Kitchen. I would scullion it with zeal. Push on!'

We were taken to the same room in

which we had received the papers concerning
our trial. As before, the Governor was
seated at his table ; beside him, as before,
sat Mr. White, the Solicitor to the Treasury.

'Prisoners,' said the Governor, 'I have
ordered you to be brought here in order that
you may receive a communication from the
Government, brought by the Solicitor to the
Treasury.'

Mr. White looked up.

'You have gone through a period of great
anxiety,' he said, 'since last you came before
me. Anxiety, I am sure that you now
acknowledge, richly deserved. But these are
my private sentiments. One cannot change
a trial for High Treason into a wedding feast,
nor turn a prison into a palace, or the condemned pew to a stall at St. George's. If you
will listen, I will now read you the paper
which sets forth His Majesty's gracious inten-
tions in your case.'

'God save the King !' said George.

'Amen,' said Mr. White, solemnly.

He then received from his clerk, who
stood behind his chair, a paper, which he read

aloud. It was like the indictment, long and full
of repetitions, and read without any stops.

He finished it at last, and laid it down.

'In other words,' he said, ' by the King's
clemency your sentences are commuted.
You, John Campbell Power, and you, Arthur
Hallett, who were simple members of this
seditious club, and are not proved to have
encouraged or advocated violent measures,
yet continued members long after you knew
the revolutionary sentiments of the members,
are to receive the King's pardon in consideration of these facts and of your youth and
inexperience, on condition of being imprisoned
in His Majesty's Gaol of Newgate for one
year, reckoning from the time of your arrest.
You will be treated as misdemeanants only.
Your chains will be knocked off, and you will
live, if you please, on the State side, or in
any other lodging that the Governor may
assign to you.'

They changed colour; they became pale;
the tears showed in their eyes. This was,
indeed, an unexpected mercy.

'Let them sit down, warder,' said the Governor, kindly. 'Give them chairs. So. They will recover immediately.'

'Yours, Nevill Comines,' continued the solicitor, 'is considered a more serious case. You were the Secretary, the most important member of the club. The evidence before the Court went to prove that you were also one of the most active. It is certain that you constantly took part in debates and proposals concerning matters of High Treason. Yet His Majesty is unwilling to take the life even of one whose projects, if successful, would have destroyed his own. He offers you a free pardon on condition of your serving him for five years in some branch of his forces, by sea or land. He gives you the choice of service.'

'I am His Majesty's grateful servant,' I replied, not knowing what else to say.

'Show your gratitude, young gentleman, by devotion to loyalty when you return to the duties of a civilian's life.'

'Lastly, George Bayssallance, I come to

you. It is true that you were the leader of the riot.'

'I was,' said George.

'You walked at the head of it carrying a drawn sword—a drawn sword—in the streets of London—on the Sunday.'

'I did,' said George. 'It is most true.'

'You have richly deserved the worst fate. Yet, His Majesty, graciously considering that no lives were lost, no property damaged, and that the riot was quelled before it became serious, offers you a free pardon on condition of being transported, for the remainder of your natural life, to one of His Majesty's settlements abroad.'

'God save the King!' said George. 'But, sir, I know not how I can accept that condition.'

'Not accept the condition?'

'Else,' said the Governor, 'you will be hanged on Monday. To-day is Thursday.'

'I am not my own master in the matter,' George explained. 'There is One higher than His Majesty. I mean the ALMIGHTY. It is His expressed will that I must die. Unless

I am assured to the contrary, I cannot accept this condition.'

'The man is mad,' cried the solicitor; George was mad, but not in the way he understood. 'Am I not here to signify the order of the King?'

'The sentence of the Judge,' said the Governor, 'expresses, when it is delivered, the will of the Lord; the pardon of the King shows the mercy of the Lord. What other assurance or revelation can you expect, Mr. Bayssallance? The days of revelation finished with the Book of Revelation.'

'No, no. I mean an inward assurance.'

'Is he of the Methodists? Is he one of those who have gone mad with enthusiasm?' asked Mr. White.

'Not to my knowledge,' said the Governor. 'Come, sir, do not stand in your own light. Transportation, to a temperate and pleasant climate, is a light punishment for a young and healthy man like yourself. Why, some of the transported convicts have sent for their sweethearts and are married. You yourself——'

'I have an express assurance,' George repeated. 'Gentlemen, in this case it is not my own life only that is concerned—it is another's.'

The Governor shook his head. 'Well,' he said, 'you will, perhaps, get that assurance after one more night in the condemned cell. Remove the prisoner, warder.' George bowed, and went off with a smiling face. 'You, gentlemen,' he turned to us, 'will go back to the State side ; you will be relieved of your fetters. You, Mr. Comines, will make your choice with as little delay as possible.'

We went back to our old quarters on the Master's side, the irons knocked off, the bitterness of death past and gone, rejoicing over our good fortune. Who so happy as three condemned convicts newly pardoned ? 'Why,' said the Templar, clapping me on the shoulder, 'you are already a free man. To serve in the King's army is liberty. Your five years of service will be nothing. Perhaps they may make you an officer. The war we are now waging promises to be long.

There will be marching to and fro and campaigning here and there. You will be winning glory on the field '—much glory, indeed, the private soldier wins !—' you will come home and tell of war's alarms.'

' As for you,' I said, ' your short imprisonment will be over in a few months. Then you will be free men.'

The first glow over, one began to examine into the situation more closely. Certainly it is better to march with a regiment than to hang on a gibbet. Life has always some sweetness. Yet at two-and-twenty, after the ease and comfort of London, the barrack has few attractions ; discipline is severe ; it is difficult to escape the lash of the cat, or at least the sergeant's stick ; drill is irksome ; a camp is rough ; the fare on a campaign is seldom abundant ; there are many fatigues and many dangers.

' When we do go out,' said the Templar, ' what shall we do next ? For my own part, I have no money and no trade ; my father hath renounced me. What shall I do ? '

' I, too, am cast away by my parents,' said

the Poet. 'Well, we will find something, I doubt not. Meantime, let us celebrate the loss of our chains with a bottle of port.'

In the end, when they came out of Newgate, they found themselves penniless and friendless in the streets. No one would employ a young gentleman fresh from prison. I found one of them a few years later when I returned home. It was the Templar. He was then employed in teaching caligraphy by day, and in the evening he played the fiddle at a drinking and dancing place near the Strand. Had it not been for the Society of Snugs, he might by this time have become a Judge, or King's Counsel at least. As for the Poet, you shall hear in due course what became of him.

The commutation of the sentence was due to none other than the Prebendary himself. With great difficulty he caused to be represented to His Majesty such extenuating facts as could be produced. He produced affidavits from three members of the club, who (under an assurance that their names would not be divulged unless under promise that no steps

should be taken) swore that the only violent
speech the day before the riot was that made
by the King's evidence himself, Richard
Archer. He also showed, by the same
evidence, that George Bayssallance had been
a member of the club no longer than that
single night, so that it was wrong to impute
unto the club the actions of this young man.
He further showed that the riot was not of a
dangerous character, but was rather a frolic
of mischievous boys, resulting in no losses,
or destruction of life or property. And then
he set forth plainly that George was a young
man of good character and loyal disposition,
who had become deranged through a love-
disappointment. In fact, his Reverence laid
before the King exactly the defence which
should have been laid before the Court, had
we engaged an attorney who knew anything
at all except the conduct of cases concerned
with burglaries, forgeries, and common shoplifting or sheep-stealing.

He prepared this case, therefore, with
great thoroughness, and caused it to be taken
in hand by one great man after another, until

it reached the King himself. And the well-known clemency of His Majesty, as well as the popular opinion that the Judge had been too severe in his charge and in his verdict, inclined him to extend his grace to the poor convicts.

'To you young gentlemen,' said the Prebendary, when he visited us on the afternoon of that day, ' you, who have still to serve an imprisonment of a few months, I recommend a course of serious self-examination. You will find that you have been betrayed by inexperience and ignorance (because even at two-and-twenty the judgment may go astray) into rashness amounting to madness ; you have foolishly tilted at strongholds which laugh at your puny efforts ; you have permitted yourselves to be allied with men of neither position, knowledge, nor character. What! You stoop to friendship with such as the man Richard Archer? These are grave offences. Ponder them, therefore.'

He shook his head, and bade them leave him alone with me.

' Nevill,' he said, ' I have taken advice, and

been at much trouble to find out what course
is best for you under the conditions of this
pardon. Five years' service in some part of
His Majesty's forces by sea or land. Consider.
Able seaman thou wilt never be. No, thou
canst not now begin to run about the rigging
of a ship, nor to learn the sailor's trade.
There are so-called landsmen on board every
ship—armourers, carpenters, cooks, and so
forth; but I think this will not do neither.
The companionship of sailors is rough and
rude; but that, I fear, one must not consider,
because, wherever we turn, the companionship is rough and rude. Let us consider the
army. It is now a time of war, and, unless
the Allies prove more successful than at
present they promise, the war may prove
long, and even disastrous. Well, if I were
a private soldier, I would rather follow the
flag afield than live in a garrison. In the
open field the living is uncertain, and the
sleeping is hard; there are many discomforts,
but to such a man as you, a man of books,
of quiet habits, the campaign will be more
tolerable than the barracks. There will be

no daily drill, no petty tyrannies of the
sergeant, no indignities to endure at the hand
of the officers; soldiers in time of war
become brothers, whether they are officers
or in the rank and file. True, one may be
shot or speared; one may take disease and
die; these are chances. Yet I think that we
may find something better than mere soldiering. Listen, therefore. I have inquired
farther; I have learned that another company
of marines is to be sent immediately to the
convict settlement of Botany Bay. They will
go out in charge of the next convict ships;
they will land with them and join the
garrison of the settlement. These men are
reported to lead a life of comparative ease
and comfort. They have few duties; the
convicts give them little trouble; some of
them live in cottages of their own; many of
them have their wives with them. I have
made application, therefore, for you to join
the regiment of Royal Marines. And I have
made further interest to have you appointed
to the company going out to New South
Wales. It will go hard, my poor boy, if I

cannot provide thee with a comfortable
voyage, an indulgent commanding officer, an
easy captain, and a sergeant whose interest it
shall be to keep thee out of trouble. If there
should chance to be an engagement or an
action, why—then I know that thou wilt do
thy duty as a man.'

I thanked him again for this fresh proof
of his kindness, which indeed knew no
bounds.

'I have again spoken to thy father, Nevill.
For the present he will not look upon thy face,
nor will he suffer any of the household to see
thee; not until the punishment is complete.
Yet his heart is softened, and I doubt not
that in the long run he may relent. I bring
thee a tender message from thy mother, with
which thou must be content. Sylvia, alas!
regardeth not anything.'

I asked him what of Archer, who had
given the evidence?

'That person,' replied the Brother of St.
Katherine's, ' disgraces the Society no longer.
We called a Chapter—it met this morning—
at which all the Brothers and Sisters were

present. We resolved that, seeing he had been for a long time, unknown to his employers, a member of a secret and seditious Society—that, by his own evidence, he had been present where violent discourses were held; that by the united testimony of three members, not arrested, and of the four prisoners, it was he himself, and none other, who had delivered the most seditious speech of all; and that it was he himself, and none other, who, knowing full well the character of the club, had persuaded George Bayssallance to become a member, and introduced him, the Society adjudged that he be forthwith expelled from his employment, and from the Precinct itself, as a person improper for the teaching of the young, and unfit to take part, even as a penitent, in the service of the Almighty.'

'That is something gained,' I said. 'He may yet learn the bitterness of the prison to which he brought us, his sworn brothers and companions.'

'The man is changed, however. He is strangely changed. He obeyed our summons,

and stood before us, but he behaved with a
new insolence. For, instead of waiting sub-
missively to hear our will, he told us that he
had come to lay down his post ; he would, he
said, be schoolmaster no longer, nor would he
play the organ any more ; henceforth the
world should hear of him in other and nobler
places—and so flung out of the room, and
hath now left the Precinct with his mother.
He will perhaps become a highwayman.
What other occupation is possible to a man
without friends, without money, and without
character ? Well, let him go for a knave.'

CHAPTER XXI

RICHARD ARCHER'S GOOD FORTUNE

THE man Archer did not propose to become a highwayman. The reason of his impudent bearing towards his employers was a thing totally unsuspected : a thing which could never have been guessed—one of those strange discoveries of which one reads in idle romances. You have read how the Wise Woman told his fortune from the cards. Wealth, rank, and authority, she said, were to come to him. You shall now hear how this part of her predictions came true. There was a sequel to the fortune, also hinted by the witch. This, also, you shall learn.

It was, again, the Wise Woman who revealed the thing to him. How she got the secret I know not ; but since I am not willing to believe that supernatural powers

can be attained by any person, I suppose
that, having been told the principal incident
by Archer's mother—that quiet and well-
behaved person, who lived with her son, and
still worked for the ladies of the Hospital—
she contrived, by means known only to
herself, to ferret out the rest. Remember
that it was Margery's business to learn everything about everybody, so that there was
not a person in the Precinct whose private
history she did not know—all the love affairs,
all the secrets, all the things—if any—of
which that person was ashamed, and would
fain conceal. Therefore I believe that, when
Mrs. Archer first came to the place with her
infant, Margery made haste to find out who
she was, and who was the father of her child.
Once you have won the confidence of a
woman, sooner or later she will tell you
everything you want to know. All that this
poor woman could tell about her husband,
therefore, she had told. If the witch knew
more, she must have ferreted it out for
herself.

Richard Archer went to her house one

evening about this time, in obedience to a message from her. But this time he went openly, and without attempt at concealment.

'Well, gammer,' he said, roughly, throwing himself into a chair. 'You want to see me. Well, I am here. What have you got to say?'

He was gloomy, because he daily expected that the Society whose servant he was would find out the part he had played at a certain trial.

'I do, young sir—young gentleman, I should say.'

'I am not a gentleman.'

'Wait, wait—many a strange thing happens. Do you remember the last time you came here? To be sure you do. You have never forgotten that evening. The old woman, to begin with, told you a great secret —a wonderful secret—a secret that made you twice the man you were before: such a secret as filled your whole soul with joy and pride. You pretended not to believe it. Well, was the old woman right? Evil Heart and Evil Eye—she said—was she right, my son? Was

the power there? Have you tried it and
proved it, and found it true? Have you ever
gone to the old woman and acknowledged
that she was right? These innocent people
whom you have yourself overwhelmed with
misfortune—do they bear witness to your
power?'

'Ay! sometimes I think it is true; but
what if I have such a power? It has proved
of no use to me. It won't bring me money or
buy anything for me.'

'Not a bit; you have used it for a vil-
lainous purpose, you see. Had you—but
never mind what you might have done. Since
you learned that you possessed that power, an
innocent girl has been afflicted with madness
—well-nigh to death, but not quite. Three
gallant young gentlemen are languishing in
prison and are disgraced for life; another
is lying in the condemned cell, and will be
hanged o' Monday, for all the world to see.
But, if I know my trade aright, he shall not
be hanged.'

'Did you send for me in order to tell me
this?'

'No; I have a great deal more to tell. Well, the Brothers and Sisters have found out at last, though none of them would read the reports of the trial, that the chief evidence was Richard Archer, their schoolmaster and organist, and to-morrow you will be haled before the Chapter and expelled. Sister Katherine came here to-day, talking about witchcraft—and told me so much. She thinks that you are bewitched as well as the rest. Ho!—ho! And what will you do when you are turned out? You cannot go into the market and be hired for your Evil Eye! And the common people in the Precinct have found out by this time that you turned informer. They swear that they will have your blood. An informer—and living in their midst! Have a care lest a bludgeon end thy days for this precious day's work.'

'Tut; do I look afraid of their bludgeons?'

She looked at him with the admiration which old women openly bestow upon young and straight-limbed men, and she laughed.

'No,' she said; 'if you have to fight, you

can protect yourself. Well, he will be satisfied
when he sees you.'

'Who is he—who is to see me?'

'Wait a bit—wait a bit.'

'They will turn me out, you say. Very
like. Will that give them back their sons?
Will that bring back things as they were
before you told me—if that was true?'

'Why, any man can compass revenge and
hatred. Love, alone, is the gift of God. Evil
Eye or not, any one can work mischief, young
gentleman——'

'Again—I am no gentleman.'

'Young gentleman, I say. Do you think
I do not mean my own words? Why, I
promised wealth, station, and authority.
These, I say, I promised; you remember so
much. Now the time has come for you to
receive them.'

'I am in no mood for trifling,' said the
man. 'Wealth will satisfy me; station is
impossible; and, for authority, why, I have
the past behind me. The former schoolmaster
of St. Katherine will hardly be received into
a place of authority. Give me the money,' he

held out his hand. 'Hand over the wealth you promise,' he added. 'What is it? A new crown-piece?'

'I mean what I say; but, on conditions.'

'What conditions?'

'Is your envy or hatred of these people satisfied?'

'That's as it may be.'

'Why, you have done as much as any reasonable man could desire for his worst enemy. You have brought them all to death's door. You should be satisfied.' The man smiled. He had certainly seen his victims overwhelmed with disaster. 'The only condition is, that you cease to compass evil for them, and think of them no longer. It will not be difficult, because you are now going to leave the Precinct; you will enter into other company much greater even than that of the Brothers. Oh! it will be easy for you to forget them—unless you are in love with Sylvia.'

'I am no longer in love with her—I never was, but I thought to spite the other man. Let them who will fall in love with her lan-

guishing blue eyes and her soft voice. Give
me a woman with a spirit of her own—a
woman I can fight and subdue.'

'Why, then, we are agreed. Give up, I
say, your malice and persecution, and suffer
them to recover in the best way they can.
Do you promise? Mind—wealth, authority,
and station, is what I have to give you. But
you must forget your rancour ; else you shall
have none of these things.'

'Why,' said Archer, slowly. 'I don't
believe you can do what you say—how can
such power be yours? But, if you make me
rich, I don't know—I say—I don't promise.'

'Then you shall not be rich,' the old
woman interrupted him ; ' go away ; remain
poor ; go out into the street and starve. You
shall have nothing. Go. You are a devil.'
She spoke so fiercely, and her eyes glittered
so terribly, that Archer was shaken.

'Is it real?' he asked.

She made no reply.

'Tell me! Is it real? Come, then, I
promise—I swear. I will pursue them with
no more animosity. From this moment I

renounce it all. If I begin again take from me that wealth which you have promised.'

'Kiss the book,' said the witch, earnestly. He took the Testament which she offered him, and kissed it solemnly. 'So, now you have sworn. If now you break that oath you will lose all. Nay,' she added, 'for aught I know you will lose all some time or other.'

'Give me a long rope, but let me feel rich once before I die! Let me know what it is to buy every pleasure and enjoy, enjoy, enjoy, if it is only for a twelvemonth. Then let me die, and it will be with a cheerful heart.'

'I will give you more, a great deal more, than you desire or expect. Listen now, young gentleman—young gentleman, I say—what did your mother teach you about her marriage?'

'She was truly married in church, but to a villain who was married already. His name was Archer, and he was a sailor. Doubtless he is dead long ago, cast away upon a cannibal coast, perhaps, and devoured by savages, for his sins.'

'Suppose he told her the truth when he

said that he was single. Suppose, therefore, that you are his legitimate son. Suppose, further, that he was not poor, but rich.'

Richard Archer sprang to his feet.

' Suppose that he is not dead, but lives, and that his wealth is of that kind which descends from father to son.'

' Is this true ? '

' It is, indeed, most true. Your mother is that man's lawful wife ; you are his lawful son and heir ; you will inherit his estates and his title.'

' His title ? '

' He is no less than a nobleman. He is a Viscount. His name is the Right Honourable the Lord Viscount Aldeburgh, formerly Rear-Admiral in His Majesty's Navy.'

' Does my mother know this ? '

' No, she does not. You shall tell her. But first see his lordship, your noble father.'

Richard Archer sat down again.

' My noble father ! my noble father !' he repeated. ' I am to see my noble father ! I am to go to him in these clothes ! I suppose he is dressed in satin, and surrounded by his

people in livery. How will he receive me?
When I tell him that I have been schoolmaster to a charity school, and that I have
been King's Evidence in a trial for High
Treason, how will he receive me then?
When he sees my boorish manners, how will
he receive me?'

'You need tell him nothing about yourself. You are educated; you will go to him
dressed as becomes your rank; you are handsome, and will become your clothes. When
you have got a sword by your side and lace
at your wrists, your manners will become as
fine as your clothes.'

'How is this story to be proved?'

'It is proved already. There is a gentleman of the law, a proctor who practises in
St. Katherine's Court, a very learned person,
who is so wise that when he wishes to learn
the future, and whether he shall be successful or no in any enterprise, he comes to ask
my advice, and as I advise him, so he acts.
A prudent, careful, and far-seeing gentleman!
He is therefore prosperous. To this gentleman, who is secret as the grave, have I

opened the business, and he has now discovered the whole. First, he knows a man
who was at the time his lordship's valet,
and remembers the circumstances ; how his
master came to the City disguised as a
merchant sea officer, in love with a City
tradesman's daughter ; and how he married
her openly in the church of All Hallows the
Great, Thames Street ; and how, after a
month or so, he went off and deserted his
wife. Now, young gentleman (who will be
a lord before many years are out), the first
wife of his lordship, from whom he was
separated, died a week or two before he
married your mother. The certificate of the
death and of the marriage prove this fact.
Believe me, your mother, if she had her rights,
would be the Lady Aldeburgh. Your mother
has letters from her lover, which are signed
with his name, Stephen Archer. But, indeed,
there is no doubt whatever.'

'No doubt,' he echoed. 'She says there
is no doubt whatever.'

'All is prepared. This good proctor first
wrote a letter to his lordship, and has since

seen him. He says that your father, who is
confined to his chair with a stroke so that he
can no longer use his legs, stand upright, or
walk, first fell into a violent rage—his temper
is well known—swearing that the thing was
a conspiracy. But he presently condescended
to listen to the facts, and though he doth not
acknowledge and confess that he was indeed
married to your mother, he is so far moved
that he consents to receive you.'

'All this without my learning anything of
the matter.'

'What need to tell you until the business
was completed? Well, to cut the story short,
my lord is now ready to be convinced, my
friend is quite sure, that you are his son, but
he will not yet acknowledge you. He will
first see you, converse with you, watch you.
It appears, luckily, that he has quarrelled
with those who look to succeed him. If you
do not please him you will have to wait until
his death, which will not be long delayed,
because he is subject to heart pains which
will kill him soon, besides his stroke. Do
your best to please him. Go gaily dressed,

let your talk be of things that most he loves :
wine and feasting, music and play acting,
singing women and dancing women. You
can play to him, and he can himself make
music on instruments—even the bloodthirsty
spider loves music ; play not the things which
you play on Sundays in the church ; Psalms
and such he does not desire ; play songs
about love and all kinds of profane delights.
And hark ye, do not hang your head ; forget
the school and the organ gallery ; show a
dancing leg and a laughing eye—— What ?
—you have too dark a look. You brood
over your lowliness. The time for hatred
and envy is gone ; you are going to become
the richest and most fortunate young gentleman in all London. Hold up your head,
therefore, and look cheerful, and above all,
show yourself a lad of mettle. Be not afraid
of him—— What ? He is a devil, as is well
known. But so are you, Richard Archer, as
I know. Stand up to him, therefore. He
cannot live more than a year or two if things
come to the worst.'

' When am I to go ? '

'You will go to-morrow. Wait,' she fumbled among the folds of her gown and produced a letter, folded. 'That is for you; it is from your friend the proctor; take it, and now go. Wealth and station and authority—all these I promised, all these I have given. How long you keep them, or how you lose them, is your own affair.'

This is the reason why, when the Chapter sent for their schoolmaster, he treated that venerable body with a disrespect the like of which they had never before experienced; but he was not, as they suspected, resolved to try his fortune as a highwayman.

That day he left the Precinct, with his mother, and never was seen in the place again.

CHAPTER XXII

A SUDDEN CHANGE

GEORGE went back to the Press Yard and
the condemned cell, his end being now
certain, and fixed for Monday morning.

As for me, I was presently transported by
boat under guard of two men belonging to
my regiment (as I must now call it) of Royal
Marines. I sat between these two fellows
and told myself that I must now put on the
scarlet coat with the stiff white collar, the
black hat with the white plume, the pipe-
clayed shoulder-belt decorated with an
anchor, and that I must now learn to hold
myself as upright as the Lieutenant, carry
a musket and bayonet, and very likely go to
sea and fight the French. But by great good
fortune I had no fighting during my time of
service. So I became a recruit, and was

placed in the awkward squad, and began to learn the drill. A man should begin soldiering early if he would enjoy the work. But one must make the best of what cannot be avoided, and I hope that I became in a few weeks a tolerable soldier. The life of the rank and file is hard, but then they are born to endure hardness. The conversation that one hears is coarse, but then these fellows are accustomed to coarseness. After Newgate, indeed, it was almost pious. At first there was a certain prejudice against me, partly because I was a gentleman, and partly because these honest lads love not the smell of prison, which still clings to the gaol bird, but they found me harmless, and this prejudice wore off.

In the barracks there were no newspapers, and I heard for some time nothing of what had happened. Moreover, as I was in some sort a prisoner, I had no liberty outside, and could not for some time learn any news. Presently, however, I procured a paper with a list of the hangings of that Monday morning when George was to have suffered. Heavens!

The name was not among them. In another place of the same paper I read as follows:

'George Bayssallance, the fortunate proprietor of Oak Apple Dock, lately mate on an East Indiaman, who was to have been hanged for High Treason, has accepted (though at first he refused) his King's clemency, and goes out to Botany Bay for life. His Dock is confiscated, and will be sold by the Crown. To a pretty market has this young man brought his pigs.'

Afterwards, I learned what happened.

George returned to the place from which he was brought, showing the same resolution as before, and the same unflagging cheerfulness. A condemned convict may be reckless; he often cracks jokes (especially in his cups) on the fate that awaits him ; he may be penitent ; he may be despairing ; he may moan and lament ; he may be insensible, until the last moment, as to his position ; but a condemned convict who is always cheerful, and apparently happy, is a thing wholly out of the common experience. No one had ever seen the like of such a convict. I suppose, however, that George is the only man who ever expected hanging with happiness, because it was the will of the Lord, and the only way to make his mistress happy.

Nay; to all the persuasion and exhortation of the Prebendary—whose advice at other times would have been a command— George turned an ear of mulish obstinacy, and in a matter of such vast importance as the Lord's will he pretended to know better than the learned Divine. It was still, 'By your leave, sir,' or, 'With submission, sir. I am inwardly assured that I am obeying orders. It is God's command, laid upon me to die—and it is not for me either to disobey or to choose the manner of my end.'

In this extremity he was visited by Sister Katherine, despite the Lieutenant, who would not so much as suffer his son's name to be mentioned any more than at the Master's house my name was tolerated. He had no longer a son.

' Try, in the name of the Lord,' said the Prebendary. ' Move him, if you can. For my part, I cannot. The boy loved you always. Go, Sister Katherine.'

The sight of the Press Yard with its crowd of wretches, both bond and free, those who were to die, and those who were to live a little longer, all drinking and roystering together, filled her soul with terror.

' Take me, boy,' she cried, ' take me from this dreadful place.'

'We have but small choice,' George replied. 'There is the Day Room, which is as crowded as the Press Yard. There is also my cell. We can sit there retired enough. It is not, to be sure, so cheerful as your own parlour, Sister Katherine. But you can sit down on the bed, and at least you will not see these poor wretches. I believe,' he added, ' that they are sometimes noisy ; but I regard them not ; besides, they are for the most part rogues, and will soon be hanged—all of them—and drinking is their only pleasure. Since they will not repent, let them drink.'

' They are wretches ! Oh ! George—to think——'

Then she burst into tears.

He led her to the gloom of his cell, and here she wept, bewailing all that had happened. When she recovered, she addressed herself to the task of persuading him to live.

'Oh! my dear,' she said at last, when all had failed, holding him by the hand, 'my own boy George, of whom we have been so proud! No one like our George in all the world—so good as well as so comely. And now, to think of it—oh! only to think of it! To end in Newgate—in this dreadful place!'

'To me it is not dreadful, because I know that it is the will of the Lord.'

'The will of the Lord! The will of the Lord! This is the hundredth time.' She flung away his hand and sprang to her feet. 'Who are you that you should know the will of the Lord better than the clergyman? How do you know this will of the Lord? Is it written on paper? How has it come to you? What angel brought the message? The Lord's will! Not so. It is your will—your own wicked, masterful, obstinate will. Will is the cause of love, they say. Well, "He

that will not when he may, When he wills
he shall have nay." For the girl's sake, say
you. How will it help the poor girl when
she recovers—if ever she does recover—to
know that you flung away your life for a
silly whim? Lord's will, indeed! Oh! grant
me patience!'

She sat down on the bed again, wringing
her hands.

'Who shall persuade this mule—this stubborn ass—this boy with a bee in his bonnet?
Women, pigs, and bees cannot be turned, they
say. What? You think Sylvia will be
pleased to hear that you have been hanged by
the neck, and your bones an anatomy at Surgeons' Hall! Why, sorrow comes unsent for,
as we all know; but sorrow pays no debt.
Grant me patience!'

'Truly,' said George, 'I am right sorry to
anger you.'

'Anger? Anger? The boy is going to
be hanged by the neck till he is dead, and he
thinks he will anger me. Child! it kills me.
I feel thy rope round my own neck: I am
ashamed to stir abroad: the rogues of St.

Katherine's Stairs look after me. They say,
" There is the woman whose nephew is to be
hanged o' Monday." It kills your father.
None of us can hold up our heads any more,
that is certain. We never can : we are ruined.
And he talks of angering us ! '

'It is worse for you than it is for me,' said
George, ' because I am doing the Lord's will ;
but you——'

' Oh ! ' she cried. ' Again ! He says it
again ! Never was there any man before who
wanted to be hanged. Art afraid of growing
old—that thou must be hanged when thou art
young ? Yet half an hour's hanging hinders
five weeks' riding, as they say. But it is no
use talking. Yet, to young and old alike, life
is sweet : while there is life there is hope.
What ? Oh ! It is horrible ! It is dreadful !
There are no words for this madness. " The
Lord's will ! The Lord's will ! " Oh !——'

' Not madness,' said George ; ' but sober
sense.'

'It is witchcraft,' said Sister Katherine.
' I said so at the very outset, and I say so
again. It is witchcraft, rank witchcraft—such

witchcraft as I never thought to see in my
lifetime. First, it is Sylvia who is bewitched.
She must hate the man she loves. Then it is
the lover who is bewitched. He must die to
make her well again. Well? What is it to
be well? It is to love him again—and he is
dead. What health is this? Then the poor
boy Nevill is bewitched, and he must needs
turn the world topsy-turvy, and so brings his
own neck into danger, and now wears the
King's uniform, and carries a pike on board
ship as a Marine. There's a fine end to come
to! And now thou art so mulish that nothing
will serve but —— Oh! lad, lad—George,
my George——' She changed her note, and
burst into weeping and sobbing. 'Live, my
dear. Only consent to live, and Sylvia will
recover. Consider, thou must go away out
of her sight. She will recover, and perhaps,
even yet, all will be well, though I know not
how. But live—if it is at the other end of the
world, among the naked savages—live. Oh!
my boy, thou must not die before me. Live!
Still 'tis day while the sun shines. Only live
—only consent to live!'

He was much moved by her tears and importunity—more moved than by anything that had been said to him. But he remained in his mulishness. It was the Lord's will. He could not fly in the face of the Lord's will; and, for Sylvia's sake, death was nothing. So she sat weeping in the dark cell for awhile longer, and then came away. That was Saturday afternoon. On the Monday he must die.

But there was to be one more suppliant, who would move his heart and change his mind.

You have seen how the man Richard Archer conversed with the old woman, and what grand things she promised him. You know what she thought : how she laid the whole burden of these woes upon an Evil Eye and an Evil Heart. I repeat that I have never been able to believe that any man should have so much power entrusted to him. We ought not to believe such things. They are pagan : they belong to the days of superstition : they consist not with the doctrines of the Christian Church. But things which happened must be related in due order.

It was on the Wednesday evening that he held the discourse with the Wise Woman. On Thursday morning he visited the proctor, of whom mention has been made. After this he attended the Chapter, and behaved with the strange insolence of which you have heard. On the same day he took his mother away with him, and returned no more.

On Friday morning Sylvia, who had gone to bed heavy and melancholy, as was her wont, slept all night long and into the morning. At seven her mother found her sleeping, and left her, being unwilling to disturb her. At nine she was still asleep, and at ten. Towards noon she awoke. Usually she awoke with a start and a sense of pain, which only increased as she returned to consciousness : usually she awoke with a memory of evil dreams and the foreboding of a miserable day. This morning she awoke gently, with the sweetness of a night undisturbed, and—what next? She sat up in bed and looked around her, wondering. She rubbed her eyes. What had happened? For she felt a strange sense of relief. Her head was light again : her heart was light : her limbs were light. She was frightened. She cried aloud.

'Ah! mother, mother—what is it? What is happening to me?'

'Child!' Her mother ran to take her hand. 'What is happening? Oh! I know not. Is there new pain?'

'No—no—— What is it? I feel no pain, but pleasure. I feel light again. The pain is gone. Mother, am I dying? Is this the beginning of sweet Heaven? I feel light again, and happy. I can speak. Something has been taken away from me. Am I dying?'

'I know not. Oh! my dear, I know not.'

'Where is George? If I am to die, let me die with my hand in his!'

'My dear, why talk of dying? There is a colour in thy cheeks again. Thy head is cool. Thy pulse is regular. Death? Nay, I think, rather, it is life.'

She brought out a bottle and gave her a few drops of cordial. Sylvia drank, and sat upright.

'If this is death——' she murmured,
waiting for her last moment.

But while she waited she became aware
that not the chill hand of death, but the warm
breath of returning life was upon her. For
the first time for six months her cheek was
touched with colour, her eyes were soft, her
head was held erect.

'Mother,' she said, 'I shall not die, but
live. I have been—I know not how—in some
strange dream, that has held me, and filled my
mind '—she shuddered—'spectres and wicked
words, and—and—I cannot remember. I
have loathed to look upon George. Now all
are gone. Oh ! will they come back again ?
Mother, mother, call George to me—quick—
quick—before they return ! There is none
but George who can save me. Oh ! bring
him soon. Where is he ? Where is he ?'

Her mother fell on her knees, and raised
her hands. 'Oh, Lord God !' she said,
humbly. 'We thank Thee—we praise Thee
—oh, we thank Thee——' and so over and over
again, being beside herself for joy and gratitude, and not able to find any other words.

Presently she called her husband, and sent for Sister Katherine, and they all rejoiced together. Then she must be fed so as to become strong, and they made an egg-posset for her, and watched while she took it, how her thin arms seemed to fill out, and her wan face to brighten, and her lips and eyes began to smile —catching each other by the hand, with joyful ejaculations and words of thanksgiving— that the child was raised from the dead.

Then she arose and dressed herself, and came downstairs walking strong and upright, and while they all rejoiced together the good Prebendary arrived, full of sorrow over George's obstinacy, and he must learn what had happened, and must share in the general joy.

'But George — where is George?' she asked again.

'My child,' said the Prebendary, as he looked at the others and no one spoke, 'much has happened since the strange and unexampled illness fell upon you.'

'Witchcraft!' said Sister Katherine, stoutly. 'Talk not to her of illness. Witch-

craft, I say, even in your presence, Prebendary. Witchcraft.'

'Indeed,' said my mother, 'it becomes
not a simple woman to believe more than
is allowed and enjoined by her spiritual pas-
tors and masters, but witchcraft it seems
to me. Nothing less than witchcraft will ex-
plain it.'

'For aught we know,' said the clergyman,
'demoniac possession may be permitted again
in these latter days. Perhaps it has been suffered to continue from primitive times. Nay,
in the Middle Ages we read of exorcisms and
the casting out of devils, a thing which we have
been too ready, perhaps, to set down among
the superstitious fables and beliefs of the time.
However, for the moment let us not consider
the cause while we solemnly thank the Father
of All for His great mercy in restoring to life
one who was well-nigh like unto the dead.
Learn, my child, without further explanation
that George is now in grievous trouble and in
great peril of his life.'

'George in trouble?'

'Briefly, the presumptuous boy took it

upon himself to construe a wild fancy of the brain into an express assurance of the Lord's will. He had the temerity, I say, to believe that the Lord, who hath spoken once for all through His own Son and the Apostles for the guidance of Holy Church, did actually speak to him, and ordered him to throw away his life.'

Sylvia understood not one word of this.

'He believed, in short, that the only way to secure thy recovery, child, was himself to lose his own life.'

'Oh! George would die for me—he would die for me?' Sylvia murmured, clasping her hands; 'for my unworthy sake?'

'I say that he conceived this belief, and still holds it. He is not a reprobate or a cast-away, and, therefore, he would not commit suicide, but he would and did expose his life to every danger. And, as each in succession was encountered with no hurt to himself at all —each escape being, rightly interpreted, a Providential rebuke—he braved the wrath of Heaven to such a height as to lead a riot in the streets of London, a mob of disorderly wretches bawling for the overthrow of the King, the Constitution, and the Church.'

'George lead a mob?'

'Even so—wherefore he now lies in New-gate Gaol.'

'George in Newgate Gaol?'

'And under sentence of death! The King's clemency he hath refused—for thy sake, Sylvia—and, if he still remains stubborn, he must die on Monday.'

Then Sylvia arose. She who but yesterday was so weak that she could not stand, was now strong and able to walk and endure fatigue. Love lent her strength.

'Let me go to him. Oh!'—she laughed and cried together—' it was for my sake. Who would think that a man would die for the sake of a foolish girl?'

'They are so made,' said Sister Katherine. 'Sit down, child. I will go to the prison and carry George the good news. Sit down and rest and get strong again.'

'I am strong—I am strong and well. Let me go to him at once. Oh, let him suffer no longer. None but I must save him from the death he would have for me. Oh!—let me go. Let me bid him live—and if he can still find it in his heart to love the unhappy girl who has caused this trouble——'

'Child,' said the Prebendary, solemnly, 'I, too, will go with thee. Thou shalt take to this thy lover the life and healing which GOD hath placed in thy hands for him.'

CHAPTER XXIII

GEORGE GIVES WAY

IT was growing towards twilight on Saturday
afternoon. The Press Yard and the Day Room
were filled with a crowd of the friends and relations of the condemned convicts, many of
whom were to suffer on the Monday morning.
As the day of execution approaches, the friends
of those about to die crowd more thickly round
them, thinking in a rude, but hearty, fashion
to console their last hour by the assurance of
friendliness, by the sympathy of their presence,
and by continual gifts of strong liquor. Besides friendship, they are actuated by the
curiosity of impending fate; round each
miserable gallows-bird, converted for the nonce
into a hero, is gathered a crowd of admirers;
they applaud his braggart resolution—his
assumed recklessness—they exhort him to

show as bold a front outside the prison as he
maintains in the Press Yard—let there be no
falling-off at the last moment; let him ap-
proach the presence of his Judge with a laugh
and an oath. So they fortify him with every
consolation except the only one of real use.
Everybody knows what such people say. We
must all die once, to-day or to-morrow, it is
small odds which. Let us be thankful for a
longish rope; your turn to-day, brother, mine
to-morrow. A short life and a merry one.
Pass the pannikin; keep it up to the end.
Why, such a day as this brings out a man's
true friends. Saw one ever such a crowd to
say good-bye? It shows the greatness of the
hero. The world will look out on Monday
morning, when there will be a gathering to
do honour to the occasion, such as was never
seen before but at a Coronation. Many a
younger man has gone before. It is a good
thing to remember what a long spell has been
your lot. To be hanged is no worse, but a
great deal better, than to die of a putrid throat
or a rheumatic fever. If everybody had his
choice, all would die by hanging when they

could no longer live in pleasure. Hanging—
mere hanging in the air by the neck—is reported, by those who have been cut down,
half-hanged, as not painful, but pleasing ; they
have spoken of sweet sounds, as of music in
the ears, and of a falling to sleep, and of
fancies, such as that one is borne upwards on
feathery clouds like downy beds, or lying in
soft waters, or floating in a bark down a gentle
stream. Such talk as this goes on for ever in
that dismal place ; while all the time the bottle
or the tankard passes round till the poor
wretches lose their wits, and forget the part
that on the morrow they must play.

One more day, and then the last look at
the light of the sun. One more chance of repentance—one more service of prayer and
contrition in the chapel, and then the Funeral
Service read before them when they shall
walk in procession through the little portico.
I have already shown that however much a
condemned convict may drink, he can never
quite forget his doom. I have seen one at his
very worst, when he reels and cannot speak or
stand, suddenly grow ashy pale, and tremble,

and pass his hands over his eyes. He has seen before him the gibbet, he has seen the dangling rope. His looks are haggard, though his words are brave ; his eyes roll in wildness, though he professes to have no fear ; because that terrible vision never leaves him.

At the end of the narrow yard, apart from the rest, George stood alone leaning against the wall. You might have taken him for a spectator—one wholly unconcerned with the place, and pleased to watch the humours of the crowd—but for his irons. On his face was stamped—not a brazen insensibility of one too stupid to be moved by any terror—but a calm serenity, a cloudless cheerfulness, as of a soul at perfect peace with its Maker and itself ; one who knows that death is best for him, and ordered by the Lord as the means by which his mistress is to recover. Nay, his very face shone in this dark court as if the rays of the sun fell upon him—it was glorified by the strength of his faith. And as for the noisy crowd around him, he looked upon them with eyes that saw, and saw not.

Those eyes of his really saw, and had seen

for a long time, nothing but a thin pale girl, propped by pillows and cushions, wasting away in her chair, silent and sad, until the knell of St. Sepulchre's, which rang him into his grave, should ring her again to life and joy. A strange fancy of the brain! But I have told you all along that this is a strange book—the history of a Marvel.

This serenity, however, was to be disturbed ; this cheerfulness was to be changed, and that in a manner the most unexpected of any.

' George ! '

He heard his name called and he lifted his head, because he knew the voice, and he thought that the call came from that spectre of the sick girl in the chair.

' George ! '

Again he moved uneasily, because the voice sounded so clear and strong, and the sick girl of his imagination showed no sign of motion and was certainly not calling him.

Before him, unregarded, stood two gentlewomen ; one middle-aged and somewhat short of stature, fat, and well-nourished, as the

physicians say ; the other a tall slight figure,
wrapped in a shawl and her face covered by
the flap of her hat. As he moved not and
made no sign, she tossed back her hat and
laid her hand in his and looked up. Then
he started and saw her and recognised her.
Heavens ! It was Sylvia's voice; it was Sylvia's
face ; it was the touch of Sylvia's hand. Not
Sylvia as he saw her last, shrinking from him
with eyes of loathing ; but his own Sylvia ;
meeting his eyes with looks of love and sweetness. Oh ! The love in those tender eyes !
The sweetness of those blue eyes ! The re-
freshment of their soft light to his poor ship-
wrecked soul ! Sylvia ! Sylvia standing before
him restored, and in her right mind !

At this unexpected sight he could not
speak. He gazed as one in a dream—nay, he
thought at first that it must be a ghost or
image of that sweet lady sent by Heaven's
grace to comfort his soul before it should leave
its earthly clay. Amidst the noise and ribaldry
of the scene around him, who could expect
that such a sight could be aught but a
vision ?

She took his silence for reproach. 'George!' she cried again, 'have you no word of welcome for me? Am I clean forgotten? Nay—nay, I deserve this silence and more. Oh, George!'—she threw herself upon her knees and caught his hand. 'Forgive me— oh! forgive me, my dear. I have been mad ; some evil spirit held my soul. But he has now left me—never to return. Oh! my poor dear, 'tis I—none other—am the cause of all. Forgive me !'

But for reply, he only stared, with open mouth. Remember that he was entirely possessed with the belief that no other way was open for Sylvia's recovery save through his own death. It was the madness of love. He still thought of the girl, pale, feeble, sitting among her pillows in her arm-chair. There, he had fully persuaded himself, she would sit until his death, when she would instantly re- cover. Well, he was not yet dead ; he had about thirty hours still to live, and yet she was before him, the colour returned to her cheek, and her eyes bright with love and sorrow and

self-reproach! Therefore he thought that he
was dreaming or gone mad.

'George,' said Sister Katherine, seizing his
arm and shaking him, 'have you become blind
and deaf and dumb? Why, here is your old
sweetheart on her knees before you. Look at
her, man—as plain as a pack-saddle! What?—
where is now the Lord's will? You must die
for Sylvia to recover—must you? Nothing
short would serve—oh! nothing short of that.
You must die! Oh, for patience!' She shook
him again by the arm.

'George!' cried the girl again.

'You must hang for her to get well!
'Twas the Lord's will!' She kept on shaking
him with both hands, because Sister Katherine
being little, and George being big, all her
efforts shook him but little. 'Look at her,
man! Why—is he mad? Does he think she
is a ghost? Look, I say—take her hand.
Stand up, Sylvia; give him both thy hands.
So, stoop down, great FOOL, and kiss thy
sweetheart.'

With these words Sister Katherine re·
called him to his senses. He obeyed. He

stooped and kissed her—once—twice—thrice——

'Sylvia!' he said, 'what does this mean? In the name of GOD, tell me what does it mean?'

'It means that you will live and not die,' said Sister Katherine. 'Quick! send for the Governor, make submission before it shall be too late. Oh! hasten! hasten.'

'George does not understand, as yet,' said Sylvia, gently. 'Take me out of this noisy place, George ; take me to some place where we can talk, and I will tell you what it means.'

He led her to his own cell. 'Twas next to that where lay a murderer doomed to die on the Monday. He was guarded by two warders, and made to live on bread and water. His groans and lamentations could be plainly heard in the next cell. Sister Katherine remained at the door while those hapless lovers talked within. Was there ever heard of so strange a place for the renewing of love as a condemned cell in Newgate?

What they said matters nothing. When

they came out, presently, Sylvia's face was full
of joy and happiness.

George it was who now looked troubled ;
he who had hitherto shown no sign of anxiety
now trembled in his limbs, and his face showed
every mark of eagerness and disquiet—even
of terror.

'Well?' said Sister Katherine. 'What
shall we say, now, of the Lord's will?'

'I must hasten to accept the King's
clemency,' said George. 'Let me see the
Governor quickly.'

'The Prebendary is now with him. There
will be no delay.'

'I stifle in this place, I cannot breathe.
The air chokes me,' he cried, who an hour before had been the most cheerful habitant of
the prison. 'The company of these wretches
drives me mad. Sylvia! my dear, this place
is not proper for thee. Leave me until I can
in some fitter spot——'

'Nay, George, what is fit for you is fit for
me.'

What more? That evening he sat again

in his former room on the State side, with two
of his former companions, the Templar and the
Oxonian, who were completing their term of
imprisonment ; his irons were knocked off; he
was once more a free man—if that can be
called freedom when one is taken to the hulks,
there to abide until the next transport should
set sail for the convict settlement across the
ocean.

It was about three weeks later that I,
being still in Deptford Dockyard, received the
news that I was ordered for active service.
At the same time I received a letter from the
Prebendary, my patron.

'I have been successful,' he told me, 'in
procuring your appointment to a company of
Marines going out as a guard on a convict
ship and as garrison of the convict settlement
of Botany Bay. This appointment will at
least save you from the dangers of war. I
have also made some interest in your behalf
with the officers under whom you will serve.
You may rely upon lenient treatment and on
such consideration as is possible for one in

your position. I need not point out to you the necessity of keeping silence on those political opinions—those Republican doctrines—which I hope you have finally abandoned ; and I hope I need not exhort you to a cheerful and ready obedience to the rules of the service and the discipline of the ship.

'I have now to convey to you the good news that your sister Sylvia has recovered her health of mind and her strength of body as miraculously and suddenly as she lost them both. This took place two days before that appointed for George's execution. The new aspect of things restored him also to a true sense of his position ; he made haste to accept the King's clemency, and is now lying in the hulks awaiting his transportation to the same place whither you are bound. The Dock at Redriff which we, in our shortness of vision, expected to make so handsome a provision for him and his family, is now confiscated, and will be sold by the Crown ; he himself is transported to the new settlements for the whole term of his natural life. How this will end as regards Sylvia I know not yet ; perhaps

he may, at some distant date, should he be
preserved from the perils which await him,
obtain a remission of this sentence; but that
will certainly not be yet.

'When your term of service expires you
must return straightway. It may be that the
righteous anger of your father will then be
softened, and that he will be disposed to
forgiveness; at present he cannot so much as
bear to think that his only son should have
been tried for High Treason.

'If an opportunity arrives of sending
letters home, do not fail to keep me acquainted
with news of your welfare. Through me you
can also communicate with your mother and
your sister.

'The settlement whither you are both
bound is laid down on the maps as it
was examined by the greatest of circumnavi-
gators as part of a prodigious great island or
continent, which may very well be considered
as the long-sought-for Terra Australis, or
southern country, but I know not of what
extent is the settlement itself. Should you
happily meet George, I hope that you will

exhort each other to patience and the en-
durance of hardships in that foreign land.

'Farewell, my son. I pray that these
trials may lead thy heart still upward.
Neglect not the duties and discipline of the
Church, and amid naked savages, wild beasts,
and torrid heats, remain resigned, patient,
and of a good heart.'

The ship on which I was placed was the
Golden Grove, 450 tons, one of the transports
purchased by the Government. She had on
board a full complement of sailors and a
guard of Marines, consisting of the captain,
two lieutenants, two sergeants, two corporals,
one drummer, and thirty-six privates, of whom
I was one. She was fitted for the accommodation of two hundred and five convicts, who
were provided with hammocks on the lower
deck, slung side by side, so that at night the
lying would be closer than is pleasant. As
yet the convicts had not come on board, nor
any of our officers except a single lieutenant
of Marines. The *Golden Grove* was one of a
fleet of six transports to be convoyed by
H.M.S. *Dædalus*, and the number of con-

victs to be sent out was in all over eight
hundred.

When all was ready the prisoners were
brought on board from the hulks, where they
lay waiting for their embarkation. They
came alongside in boats well guarded, and a
miserable-looking company they were, unshaven, unwashed, pale with their long con-
finement in prison, ragged, and half fed.
Some of them, though we were supposed to
take none with us but the able-bodied and
the strong, were so reduced that they had to
be carried up the companion. Sea-sickness
finished off most of them a few days later.
My post, while they embarked, was on the top
of the ladder, armed with a loaded musket
and fixed bayonet. Now, as the men came
up one after the other, I espied among them
—indeed, I was not surprised at all—none
other than George himself. He who had
gone through the horrors of the condemned
cell with cheerfulness and no apparent loss of
health, now, when there was no longer a
gallows at the end, came slowly up the ladder,
the pale ghost of himself. Fever was on his

brow, and misery in his eyes. The convict companions among whom he had to pass his days and nights shamed him; his exile weighed upon him. He who had faced death cheerfully because he was dying for Sylvia, was now in danger of despair because he was going to the uttermost parts of the earth without her.

'Courage, George!' I whispered as he passed.

He started. He hardly knew me in my uniform—stiff and pipe-clayed.

'Do not speak,' I went on. 'Cheer up. We are on board the same ship; we shall find an opportunity; we are bound to the same place.'

'Pass on, prisoners. Pass on——' cried the sergeant.

CHAPTER XXIV

LORD ALDEBURGH

RICHARD ARCHER, therefore, left the Precinct, accompanied by his mother, and took boat to the Temple Stairs, carrying such slender baggage as constituted their whole worldly effects. He was now about to commence as fine gentleman—a new trade, and one to which he had never been apprenticed. He first took a decent and respectable lodging in King Street, Covent Garden. Here he placed his mother; he then laid out the greater part of his small stock of money in providing himself with apparel more becoming to his new pretensions than the plain brown coat of the schoolmaster. He returned to the lodging, his hair powdered and tied with a black silk ribbon, a waistcoat of flowered silk, black satin breeches, white silk stockings, a blue coat, and a great muslin cravat, so that he really seemed to be a young gentleman of fortune.

'Mother,' he said, pranking and pea-cocking about as those do who, for the first time, find themselves in fine clothes, 'am I dressed to your liking?'

'La, Richard!' she replied—the poor woman was but a homely body, as you may understand—'you are fine indeed.' I dare say that, being a personable and straight man, with regular features and black eyes, he did look very fine. 'Who would think,' she went on, being one of those persons who can never adapt their minds to new circumstances, and are, therefore, awkward in unexpected changes of fortune, 'who would think, my son, that only yesterday you went in homely brown and flourished a cane and flogged the boys?'

'Tut—tut,' he replied, changing colour; 'we must forget yesterday—no matter what I did yesterday. Let me never hear a word of what has been; never a word again, not even in a whisper. Remember, walls have ears;

people are curious. Already they are asking
who I am and what is my calling. Mind
what I say, mother. The past is gone—
dead and gone. Mind!—dead and gone and
clean forgotten.'

'Very well, Richard. Though if you
suppose that I am going to forget how my
husband left me to starve with a babe at the
breast——'

'The past is gone, mother!—gone and forgotten, I say,' he repeated, raising his voice.

'Nor how I was thankful and glad to get
a little work from the ladies of the Hospital——'

'The past is gone, I tell you,' he repeated;
with sudden anger.

'Let it go, then. But it can't be forgotten.
No, never. Lord! Richard, just so your
father would fly out before we were married
a week.'

'Just so you provoked him, no doubt,' returned her son, 'letting out things with your
silly old tongue. Now, mother, try to understand you are henceforth a lady—yes—you
are the Lady Aldeburgh—nothing short of

that, and I am the only son of your ladyship. There is no doubt whatever about it.'

The good homely body, who had now lost whatever comeliness she might have had in youth, and looked what she was, a respectable sewing woman, short and thick-set, with a face to suit her figure, was as fit to be a Peeress as to be a Queen. She laughed at the thing.

'Lady or no lady,' she said, 'I am a plain tradesman's daughter, and never thought either to marry above an honest man of my own condition (as I did to the best of my belief) or to sink down to Cat's Hole in the Precinct there to take in——'

He stamped his foot and swore aloud.

'Have a care, Richard,' she replied, tranquilly, 'have a care, my son. If my husband (who, it seems, is really my husband after all) still lives he will not have changed his temper, which was as much a part of him as his nose —Old Horny himself hath not such a temper. And if you think to get anything from his generosity you must subdue your temper, and go humble.'

'Not I,' said Richard. 'I have had enough of humbleness.'

'As for me, I have lived so long without him that I want nothing from him, not even a noble name. And what—oh! my dear—whatever is the good of being his son if he refuses to own it?'

'There is the Law, mother. The Law of the land shall compel him to own it. Ay! whether he will or no—like it or lump it. There's a law for a nobleman as well as for a poor man. Come to that, I'm a nobleman now.'

'The Law? Oh!' she laughed, like Sarai the incredulous. 'You think that any law of man, or even of God Himself, would bind that man? Laws are not made for noblemen. Besides, he was always masterful, and is now, I take it, too powerful to be touched by any law ever made.'

'That we shall see.'

'No—no—if he refuse to own—why, he will certainly refuse—we are no more forwarded than before. Son, be persuaded. Put off those fine clothes—they become you

hugely, but they are above our station—
and become again a sober schoolmaster and
organist. No one plays better, I am sure.
Humble thyself to the Chapter, and let us go
back to the old place again—where I was
comfortable, and we had a good house and
enough to eat.'

Her son laughed scornfully.

'Back to the old place again? Back to
their insolent airs and their pride?' Thus
he spoke of his benefactors. 'No, no. Listen,
mother. It is now certain that I am nothing
less than the Honourable Richard Archer, son
of Stephen Lord Aldeburgh, married to you,
his first wife being three or four days dead,
twenty-three years ago, under his own
name of Stephen Archer, described as master-
mariner. This can be proved. My friend
the proctor—whom yesterday I should have
called my patron, to-day is my friend, and to-
morrow shall be my servant—is a sharp and
keen man, and has all the evidence in his
hands. He is to be paid a great sum when
I come into my own. Suppose my father
should refuse to acknowledge me, what then?

He is old : he is already paralysed, and cannot move his legs : he will before long die.
Then I am the heir to all his estates. That,
I say, can be proved. His other property he
may give to anyone he pleases ; but his lands
are mine—all mine. Fifteen thousand pounds
a year, at least—fifteen thousand pounds a
year! Then, you ask, how are we to live
meanwhile ? It is not fitting that the heir to
so great an estate should live by his own
handiwork. No, no ; he must live on his
fortune. There are plenty of people in the
City, however, will lend me money—all the
money I want—on what they call a *post obit*,
or reversion. The proctor himself will procure for me, if necessary, as much as three
hundred pounds a year. Think of three
hundred—three hundred pounds—a year!
I shall have no less than three hundred pounds
a year to live on until my father dies. With
swinging interest, I understand. Oh! yes—
swinging interest. Well, the estate will stand
it. But I shall not borrow too much. Not I.
No, no ; I am a prudent man. Thus I march
into the world of fashion, as bold as any of

them. I am Mr. Archer, son of Lord Aldeburgh. But the old lord is peevish and
stubborn : he will not own me, yet his son, as
all the world knows very well, and as like
him as one pea is like another. Then I look
out for an heiress. There are hundreds of
heiresses, all ready and eager to marry a lord,
or a man about to become a lord. I am not
yet proud ; though, when I get the title, I
mean to be as proud as Lucifer. The daughter
of an alderman will do for me meanwhile,
provided she bring me a plum—a lovely, ripe,
and melting plum—a hundred thousand clear.'
Yet only yesterday this man had been rich on
forty pounds a year. 'No one will know
anything of the past. That is clean gone.
In the Precinct the name of Richard Archer
will be forgotten. Out of the Precinct
nobody has ever heard of it.'

'No, no,' said his mother. 'Alas ! I
wish I could think it would be forgotten. It
will be remembered so long as the trial of
those poor young gentlemen is remembered.'

'Everyone for himself. Should I hang ?
Should I turn King's evidence, or should I

hang? Why, I was but just in time.
George Bayssallance was about to offer himself, as I heard in the very nick of time.'
(Here was a liar for you!) 'And I let him
off as easily as I could.' (Another bouncing
lie!)

'Is the past forgotten?' the mother per-
sisted. 'Richard, is that poor girl forgotten
—the girl? Oh, how could you dare to
raise your eyes so high! Who turned your
head and made you hate that young gentleman, and filled your heart with such bitterness, that I wonder you could live?'

'Forgotten? Why, I now marvel that I
ever thought of her! A fine rich lady—
Court or City madam, I care not—shall be
my next; one who can choose and wear her
feathers and her lace; such an one as I have
seen in these streets. That girl! Why, there
are thousands better even in the City! What
is she? A girl with pink and white cheeks,
and fair, curly hair. Thousands better than
Sylvia even in the City. Her father is but
High Bailiff to the Hospital—servant to a
Charity. She is neither gentlewoman nor

shepherdess; neither citizen's daughter nor of the gentry. She is now clean forgotten and out of my mind. A nobleman that is to be would scorn to marry a woman from the Precinct of St. Katherine's. He would be ashamed to speak of her origin. As lief marry a Wappineer!'

'The better for her, Richard, that she is clean forgotten; for, to say the truth, there is too much of thy father in thee to make the happiness of any woman, unless such as are like the walnut-tree, and improve and grow happier with every cuff and kick and savage oath.'

'I am glad there is in me so much of my father; I would be all my father.'

'Ay, but he is a proud man and a hard man.'

'For his pride I honour him; a noble lord ought to be proud. For his hardness, I can be as hard, or harder, and so I shall let him understand. It will all come right when he is dead. You shall then be the Dowager Lady Aldeburgh, and have a hundred servants at your call.'

She shook her head.

'No,' she said, 'I am not fit to become a

great lady. I married a plain sailor, as I
thought, being myself little better. He must
have known from the outset that I had no
fine manners. No, no, he meant all along to
leave me when he was tired. Then I became
a sempstress.'

Her son stamped his foot, and swore at
her for a chattering old fool.

'Ay,' said his mother, 'so stamped and roared
and swore, so looked your father before you.
Could he see you as you are, he could not
choose but acknowledge thee to be his son.'

'Well then, if that is all, he *shall* see me
as I am,' said Richard, mollified. 'I will
show him that I am indeed his son—all his
blood—none of the City puddle in my veins.
Ha! I feel myself every inch a lord. I was
born with a contempt of the people around
me—from the Prebendary to the Apparitor,
I have ever despised them all. Nature will
out. Thus do sons still follow their sires,
although they know them not.'

There sat all day long in a round or
bow window on the first floor of a house in

Bond Street a man, now in years, upon whom had fallen the affliction of paralysis. He sat in a chair, his feet propped up on cushions; behind him stood a valet, always ready to obey at a moment; on the table were books, chiefly in the French language, in the reading of which he found his greatest pleasure; there were also cards, in case he chose to play a game with his man; mostly he looked out of the window upon the gay world below, the fine ladies in the chariots, the gentlemen riding and caracolling or lounging along the pavement. He belonged to the world no longer; he had dropped out of it suddenly and without warning, at the age of fifty-five years, and after thirty-five spent in feasting, love-making, dicing, and drinking, except when he was at sea, for he had formerly been a Post Captain in the King's Navy, where he was, I believe, a gallant officer and an able commander.

While he was well, Lord Aldeburgh had many companions. One who is rich and lavish can command companions. There are many men in London, I am told, who live—or rather

prey—upon those who are rich and lavish ;
feast with them ; win their money at cards ;
receive gifts from them ; the trade of parasite
has never, since great men began, been without its followers. His lordship freely gave
to them, his parasites, suppers and feasts ; he
was a generous patron of all those people
who live by making amusement for the great ;
such as jockeys, horse-trainers, cock-fighters,
prize-fighters, singing men and women, dancing women, actors, painters, sculptors, and
the like. But he had now few friends,
because his temper was notorious. Men do
not willingly enter into close friendship with
the possessor of such a temper. Such friend-
ships too often end in the Field of Forty
Footsteps. Therefore, when Lord Aldeburgh
was stricken with paralysis, such people as
these playing and racing folk, to whom he
had been so good a patron, were sincerely
and deeply grieved ; the noble army of parasites were truly afflicted ; but of friends who
came to the sick man's room there were few
indeed. Those who did come reported that
his lordship's temper had now grown worse

than ever; that he lay in a rage which knew neither beginning nor end; that he cursed and swore by night as well as by day.

Concerning the life of pleasure and the fashionable world, I know nothing. Rumours have reached my ears in the Precinct, which is far removed from that giddy throng; but I know nothing certain. Yet I can very well understand that one to whom earthly joys are all in all would be like unto Tantalus standing in his stream and catching at the flowing water with dry lips and parched throat, when he could no more enjoy any of them; when the only thing left for him was to sit at the window and watch the gay procession, and remember the past, when he too had formed a part, and pranked it with the best.

Lord Aldeburgh presented in his appearance a wonderful resemblance to Richard Archer, allowance being made for the difference of years. His face was filled out now, his cheeks red, and his nose, which had formerly been straight and narrow, had now broadened. His eyes were black and piercing; his mouth was firm, and his chin square. He had been tall, but, as you have heard, he could no longer stand.

It was nearly noon, and a clear day, although the month was November; the sunshine fell warm and bright upon the street below, filled with dandies and fine ladies. The old lord lay back in his chair grumbling and growling. On the table before him was a book by one of the French philosophers.

The door was pushed open gently, and one of his valets walked noiselessly across the thick carpet, bearing a letter on a silver tray.

'The gentleman waits your lordship's pleasure,' said the man.

Lord Aldeburgh opened the letter.

'My Lord,—The bearer is the young gentleman concerning whom I have already had the honour to communicate with your lordship. I venture to remind your lordship of your permission that he should wait upon you personally.

'I remain, my lord,
'Your obedient servant,
'Aaron Teller,
'*Proctor, Solicitor, and Attorney-at-Law.*'

'Well,' said Lord Aldeburgh, 'I promised the man—I was curious to find out what kind of creature—— I will see him. Tell him he may come upstairs. Do you wait outside. I will ring the bell when I want you.'

The gentleman who entered the room as the valet left it was none other than our friend Richard Archer, dressed as you have seen. He bowed low and stood waiting to be addressed. But he stood his ground courageously, as one who is not embarrassed or afraid.

'Well, sir,' said his lordship, after looking at him curiously for a few moments, 'why have you come to me?'

'I have come to pay my respects to my father, whom I have at last discovered.'

'Dutiful boy. Wise, too, above the generality of mankind.'

'Your lordship has heard the history of my mother, and what befel her when you deserted her.'

'So we can use plain words as well as pay respects, can we?'

'Plain words are best,' said Archer, with
some dignity. 'I am not come as a beggar.
My lawyer has completed the proofs of my
case. If your lordship acknowledges me so
much the better for me—and for you and
everybody. Then the story will not be made
public. If you do not, so much the worse
for me—and for your memory, because the
story will be told after your death.'

'You crow too loud, young sir.' But he
did not fall into a rage ; he even smiled.

'Not so, my lord, with submission. I do
but state my case plainly. Permit me to go
on. I am in hopes that you may acknowledge me before all the world as your son
and heir, born in wedlock. I am told that
your temper is irritable : on that point I am
your equal—I am my father's son. Nay,' he
stepped forward into the full light of the
window. 'Look at me—whose son am I ?
My father shows in every feature—in my
voice, in my eyes, in my shape—whose son
am I ? '

Lord Aldeburgh leaned his chin upon his
hand and gazed upon his face and figure as

one examines a horse put up for sale. Then he laughed gently.

'Why,' he said, 'if looks go for anything in this world, I dare say you are, indeed, my son. I recognise in your face more than something of my own. Why not my son? Yet, Mr. Richard Archer, that is a long way from being my lawful heir and successor. A very long way, young gamecock. The inheritance, you will find, is quite another thing.'

'Acknowledge me to be your son, my lord, and the rest I can myself manage.'

'After my death, you mean. Well, every one who has rank and wealth expects heirs, and those who would be heirs if they could: it is natural that these should most ardently desire the death of the man from whom they will inherit. You will advance a claim to legitimacy after my death. Very good. I see no reason why that promise—or threat—should move me in the least.'

'I say, my lord, only acknowledge me to be your own son, and the rest can wait. You will have a son who will obey you in all things reasonable. If you swear at him, he will swear in return ; he will give you like for like ; he will not be afraid of you, but he will do his best to meet your wishes and to keep you amused. Do this, my lord, and you will never regret it.'

'You are the son of a certain London girl —daughter of a poulterer or a pepperer or a saddler—I know not what—who went through a form of marriage——'

'A real marriage——'

'With me in a City church. I remember her. She had a pretty face, but no manners, and a tongue that never stopped.'

'Does your lordship desire to see my mother again ? '

He shuddered. 'What? See a woman whom I fancied for a month twenty years ago and more ? See that woman again? Name her not, young man. What is your Christian name ? '

'Richard.'

'What have you been doing? How living ? '

'I would not presume to inquire into your

lordship's way of life, and since you deserted me and have done nothing for my education, my maintenance, or my present position'—his lordship smiled at the word—'I submit with respect that you have no right to inquire into my way of life.'

'This is very true. As I knew not that I had a son I could not educate or maintain him. Nevertheless, when one is asked to acknowledge a son—you are perhaps an apprentice to this pepperer or saddler.'

'I am no 'prentice, my lord.'

'You may be a highwayman for aught I know.'

'I am no highwayman. I am a scholar. I have been educated by Churchmen in the hope of myself entering into Holy Orders.' This, I take it, was a figurative way of putting the truth.

'Pray do not let me stand in the way of so laudable an ambition.'

'I have abandoned that hope.'

'You have studied at Oxford or Cambridge?'

'No, my lord, my slender means forbade.

My utmost ambition was to obtain Holy Orders through the interest of friends, and so get a curacy or evening lecturer—a humble ambition, so long as I knew not my parentage.'

'Humph! I suppose you are surrounded by low companions and friends?'

'I have never been able to afford to consort with gentlemen, and with the baser kind I would not consort—I have no companions and no friends. None, that is, who will hinder me or keep me down, or make me ashamed of the past.'

His lordship kept looking at him steadily and curiously. 'I *believe* you are my son,' he said. 'I repeat that I believe so much. As to being my lawful son—well—that is different. What have you learned? What can you do? How do I know whether I shall tolerate you about me? There are not many whom I endure near me. I am exacting. I want to be pleased. What are your arts or accomplishments, if you have any?'

'I confess, my lord, that I am ignorant of the polite world. But I can learn its manners. Meantime, I am not without accomplishment.

I can play cards with you, if you want amusement. I can read French to you, if you want reading. I can play or sing to you. Would you like to hear me?'

'In my youth I loved music, and excelled in it. I am now old, and my fingers are stiff. You may play me something.'

There was a harpsichord in the room. Richard Archer sat down and struck the keys with a masterly hand. Then he sang a song —one of the old rollicking love-ditties which used to be popular.

When he had finished, Lord Aldeburgh nodded, still looking thoughtfully. Richard Archer rose. He saw lying on a chair a violin-case. He opened it, and took out the violin. 'Ah!' he said, 'this is a finer instrument than I have ever had in my hands before.' He began to tune it. 'I will now play your lordship a very different thing.'

He did: he played some piece which he had learned, I know not where—some piece of Italian music, full of passion and of tenderness. When he had finished he made a low bow, holding the violin in one hand and the bow in another.

'Ah!' said his lordship, 'it is long since I heard that piece. Hark ye, Mr. Richard Archer: I like your music. Sit down opposite me—there. You are poor, I suppose?'

'Your lordship is always right.'

'Such playing as this should, with some further tuition, make thee fit to play in concerts and operas. Would that suit your ambition?'

'My lord, I would be a gentleman.'

'You want money? Of course you want money.' He lugged out his purse, which, not because he wanted it, but from old habit, he kept full. 'Here is all I have with me. I think there are ninety guineas.'

Richard's eyes sparkled. Ninety guineas! He bowed, and took the purse.

'Does that content you?'

'By no means, my lord. I would be a gentleman.'

'I will give you more money if you will come and play to me often. Oh! I can get musicians, singing women, dancing women—

what not—to amuse me. I will pay you instead.'

Richard bowed.

'Your lordship means that you can command me. But—I wish to be a gentleman.'

'If you will play cards with me I will give you more money; if you will talk to me —but you know nothing about polite society.'

'Nothing at all. It will be an amusement for your lordship to instruct me; it will help to make me a gentleman.'

Lord Aldeburgh inclined his head gravely, never taking his eyes from the young man's face.

'Well, what will satisfy you? I would willingly do something for you, short of—— But that you cannot expect. What is the least that will satisfy you?'

'For the present your recognition. Let the world know that I am your son; let them think, if you please, that I am your natural son; with that, for the time, I shall be well content. Then I can be received as a gentleman.'

'Have your own way, then. Call yourself
my son. It will not hurt me if a dozen
young men call themselves my sons, so long
as they do not also call themselves my heirs.'

His lordship rang the small silver bell that
stood on the table.

'Tell the people,' he spoke to his valet,
'that this young gentleman is my son—you
hear?—my son.' The man bowed respect-
fully. 'He must receive the respect due to
—my son. He will have a room here, if he
pleases. He will come and go as he pleases.
You will obey his orders as if they were my
own. Richard Archer, if you please, you can
call yourself the son of a nobleman. You
can imagine to yourself that this makes you a
gentleman. Are you content?'

He held out his hand, and his son rose
and took it, bending low.

CHAPTER XXV

SISTER KATHERINE FINDS OUT

'LORD ha' mercy! who would dream, Sylvia, that you were at death's door for six long months and more?'

'Was it so long, Sister Katherine?'

'So thin that a body could see through you, as they say, and so feeble that you could hardly stand, and never without tears in your eyes and despair in your face; and now you are rosy and strong, and can sing again and laugh, although we have lost the boys, and your lover has gone out to the other end of the world, and will be eaten by cannibals, for all you know.'

'Sister, I laugh and sing, because whatever has happened to them, all will come right in the end—I know it.'

'Has old Margery foretold it?'

'Nay, I have not gone to the fortune-teller. Nevertheless I am assured. Yet a year or two, and all will be well.'

'Tell me, child, if you can, what caused it? For out of this trouble sprang all the rest.'

'I know not, indeed. I was as one encompassed with an evil spirit, so that I could neither say nor do the things which I wished. I was, I say, possessed by an evil spirit. That is certain. But Dame Margery knows more than most about it. I like not to think of that time. I cannot look behind me. It terrifies me. I look forward. George —I say to myself—will come back again. Somehow, we shall all be happy yet.'

There was certainly room for improvement in the point of happiness. An abiding sadness now lay upon the two families, affected by the events already narrated. The Lieutenant, always a silent man, now sat in gloom; he could neither forgive his son, nor could he find it in his heart to condemn him, seeing that he had been touched in his mind, and was not himself. Moreover, he had been heavily punished. Yet, his own son was a rebel and a traitor ; he had been tried and sentenced as such ; he was close to hanging, almost as close as any man ever was ; this disgrace affected him profoundly ; it was a family disgrace.

Observe. The family named Bayssallance has lived in St. Katherine's Precinct for two hundred and fifty years. It has hardly ever left this part of London ; it is not connected with any great house, or even with the substantial merchants of the City ; the Lieutenant who bore His Majesty's Commission was the first of the family who could write himself gentleman. The disgrace to the family could, therefore, be felt by few or none, except himself and Sister Katherine. Nobody in the Precinct heeded any disgrace ; nay, I think that the humble folk in their ignorance thought it was a great day for the House of Bayssallance, when one of their number was put up to a public trial on such a grand charge as that of High Treason. Many of them went in daily danger of a trial for theft—which

also led to the gallows. But High Treason
—Rebellion—that was another thing ! '

Again, the family named Comines, or De
Comines, commonly called Cummins, was
equally unknown outside the Precinct, where
they, too, had lived for two hundred and fifty
years. Such disgrace as was involved in my
own trial, was felt by none outside the walls
of the Hospital. Yet they were all disgraced.

'It is not, Lieutenant,' said my father,
'the exile of the boys that weighs upon me.
In that respect they are little worse than
when you went to fight His Majesty's battles.
It is the family disgrace.'

'It is the family disgrace, Mr. Comines.'

'If I walk abroad, the people look after
me. When I visit the City, which is not
often, they turn to look upon a man whose
son is a traitor. Last week I was as far west
as Charing Cross. Even there they pointed
to me as the father of a traitor.'

The Lieutenant nodded gloomily. It was
the disgrace—the family disgrace—that he
felt.

'Sylvia, child,' said Sister Katherine, 'what made you say, just now, that the old woman, Margery Habbijam, knew more than most?'

'Because she comes and looks upon me curiously; and she asks me questions as to when the fit left me, when I ceased to feel the oppression, and the like. And she asks if all is as it was before with me, meaning if I am in the same mind as regards George. Then she nods her head and winks, and says that since he has gone away all will be well.'

'Who is he?'

'I know not; but she knows.'

'If Margery Habbijam knows anything about it, she will have to tell me,' said Sister Katherine, resolutely; 'I will tear it out of her.'

She walked to the Wise Woman's house in Helmet Court. It was in the morning, when the old woman sat for the most part alone with her pipe and her cards.

'Dame,' said Sister Katherine, 'I am come to ask a question.'

'Is it of the future or of the present?'

asked the witch. 'Shall I tell you, madam, of the safety of your nephew and Master Nevill? Last night I inquired of the cards, and I found they were in a storm. I inquired further, and I learned that they will get through safely, and presently land on the foreign coast.'

'Never mind your fortune-telling, though you may be as wise as a wisp and as cunning as Captain Drake. Come, dame, they say you know one point more than the devil. Tell me, and tell me true, who bewitched Sylvia Comines?'

The old lady made no reply.

'Tell me, I say, who did the mischief? Bewitched she was. Of that there is no doubt, whatever they say. A girl does not fall into a fit of loathing, and remain in it against her will for six months, and sink into the very jaws of death, and then suddenly recover and be strong again in a single day, by any natural disorder. Sylvia says you know more about it than most. Well, I have had my suspicions all along. Out with it, therefore. If you think to escape, you will find you have put your dish at the wrong man's door. No, no. I've got this crow to pluck with you. Ease your mind therefore, and out with all.'

'What should I know about the girl's fancies?'

'Hark ye, dame, it is an open shame— and one that should be looked into—that in a religious foundation like St. Katherine's, a witch should be suffered to live. This, I say, must be seen into. Thou art old now, and to turn thee out of the Precinct—yea, and out of the parts around the Precinct, which might also be done—would deprive thee of thy daily bread. Look to it, therefore.'

'You are hard on me, madam,' said the dame. 'You are cruel hard. What have I to do with Sylvia Comines? I have never so much as wished harm to that poor child.'

'Clear thyself, therefore. Nay, now I think of it, the High Bailiff himself shall deal with the case in our Ecclesiastical Court, which is ordered and provided for all such offences against Holy Church. It cannot be denied that for many years thy livelihood hath been that of a witch, or wise woman. This may be winked at by the law, but it is not allowed. The clink of the Precinct has not seen a prisoner within its walls for many years, but still it stands, and there is still a servant of the Hospital called the gaoler. Think, therefore.'

'The man who did it is gone away. He will do no more harm. But if he knew that I had told, there might be more mischief— oh, much more. He is a bad and wicked man; he has no fear of the Lord.'

'Who is the man?'

'Richard Archer,' she replied, thus driven into a corner out of which there was no escape.

'What had Richard Archer to do with Sylvia?'

'He fell in love with her, and she was promised to another man—and she was too high for him at that time.'

'Hoity-toity! Richard Archer, the schoolmaster, fall in love with the daughter of Mr. Comines? Heard one ever the like? What did Sylvia say to this?'

'She said nothing. She knew and sus-pected nothing.'

'Well. But even if he ventured to think such thoughts—fancy is free—though from golden dreams we wake up hungry, and hasty climbers have sudden falls, and the higher gets the ape the more he shows his tail—yet a cat may look at a king; well, if she knew nothing, no harm was done.'

'Nay, but he fell into envy and hatred. He hated everybody about the girl—the man whom she loved, her brother, her father, her friends.'

'Oh! And it was for this that he turned King's evidence—the villain!'

'Nay, more, madam,' said the old witch, earnestly. 'It was this man, Archer—Richard Archer himself—and none other bewitched the girl, if you call that witchcraft, which was only the Evil Eye. Yes, Evil Eye and Evil Heart—nothing but that.'

'What do you mean?' cried Sister Katherine, startled. 'What is that?'

Margery told her what you have heard already.

I have said before, and again I say it, that I do not believe in this alleged witchcraft of any man's eye ; nor can I believe that the Lord would entrust any man, even the most saintly, with such power, by the exercise of which he might overwhelm the people around him—nay, his town, his country, the whole world—where shall we stop ?—in ruin and destruction.

Yet it is true that the first fit into which Sylvia fell corresponds with the time when this man learned the secret (or thought he learned it) of his dreadful power to work mischief. I say again, I cannot believe it. Think of being born with the power to cause evil—evil perpetually—as much evil and disaster as you please—but never any good whatever ! This—apart from the agonies of the flames—is to be damned. Nothing less. I cannot believe it ; yet the time corresponded. Also, it was not until then that disaster fell upon George, or upon me, who might have continued unmolested and unsuspected in my obscure club of Snugs. And the end of it— the reprieve, the King's clemency, and Sylvia's recovery—also strangely corresponded. Yet, I cannot believe it.

'I am in amazement,' said Sister Katherine. 'What? Richard Archer the cause of all? Why not tell us at once?'

'Because I could prove nothing. Who would have believed me?'

'Richard Archer! I remember him, a barefoot boy, sitting on a door-step. Richard Archer!'

So one might remember a torch when it was but a bit of resinous pine; yet it has burned down a great Cathedral.

'Evil Eye and Evil Heart,' said the old woman.

'I cannot believe it. The thing is monstrous.'

'Yet it is true. Madam,' said Dame Margery, 'we have been wise women, from mother to daughter, for six generations at least. I learned the signs of Evil Eye long ago; yet never before have I met a case. It is rare in this country. Yet——'

'Evil Eye! How can one believe that a

man with such a fatal power would use it
with such wickedness?'

'Richard Archer is now another man,' the
dame concluded. 'He is in prosperity. His
father, who is a great lord, hath recognised
him. He will be the heir—at least, I hear
as much. His mother, your honour's needlewoman, is now, I suppose—for I have not
heard how she fares—a fine madam, and may
call herself "ladyship," if she so pleases.
He now wishes evil to no one. Nay, if he
wished ill to Sylvia again, nothing would
come of it, because he has gone away. She
is no longer within his power.'

'I am in amazement,' said Sister Katherine.
'I know not what to say, nor what to think.
Richard Archer a great man! Richard
Archer to have the power—what do you call
it?—the power of the Evil Eye! And we
who sat in the church every Sunday to hear
him play! Why, the Devil himself——'
Here she stopped, overwhelmed.

'What think you now, madam? Had I
not cause to say, when I did say it, that

they who caused might cure? Would their reverences of the Chapter House believe me if I were to tell them this story?'

Sister Katherine rose slowly.

'I know not what to think,' she replied: 'except, as the old saw says, "GOD is still where He was before."'

CHAPTER XXVI

PARAMATTA

Two years and a half elapsed before any
letters or news from England reached us.
Ships arrived bringing out more convicts; we
learned by them the progress of the war, of
which there seemed to promise no ending; of
private news or letters we had none.

The settlement of Sydney (wrongly spoken
of as Botany Bay) lies in a part of the world
as remote from the British shores, unless it be
some island of the Pacific Ocean, as can anywhere be found. That is reckoned a fair
voyage when no more than eight months are
spent at sea; our own voyage out took eight
months and a half. One sails, indeed, half
round the world when one goes to Australia.
This is a very great undertaking, and we may
admire the ingenuity of man in devising a

N 2

machine so perfectly adapted to its purpose as a ship which shall traverse this vast extent of water with no more risk than that of storm or sunken rock, and which shall carry on board provisions for three hundred men during this long period.

One cannot pretend that a voyage on board a convict transport is the most agreeable mode of travelling ; nor that one would choose the rank and position of a private in the regiment of Royal Marines for such a voyage ; but some of those on board the *Golden Grove* had no choice—of these, I was one. My lot might have been harder, for I might, like George, have had to herd with the wretches whom we were conveying to a condition as near slavery as the laws of the country will allow.

The chief duty of the Marines was to guard the ship, to preserve order, and to keep the convicts in safety. We were on guard day and night ; when the convicts were taking the air on deck the guard was trebled ; on the quarter-deck three carronades were placed loaded with grape and commanding

the whole deck; the officers of the ship, as
well as the Marines, went about their work
armed with pistol and hanger; the sentries
had loaded guns and fixed bayonets. There
were but six-and-thirty Marines for this
service, so that—with the polishing of arms
and accoutrements, and such drill as was held
on board—there was not much time for
repining over hardships. Nay, I felt no hardships; there were none of which a young
fellow could complain; I have already
explained how my officers had been influenced
in my behalf; I was neither bullied nor
treated with more severity than the rest; and,
as for companions, mine were the most honest
fellows in the world; some were veterans, who
took out their wives and families, and intended
to make the Settlement their home; some
were young fellows—country lads—drafted
upon this service. Those who proposed to
become settlers were full of hope: the climate
of Australia, they said, was beautiful; the soil
was fertile beyond all belief; it was a land of
plenty; it was another Canaan.

The provisions on board were wholesome

and abundant; salt junk, pork, and biscuit
do very well for hungry men at sea; one
quickly learns to relish the ration of rum.
When we put in at Santa Cruz and at the Cape
of Good Hope, we took on board fresh water,
vegetables, fruit, and fish. Sometimes we
hooked a shark; we had no scurvy on board
during the whole voyage, nor any sickness,
except among the convicts, some of whom
came on board rotten already, and ripe for
death. And for the most part we had fine
weather. If I try to recollect the voyage, I
find in my mind a memory of smooth ocean,
but with a roll upon it, of a ship under full
sail, softly gliding over the water, of blue skies
and a hot sun. One day is exactly like
another. On the quarter-deck stand the
captain of the ship and the Captain of
Marines; one or two lieutenants or midship-
men are with them; the three carronades
point their mouths at the deck below; and in
the waist the convicts are lying or sitting
about, ragged and dirty, unshaven and
unwashed. Some of them are wounded,
because they quarrel down below, and have

fierce fights. After a spell of fresh air they
go below, and another batch comes up. And
so on all day long. When night arrives they
go below and are made safe till the next
morning. There cannot be anywhere a more
horrible place than the convicts' quarters at
night on a transport. They are left in the
dark, secured; in the tropics the heat is
stifling and insupportable; the talk is of
nothing but of past villanies, each man
making himself out to be the worst man on
board the ship; or, if he can, the very
wickedest man in the whole world. They
were brought on board from the hulks, which
surely contain the finest school of wickedness
ever created for the service of the Devil.
They were mostly lost to any feelings of
decency; they made each other worse; their
language was as ribald as their actions were
wicked. I had seen the common felon's side,
and the Press Yard of Newgate, but these
transported convicts were far worse than even
the sturdy rogues and gin-sodden drabs of that
horrible prison.

There is a dreadful uniformity, I have

learned, in such voyages as this. At some
time or other a few of the more desperate
form a plot to seize the ship; it is always
discovered in time, and the ringleaders are
flogged, or hanged. Two years before I went
out, there was a ship, the *Albemarle*, on board
of which the plot actually went as far as a
rising of the convicts and a fight with the
crew; this was owing to the treachery of a
sailor who gave the men a file to get rid of
their irons—the ringleader was wounded in
the shoulder by the Captain, who fired his
blunderbuss at him; the rest were driven
below, and the next day two were hanged.
On board the *Golden Grove* the conspiracy got
very little way, because George himself, who
had been invited to join in it, publicly
revealed the whole plot. It was after we left
the Cape of Good Hope, the time being fore-
noon. I was on guard on the quarter-deck,
the convicts were in their place, the day was
bright and fine, with a fresh breeze and a
rolling sea.

Suddenly a man among the convicts stood
up. It was George. He called the Bo'sun,

'Hark ye,' he said ; 'I must speak with the Captain.'

'Must ye? Ah, must ye, then? You to speak with the Captain? Sit quiet, or the Captain will speak to your bare back, ye mutinous scoundrel.'

'If I were to be flogged for it, I must speak!'

One of the officers overheard this, and ordered the man to be brought aft. So he came and told the officer what he had to say.

The plot was ready, and would that day have been attempted. What need to tell the old story? There were four men who were the leaders. They proposed to seize the arms, kill the officers, and drive the crew and the Marines overboard unless they submitted and joined. These men, their guilt clearly proved, were tied up, and had two hundred lashes each. After this example we had no further trouble, but this circumstance procured George his freedom. He could not very well be sent back among the convicts, who would have murdered him the moment he set foot among them. The Captain of the Marines, therefore, who was in charge of the convicts, consented that he should be placed, being a good sailor, in the fo'ksle, and rated as an able seaman. To this he was the more inclined as I had already told my friend, the Sergeant, something of his history, and how it was from love and madness that he fell into trouble. So George put off very willingly his convict garb, and continued until the end of the voyage as a common sailor, and a most handy, willing sailor he proved. From time to time, but not often, I had private speech with him, and I found that though he bore his lot with fortitude, he no longer showed the cheerfulness which had marked his demeanour when he thought himself called upon to die for the sake of Sylvia. He now cursed his own folly and the credulity which caused him to fall an easy prey to the villain who compassed his destruction, whereas, if he had possessed his soul in patience, Sylvia would have returned to him, the fit of madness spent, his mistress and his sweetheart once more.

We sailed from London at the end of

December. It was in August or September
that we arrived at Port Jackson, where lies
the Settlement called Sydney, in New South
Wales, which is a part of the great island (or
the continent) of Australia. Strange though
it sounds to our ears, this time of year is in
that climate (where everything is upside down
or reversed) the depth of winter, but such
a winter as we cannot imagine—a winter
without frost or snow—when the sun is warm
all day and only the nights are cold. If
August is winter, November is spring and
Christmas is summer.

The Settlement of Sydney is as yet wholly
inhabited by convicts (those whose terms have
expired and continue here as settlers) and a
few old Marines, who have no wish to leave
a place so delightful both for situation and
for climate. It lies on the south side of the
great creek which here runs inland; a noble
piece of water, with beautiful bays, hanging
woods, rising grounds, capes, and headlands.
The place was first settled five years before
we landed. It had by this time well-nigh sur-
mounted its early difficulties; there was no

longer fear of famine; the country was
planted; there were many farms, and already
a good show of live stock. But the majority
of the people are transported convicts. They
are not kept in prisons (except the unruly
and the hardened), but scattered about in
cottages and on farms. There is among them
a great deal of crime; floggings are adminis-
tered every day, and no one is allowed to
forget that he is in a penal settlement. This,
and nothing else, makes the colony sad to
those who live in it; for I do not think that
anywhere in the world can there be an air
more delightful; warm, yet not enfeebling;
breezes purer or fresher; a soil more fertile;
fields and gardens more smiling, when once
the settler has cleared the surface and
ploughed the earth.

Natives there are—naked blacks who
cannot be tamed, and who spear any white
man they find straggling in the woods. But
these (like foxes at home) come not near the
settled parts. Wild creatures are there—
none to hurt, but plenty of curious creatures
and strange birds. In the woods there are a

great quantity of snakes, and these are said to
be venomous, yet did I never hear of any one
dying in consequence of a bite from them ;
whereas, to my certain knowledge, a worthy
citizen of London, some years ago, lost his
life from the bite of a viper on Hampstead
Heath ; thus you may see that some dangers
at home are equal to those abroad. Other
inconveniences are there none, unless a certain
hot wind which prevails in the summer may
be counted.

This Settlement is surely the most lovely
of all the outposts of Great Britain. It stands
alone on a coast which Captain Cook has
explored, and none but he ; the untrodden
beach stretches a thousand miles north and
a thousand miles south ; behind it lies a great
unknown forest in which many men have lost
their lives ; behind the forest lies—one knows
not what—the interior of the great island,
which may contain, for all we know, people
with a civilisation, with arts, even with a
religion, all their own.

It is almost unnecessary to state that the
convicts, on first landing, are always trying to

escape. Once five men seized a boat, and stole away, at night, 'twas said; they intended to make Otaheite, where Cook's sailors found hospitality so unbounded. They were never heard of again. Then one Bryant, with a dozen others, including a woman and two children, escaped in a boat; they got to Timor in safety, and were there put on board an English ship, but Bryant and eight of the others died of their sufferings. Once, a whole party of thirty walked out into the woods, intending (such was their ignorance) to walk to China! Most of them perished miserably, but a few were picked up and brought back, well-nigh starved.

Those who do not try to escape are prone to theft and drunkenness. They steal everything; the vegetables in the Governor's garden, the Indian corn before it is cut, the fruit on the trees; they break open the stores and steal the rum, and indeed everything else.

The things they steal they exchange, or try to exchange, for drink. They start stills to make rum for themselves; they collect gum in the woods, and shells by the sea-shore, and offer them to the sailors of transports, for rum.

Their dress consists—for the men—of an Osnaburg frock and trousers, yarn stockings, a hat and shoes; and for the women, of a cloth petticoat, a coarse shift, yarn stockings, and shoes; they have allowances and rations from the public stores; they have to do a certain amount of daily labour; they lived at first in huts, built of the cabbage-tree, and afterwards, in wooden-frame houses, thatched with grass of the gum-rush. But before we arrived they had begun the making of bricks.

When a man becomes a settler, that is to say, takes up a piece of ground and begins to farm it, he receives a plot of about thirty acres; if he is a Marine whose time has expired, he gets from eighty to two hundred acres, according to his rank. And these men, when they are industrious and sober, are now fast becoming wealthy, as they have long since been independent. I can conceive of no happier condition for a man than to be the owner of a farm large enough to keep him and his family in comfort and plenty. There is no money as yet among these settlers. May God long postpone the day when the town of Sydney shall become great and rich!

You must not think that George, on arriving in this country, was treated like an ordinary criminal, and made to work in a gang. Not at all. The Governor sent for him, and informed him that he must not expect any reversal of his sentence, that he must make up his mind to living in the colony, but that he should, if he were wise, make the best of it.

He therefore offered him a piece of ground of some thirty or forty acres, very fine ground, lying in that part of the creek where the newer settlement or township, called at first Rose Hill, and afterwards by the native name of Paramatta, is situated. He also offered to assist him at the commencement with seeds and instruments.

George accepted the offer with gratitude. He exchanged the anchor for the plough, and became a farmer; and since he was one of those men who bring to every task of life the utmost zeal, he became a very good farmer indeed, and now has one of the largest farms in the colony, well stocked with cattle, sheep, and poultry of all kinds, with orchards and fruit-trees and gardens, with fields arable and pasture, and with farm-buildings which would delight even a yeoman of Essex. I suppose, some of the convicts, his servants, must have taught him the art of agriculture, because, up to the moment when he accepted the grant of land, he had never, I believe, so much as seen a plough, or handled a spade, or wielded a flail.

I have said that it was two years and a half from the day that we left Great Britain before any news came to us from home. Others received letters, even the convicts, but to George or to myself there came none.

At that time I was stationed at Paramatta, where there were a good many convicts, and a company of Marines. At the time when the letter came with the joyful news which I am about to tell you, I was off duty, and sitting, in the hot afternoon (for it was in January), under the shade of the verandah (which is a sort of linney or lean-to in front of a house, put up for shade) of George's cottage. The day was drowsy, and I lay half asleep, listening to the grinding of the wheel at which George, his shirt sleeves rolled up, was sharpening his axe. Thus to sit idly in the shade while the pleasant heat warms a man through and through, and when one has had an abundant dinner and there is no work to be done before sundown, is happiness in itself. Such genial warmth we can never feel at home, where it is only hot for about three days, and before we have grown accustomed to the change there comes a thunderstorm, and it is again cold and damp.

Why, what punishment is it for a man to be sent into such a country with such a climate? It should be a reward; we should keep our most gloomy islands, our Shetlands and Orkneys and Hebrides, for our convicts, and this lovely country, these soft airs, this fertile soil, and this land of milk and honey, we should keep for the honest and industrious; we should make them yeomen in the new land.

Alas! there can be but little wisdom in a people whose statesmen thus bestow the choicest gifts and blessings which the Lord hath placed in their hands upon the most worthless. Yet with every transport there never failed to arrive three or four honest artificers as settlers, free and worthy men, from whom there will surely spring a sturdy stock. And as for these convicts, the worst of them die quickly, their bodies being corrupted by evil courses and strong drink, the worst that can be made. Those who settle in the place, and marry and live soberly, must be held to have redeemed their characters, and so are the equals of those who have always been free.

While, therefore, I was lying thus, half asleep, there came to the cottage the Captain's orderly, with a summons for me. I arose quickly, put on my stock, which for coolness I had thrown off, buckled my belt and followed, wondering what the Captain wanted me for, half afraid that there might have been some infraction of discipline. The Captain was sitting at his ease in a long chair

made of canes, more like a bed than a chair.
He rose, however, and took from the table
a great sheet of written paper with a seal
upon it.

'Private Comines,' he said, 'I have a communication from His Excellency the Governor.
Here is the essential part of it.' He read from
the paper :

'In consideration of the said Nevill
Comines' youth, and of his previous good
character, His Gracious Majesty the King has
consented to remit the remainder of the term
for which the said Nevill Comines is now
serving in the regiment of Royal Marines,
and to allow the said Nevill Comines to return
to his own home, or to reside in any part of
His Majesty's dominions that he may choose ;
always provided that His Majesty's service
suffers no detriment by the retirement of the
said Nevill Comines, and that his commanding
officer shall have power, should the service
require, to retain the said Nevill Comines in
the force.'

'That is the communcation which His
Excellency sends to me ; I could, I believe,
insist upon keeping you by the terms of this

document, and indeed I am loth to suffer so
excellent a soldier, and so well-behaved a
man, whose example has proved of great
benefit, to depart. But I will not stand in
your way. You are no longer a Royal Marine.
Go to Sydney, get a civilian dress ; pay your
respects to His Excellency, and depart in
peace as soon as the ship leaves port.'

I stood stupefied.

'Since you are no longer under my command, Mr. Nevill Comines,' the Captain continued, 'I may now shake hands with you as
one gentleman with another.' He very kindly
did so. 'I have next to give you a packet
which also arrived in the mail. I hope, sir,
that it contains good news. When you have
put off your uniform I shall be very glad of
your company to crack a bottle.'

So, I was free.

I ran to tell the good news to George.

'I am released, George,' I cried. 'I can
quit the service and go home—I am pardoned.'

'And I ?' he asked.

We are selfish creatures. I thought only
of my own freedom.

CHAPTER XXVII

LETTERS FROM HOME

'You are free, at least, lad,' said George,
after a moment. 'You will go home, and I—
I must remain here for the whole term of my
natural life. The place is a paradise; I have
all that a man can ask, but for one thing, and
that turns heaven into hell.'

There was no word of comfort or of consolation to be said; for the one thing which
was wanted—how could that be attained?

Then I opened the packet given to me by
the Captain; there were one, two, three, four,
five letters in it, two for George and three for
myself.

The first was from the Prebendary.

'My dear Nevill,' he said, 'you should
receive this letter, unless the ship founders on

the ocean, about the same time, or shortly
after, the good news which the Governor of
the Settlement, or your commanding officer,
will have communicated to you.

'Your pardon has been obtained, not
without difficulty, because other and more
heinous offenders have been tried for similar
incitements to sedition, and the temper of
the country against all such is strong, and
growing, thank God, stronger. Nevertheless,
through the good offices of the Master of
St. Katherine's and the favourable report
received from the Governor of your Settlement, we have at length obtained permission
for you to leave the service and to return
home.

'We have been equally anxious to obtain
pardon for George, but hitherto without
avail. It has been decided, one must admit
with wisdom, that a young man so hot-
headed as to lead a party of rioters, crying
out for the downfall of the King, is best
bestowed in a place where he will not be again
tempted, and where, should he unhappily
be tempted and fall, he will certainly be

hanged. Therefore, inform George that he must resign himself to continuing where he is, and must make the best of it. From the last advices' (we had both written letters home to which no answer had come) 'it appears that he is in good condition, flourishing in worldly affairs, and in good heart. Therefore, I am under little anxiety concerning him. Should he obtain a pardon and come home, what would he do? He must go back to his old trade and begin that again, for the Crown hath confiscated his property. Oak Apple Dock, that possession which was to make his fortune and enable him to marry and live as a respectable and substantial citizen, is now sold to another man. See how the plans of mortals are destroyed. Sylvia, poor child! already saw herself the wife of such a man, sober, worthy, respected by all. I, who have no children of my own, and therefore love the children of my neighbours, thought to increase their happiness by gifts of my own; I would present George with the redemption of his Livery in my own Company; I would be godfather to their

children, and remember them in my last
Will and Testament. Now, what can I do?

'Sylvia, whose strange possession (if I
may so call it) was the beginning of all this
trouble, is now as love-sick as she was formerly
filled with unnatural loathing. Nothing will
serve her—but she hath written a letter in
her own hand which will inform you of her
desires.

'We shall expect your return, if Heaven
send you safe home, in a year and a half, or
thereabouts. Your mother is greatly changed
for the better since the good news, and your
father, who himself writes with this, has
resumed his former cheerfulness. Now for
the future. Since your place in the Admiralty
is lost, I have considered what will be best;
I can think of nothing better than the
Hospital itself, and the succession to your
father's post when he vacates it. It is a
peaceful and honourable employment. You
will live retired. Should you embrace any
calling which would take you much into
the company of men, you would be annoyed
continually by questions concerning Botany

Bay and the service of the Royal Marines, and you would hear references by the unfeeling and the cruel to trials at the Old Bailey and the condemned cell; from these and like rubs and annoyances I would willingly save thee.'

More this good and kind patron added by way of exhortation.

Then I opened and read the other letters in the packet.

The first was from my father, in which he conveyed to me his forgiveness for the past, and his blessing for the future. There was also enclosed a draft upon His Excellency the Governor for fifty pounds, which was as welcome as the roses in June.

The second was from none other than the old Marquis:

'My dear young friend,' he said, 'you will, by the time you read these lines, have received your pardon; we may, therefore, expect you home once more, though not at the same time your partner in misfortune. Reasons which you may understand prevented

me from visiting you in prison ; I could not,
at my age, expose myself to the risk of
recognition as a former member (or brother)
of the Sublime Society of Snugs. Alas! I
have been disappointed in my Snugs. I
thought I had chanced upon the Jacobins at
least. Where are they now? Denounced
by their most zealous member ; scattered,
dispersed. There is no longer a Club of
Snugs. The landlord, with whom I conversed
the other day, has now established a new
club. They are called the Merry Mummers.
Every Saturday evening they meet in the
room sacred to the memory of the departed
Snugs ; they drink, they talk, they smoke
tobacco, they sing, they get fuddled ; but, my
friend, always with the doors wide open.

'Since, therefore, I am unable to watch the
progress of the English Revolution as I once
expected, nothing remains but to consider
that of my own country. There is presented
before the eyes of the world at this moment
the most interesting of all experiments. The
French people, for whom your generous heart
once bled, have at last become convinced that

they have all the power and all the liberty that exists. Under this belief, having finished the little excesses with which they naturally began, they are doing great things. I know not what greater things they will do, or what will be the end. Certain it is that the mass of mankind, who speedily grow tired with shouting for liberty, settle down with patience under the rule of new masters. It is the law of man to obey; the exceptions are those who are born to command. When such an exception is found within the rank and file he becomes a mutinous rascal, and is flogged, shot, or hanged. Come back, my generous young friend, before I die. Let us together witness the triumphs of the people under their new mistress, whom they call Liberty. This sweet Princess will, in a short time, I clearly perceive, put on a masculine visage and male attire; already she carries a naked sword. She will then assume a crown (one of the old crowns), and she will be called Imperator, or Dictator, or Consul, anything but Rex. She will become Absolute; and the people—the people—they will still rejoice in

their newly-acquired liberty. As for me,
though I am now old, and can live but a
short time longer, it is pleasing to have
seen realised the dreams of so many wise
men, philosophers, freethinkers, and generous
youth. To this have the dreams brought
us.

'Come quickly home, my friend. We
are *tristes*. The Precinct, never lively, is now
unspeakably melancholy. The new schoolmaster is a young man of modesty and worth;
I miss the turbulent, wrathful soul and the
flashing eye (the Evil Eye) of his predecessor.
Your father, who has been more than Roman
(Gallo-Roman) in his treatment of a son who
has sinned against the State, has now signi-
fied his forgiveness. The period of Family
Mourning has spent itself. We, therefore,
resume our party of whist.

'Last night—to you it will be eight
months ago—I met once more that fiery soul
who caused so much private mischief with
his devil of an Eye, proclaimed the British
Republic for the destruction of his friends,
and betrayed them to the Government. A

good hater, this man! I saw him at a hell
in St. James's Street, a place where, when by
chance I find myself possessed of a few pieces,
I repair for the purpose of increasing their
number if fortune favours me. The man,
Richard Archer, has turned out to be the son
of a noble lord—some say, his lawful son and
heir, but that is not certain. This fact may
account for his ambition, his hatred, and his
malignity. He is now, it is stated, acknowledged to be the son of this great personage,
and keeps up a fine state, though his mother
has returned to the Precinct, where, after
making due submission, she is allowed by the
ladies once more to make and mend their
frocks. So that I believe nothing concerning
his legitimacy. He was dressed like a young
man of fortune, and was playing at the table
with great success. Round him were gathered
the usual throng of those who cluster about
a winning gamester. From their conversation I gathered that he is a successful
player.

'I waited and watched. When he left
the table he must have won more than a

"He was fighting all the ...   the ... ..."

thousand pounds.   As he passed me I saluted him gravely.

' " Have you forgotten me, Mr. Archer ? "

' He changed colour and started, but presently recovered himself, and attempted to laugh.

' " I did not expect to meet you here, Marquis.   I wish you good luck."

' " Where did we meet last, Mr. Archer ? " I asked him.

' " In a part of the town which need not be mentioned, Marquis," he replied with an impudent laugh.

' I might have reminded him that it was in a certain Society of Republican principles, against whose members he afterwards turned informer.   But, I could not—first, because it was not convenient in such a company to acknowledge that I too frequented the club, even as a philosopher.   The actions of philosophers are sometimes misunderstood. Next, I could not so remind him, because I can no longer use my sword arm, and a man who cannot fight must not insult any other man.   To tell a villain the plain truth is a

privilege which I lost for ever about the age
of seventy-five. The extermination of vermin
is the work of younger men.

'He waited a moment, but I made no
reply. Therefore the company laughed,
thinking no doubt that we had last met in
some place of assignation and intrigue, and
our friend the villain walked away, jingling
his guineas in his pocket.

'His appearance and manners are those
of the bold highwayman, the ruffling swash-
buckler, the led captain, the bully of the
coffee-house. Yet, he boasts that he is the
lawful son and heir of a noble lord. He is a
lucky player. He has the devil's luck, which
carries a man along triumphantly for a year
and a day and then changes. He will arrive,
I doubt not, at some bad end. Most likely
he will die in a duel.

'Come home quickly, Nevill, if it be only
to seek out this man and to insult him before all the brave company as King's evidence
—informer—spy—and former conspirator.
Come home. Insult him. Fight him. Kill
him. It is your duty. I long to see this

man either killed or hurled back again into
the mud and gutter to which he belongs.

'I remain, my dear young friend,
'Your devoted,
'   'De Rosnay.'

I read this letter through, slowly. Archer
was the son of a great lord. Well, life is full
of changes and chances. Yet, the higher a
man climbs the more conspicuous is his
history. When such as he lie hidden in
obscurity, who inquires whether or no they
have at one time been King's evidence,
Government informers, or spies?

There was one more letter. It was from
Sylvia.

'Dear Brother,' she said, 'it is two years
since you sailed away—you and George. We
are sad without you. I think of you and
pray for you every day. And now you have
been pardoned and are coming home. But
George must remain behind. Dear brother,
I cannot bear that he should be alone in that
distant country. Yet you must come home

for my mother's sake. She has suffered more
than any one over this business. I cannot
bear to think that he should be left quite
alone without a single friend among the black
savages and wretched convicts. Who will
care for him ?   Who will attend to him and
work for him ?

'Dear brother, I have made up my mind
what is my bounden duty in this matter.   It
is that I should brave the long voyage and
leave my father and my mother, and go out
to George.   I am persuaded that this is right
for me to do.   Consider—I love him so, that
I am always thinking about him.   No other
man could I endure even to think of as my
husband.   And there is no one in Australia
(of that I am sure) whom he could marry.
Thus, if I go not out to him, I remain without a husband and he without a wife.   I am
a charge to you, who will, doubtless, in due
course, have your own wife and children, and
he will be solitary and unhappy to the end of
his days.   I have opened the matter to Sister
Katherine, who weeps to think that she shall
never see the boy again, and to Dr. Lorrymore,

who hath not yet given me his opinion, but is much moved at my proposal.

'Dear brother—help me in this matter. It may be that my father and mother will give me the permission which I seek. It is a terrible thing to ask, because I may never hope to see again any of my own kith and kin. Yet it is my duty to my lover. Help me thus. Sit down and write to mother. Tell her that George being left alone, and refused any hope of pardon, must needs have a wife; and that he will take no other wife but me—Sylvia. Therefore, that I—Sylvia— who is promised to him, must go on board ship—the first convict transport that sails, and so join my lover and be married to him by the Chaplain of the Settlement. Tell her, further, that you cannot leave George alone, and that you will wait with him until your sister arrives. I think that then they will not refuse, but for the sake of getting you home again they will let me go. Farewell.'

When I had read this letter I looked up. George had a letter in his hand—also in

Sylvia's writing—and was staring straight before him across the creek, the tears in his eyes.

'What does she say, George?' I asked. 'Nay, I seek not to know the contents of your letter, which are all for your own eyes, but you shall hear what Sylvia says to me.'

With that I read her letter to me.

'How can I suffer this sacrifice?' he cried. 'That she should leave her home and endure the hardships of the long voyage, and come out to live with me in this rude place! No, no—I cannot—I must not—suffer it.'

Well, we talked it over. As for me, I perceived at the outset that Sylvia's project must be carried into effect. Why, all this trouble—the whole trouble—was begun by her strange conduct: it was due to George, if only by way of reparation, that she should come out to him. In no other way would he ever enjoy any happiness.

'But Sylvia—my tender Sylvia,' he said. 'Can she live in a hut such as this?'

'Your tender Sylvia,' I replied, 'who at home gets up at six, makes the puddings and

the pies, the cakes and the preserves and the
wine, can do all that you want here. What
else is there for her to do? Then this hut,
which is as comfortable a frame-house as
there is in the Settlement, can be built bigger
when you grow richer. Why, already you
have a farmyard which would look well in
England : there are your cattle, your sheep,
and your pigs, your geese, and your fowls.
Every year you will extend your borders ;
you will sell your produce to the Settlement ;
you will add to the number of your servants ;
this hut shall become a substantial dwelling-
house of brick, as big as the Governor's ; this
garden in front shall become a spacious lawn ;
you, who now dress in rough Osnaburg, little
better than the convicts, your servants, will
go in broadcloth. You will grow rich here,
George. Hardship? What hardship to
breathe this fragrant air ; to watch yonder
lovely creek ; to eat the fruits of your own
country in this distant land? Is there any
hardship in love? Talk not to me of hardship. There will be none, believe me, except
the separation from her parents and friends.

And this, George, by the beneficent operation of Nature, will be speedily made up to her by new ties, more tender still.'

'But the voyage. How will she endure the voyage? Who will take care of her?'

'The captain of the ship, the officers of the ship, and the officers of the Marines on board will be as tender over her as over a baby. And among the wives of the Marines or the free-settlers there will surely be some honest woman who will become her maid, or her nurse, whichever you please. No more words, George,' I cried, clapping my hand upon his shoulder. 'She must come. When you are fairly married, then—and not before —with a contented heart will I leave this place and go home again, if I am permitted to win my native shores in safety.'

CHAPTER XXVIII

THE DEVIL'S LUCK

THE Devil's luck—which, as the Marquis said,
would run for a year and a day—came, in
fact, to a sudden end. I know not what part
the Devil plays in these affairs; but certainly
the profligate, the gambler, the robber—he
who pursues any course of crime or madness
—seems always allowed at the outset a clear
course. He is overtaken by no punishment
for his profligacy; he wins when he gambles:
he is not detected when he robs—for a time.
Then—crash!—comes the end of it, with de-
tection, ruin, or bodily disease. The thread is
cut: the course is run: *exit* prodigal son.

So complete an end was put to Richard
Archer's course, that when I came home, resolved upon finding out the man, and, if possible, upon exposing him before some great

company, behold! there was no Richard Archer left. He was gone. The toils that he had laid for others caught his feet too. But, while we escaped with grievous wounds, he was entirely destroyed. The Wise Woman prophesied true things ; so that I am the more convinced, the longer I think of this strange story, of what I said at the outset, that the gift of prophecy is the power of reading a man's character and disposition with the knowledge of what will result, given such a character and such a disposition. This spoiled darling of Fortune continued his victorious career, therefore, for a certain time. During this interval everything went well with him. He grew—or seemed to grow—in daily favour with his father, who gave him money in abundance—money as much as he asked for : but promised nothing, and entered into no engagement with him for the future, so that he was, in reality, little advanced in his main purpose, which was the succession, not only to what he considered certain, the title and the lands, but also to the great personal property of his father.

With this object he was assiduous in his
court, visiting the old lord daily, making music
for him, conversing with him, playing cards
with him, and telling him stories and scandals
of the company with whom he consorted.
Lord Aldeburgh treated him with indulgence,
watching him, listening curiously, smiling at
his adventures, and pushing him gently down
the flowery slope on which the young man
was eagerly devouring the fruits which poison
the soul. So that for two short years there
was no pleasure which Richard Archer desired
but he was provided with the money at least
to buy it. As for his mother, he very soon
neglected her, and suffered her to go back
again to the Precinct, where she returned to
her old work for the ladies of the Hospital.

At this time he went about the town
dressed in what is called the ' high kick ' of
fashion ; his friends, of like mind with himself,
committed a thousand follies and extrava-
gances ; they were all young gentlemen of
fashion and rank, among whom he was admitted as the son (and perhaps the heir) of
Lord Aldeburgh. He drove a curricle, hand-

ling the ribbons to general admiration; he
rode a fiery horse; he learned to fence
adroitly; in short, there was not to be seen in
the whole of Bond Street a more fashionable,
flaunting, swaggering, fine young gentleman.
No one to look at him would have thought
that this splendid creature had formerly been
the humble master of St. Katherine's Charity
School.

If he was handsome, dexterous, and auda-
cious—qualities which were found, I believe,
well able to please many fine ladies—he could
also drink, which gratified the men. Others
drank and got fuddled, this man drank and
his wits grew clearer; that is to say, during
his period of success. He was always ready
to gamble, and, a thing almost incredible, he
always won. It is strange how men should
be found to play with one whose luck is pro-
verbial; perhaps they look for the turn of
the tide. No one ever heard of a gamester
continuing all his life to win. He played at
the public hells, or gaming-tables, of which
there are so many, and he won constantly; he
frequented the houses of those great ladies who

keep a kind of public bank, and he won there ;
he played in private with his friends, and
he always won of them.

Every year, I am told, there are seen in
Bond Street, the Park, and Piccadilly, at the
opera and the theatres, on the racecourses and
in the hells, and wheresoever the profligate
resort, two or three young men, who appear
for a time, dazzle the beholders, and then
vanish, and are no more seen. No one knows
what becomes of them, or where they hide
their heads when their little flight is finished.
Mostly, it is believed, they languish in the
King's Bench, the Marshalsea, and the Fleet.
They are the dragon-flies of Society, not its
butterflies. I do not suppose that there was
ever a dragon-fly with a previous history such
as Richard Archer's. Yet no one knew it—
no one would suspect such a history ; they
might believe that for his own reasons Lord
Aldeburgh had brought up his son in the country ; no one certainly could possibly suspect the
truth. It might be urged that the Court was
crowded during the trials of the four men
charged with High Treason, for belonging to

an obscure little club, and for being concerned
in a petty riot which led to nothing. Some
one may have remembered the face of the informer and King's evidence; but consider, his
new dress had so altered the man that nobody
could possibly recognise him. Nothing of the
grub was left in this splendid dragon-fly. Nay,
I suppose that he thought himself quite safe from
discovery. St. Katherine's is a most obscure
place. The world of fashion finds not its way
there; one trembles to think what would become of a Beau, Jessamy, Maccaroni, Smart, or
Dandy (the creature changes his name yearly)
were he to stand alone or unprotected among
the tarpaulins and mudlarks at the head of
St. Katherine's Stairs. And if the world of
fashion never gets as far East as the Precinct,
never do the residents of the Precinct get as
far West as the Park, or even Vauxhall.

But a man can never escape his past.
From his birth and the station to which he is
ordained and called into being, unto his death,
the whole of his history is always ready to be
unfolded and disclosed. He can count upon
hiding nothing, principally because there are

few things which a man does absolutely alone and unnoticed. His past clings to him; it follows him; it is like a lengthening shadow; it is like a chain which he drags after him; it takes shapes; to some it becomes an angel of light to lead him upwards; it cuts out a way for him through the wood and lays low the thorns; it strengthens and supports him. To others it lies as a net about his feet to trip him up and lay him low; it may become a Devil with a scourge; it may take the shape of an executioner with a torture-chamber and a gibbet. Physician and philosopher have held that every moment of a man's life is remembered and may be recalled by a trick of memory or some sudden association of ideas. Thus may we understand how a man may be judged by his own memory, by his own mind, and out of his own mouth.

The gardens at Vauxhall which open for the season about the middle of May were crowded one evening towards the end of that month for the first warm and fine evening of the year. By daylight the grounds and beds were splendid with spring flowers and flowering bushes; after dusk the air was laden with the fragrance of the lilac bushes; and the gardens were brilliant with the coloured light of ten thousand lamps. Among the gay and animated company were merry parties from the City, the sober merchant with wife and daughters, and their attendant swains, come to hear the singing and music, to look on at the dancing, and to take their supper, with a bowl of Vauxhall punch, in one of the alcoves or rustic retreats, contrived for the purpose. There were gallant young Templars looking boldly in the girls' faces, ready for adventures; there were ladies exhibiting their charms along the walks; there were others dancing, who seemed not unwilling to attract attention; in the more retired walks roamed couples amorously discoursing, giggling, and whispering; there were supper-parties merrily feasting, laughing, and drinking in every alcove. Who, in short, does not know the humours of Vauxhall?

There had already been omens on this day

which should have pointed it out to Richard
Archer as a day of disaster. He knew as well
as any one the signs of good and bad luck ; he
had learned the old women's sayings ; he
should have observed their rules and kept at
home. But whom the Gods intend to destroy
they first make mad.

For instance, at the moment when the day
began, at stroke of twelve, he, who was then
in a certain hell or gambling-house in St.
James's Street, began to lose.

Up to that moment he had already won a
goodly sum of money. Had he left the place
at midnight, he would have gone home with
thousands of pounds in his pocket. He did
not ; then he began to lose. His luck changed
suddenly at the stroke of midnight. Now, he
was so little accustomed to lose, that he continued to play, being surprised, but confident
that the luck would turn : the cautious player,
when he finds the luck persistent against him,
retires—hastens to retire. He bows to Fortune ; he does not tempt and defy her.
Archer, who was the spoiled child of Fortune,
could not understand that he might go on

losing. He continued to play; when he got up from the table, at four in the morning, he had lost, not only all his winnings of the evening, but a great sum in addition. The credit that he enjoyed as Lord Aldeburgh's son, and the figure that he cut, are shown by the fact that he was able to borrow of the proprietor this great sum, all to be lost at the table immediately afterwards.

During the night he drank a vast quantity of wine, the fumes of which rose to his head and made him stagger. This was a new thing for him, because, in general, his head was so strong, that he could drink the company under the table and feel no worse. To go home reeling drunk astonished him. But he was not so drunk as to forget his losses. In the morning, when he awoke with a heavy head and a grievous thirst, he remembered that he had borrowed, and given a note of hand for, a much larger sum of money than he owned in the world. Well, his father would help him out.

But then there happened a thing that should have made him reflect. If the old

woman's story is true—I say nothing for or
against it—then all the troubles were begun
by his own action; he cast the Evil Eye on
Sylvia; he caused her to feel an unnatural
loathing for her lover. The rest followed as
you have seen. Now, this man had a mistress.
How much or how little this cruel and selfish
nature could feel the passion of love I cannot
pretend to know. This mistress of his, however, wrote him a letter, which his servant—
this young gentleman of fashion, who had
been schoolmaster to St. Katherine's, had now
a servant of his own—brought him before he
dressed. She informed him that she could no
longer abide the sight, or the touch, or the
voice of him. She was going away where he
should never be able to find her. Observe,
therefore, that the same thing happened to
him as had happened to George. Remember
what the Wise Woman had warned him. His
sweetheart now loathed him who had professed
to love him.

He read it, hardly understanding it, so
strange, and sudden, and unexpected was the
letter. His mistress was gone, and his money

was gone. He swore aloud, after the old fashion of St. Katherine's Stairs, which came more natural to him than the finer oaths of Bond Street. He drank a tankard of small ale for his thirst, and he cursed the girl again.

He sat down to breakfast, but could eat little, being smitten with a dismal gloom of spirits. While he sat at table another letter came to him from one of his friends of the racecourse. A certain racehorse, on which they both expected to win, and had staked large sums of money upon the event, had gone dead lame. He could not run.

Archer was not one of those who can take misfortunes with an appearance of lightness. Only a gentleman of breeding can do this. It is, indeed, one of the marks of a gentleman to meet the blows of Fate with courage.

'This seems a day of misfortune,' he said, with more truth than he suspected. 'By Gad, it begins well. What next?'

Now on a day of bad luck, as this clearly promised to be, no wise man enters on any business whatever, nor does he mix with other men more than he must: he stays at home, and

keeps quiet. Next day another sun rises, and
Fortune smiles. Even if he stays at home on
such a day, some accident will happen to him
—a chimney on fire, the breaking of his best
punchbowl, a gash in his chin when he shaves,
or something. Richard Archer should have
kept quiet and snug.

Unfortunately he did not. He was in a
desperate, savage mood, ready to quarrel with
anyone. Yet he went to visit his father. And,
as a part of the bad luck, my lord was also on
that day in a mood as savage and as ready for
a quarrel as his son. Nothing went well.
First, he began to play to his father; but a
string snapped, and he laid the violin down
with a curse.

He sat down, and began to tell of his last
night's losses.

' Three thousand I left behind me,' he said,
' in notes of hand ; and this morning I hear
that Œdipus is gone lame, and scratched for
all his engagements. That makes five thousand
more—eight thousand dropped in one day.
And all I have is two thousand.'

' How do you propose to pay the money?'

'Well, my lord, if you will not pay my debts of honour for me, I must vanish and go away.'

'Humph! A pretty expensive son you are!'

'Come, it's the first time I've lost.'

'Mind it's the last, then.'

The son restrained himself with an effort. 'Will you choose to play a game?' he asked, taking up the cards.

They played one game and then another. Each time the son lost. The moment came when he lost his temper as well, and threw down the cards, swearing that the Devil was in them, and sprang to his feet.

Then his father flamed up.

When two men, both of ungovernable passion, fall at the same moment into wrath, the quarrel is one which affects both lives afterwards to the end.

'You?' cried the son, 'you to talk about filial respect? You, who suffered your own wife to go away and starve!'

The old man's face was now purple.

'You—you—who are you, sir? My son?
You? No. I, your father? No—no—you
are the son of nobody. You have no father.
Did I speak of filial duty? I mistook. Forget
that I used the word. You are no son of
mine!'

'I will show your lawyers, when you are
dead, whose son I am.'

'As for your pretended discovery, learn,
once for all, that it is false. My wife—my
only true and legal wife—did not die a week
before the sham marriage, but six weeks after
that event—six weeks after, sir, as will be
proved when the time comes.'

'Then,' replied his son, with filial piety,
'either you lied to my mother or you lie to me.'

The old man now became quite calm in his
manner. This was dangerous, if the son knew
it. 'Sir,' he said, 'do you believe that at any
time I could make your mother—your mother
—Lady Aldeburgh? I beg you to consider.
She was more in her place as a washerwoman
or needlewoman of St. Katherine's Precinct.
Oh! I know,' for here Richard started and
changed colour. 'I found out all about you

when first I heard from your lawyer, who hopes to make a good thing by his pretended discovery. Barefooted beggar-boy, gutter-boy, charity-school-boy, schoolmaster to St. Katherine's Hospital, organist to the church, member of a seditious club, one of a gang of rascals, informer for the Government and King's evidence—this is your history. And you think you are going to be Lord Aldeburgh when I die? Never—sir—never.'

'I think—nay, I am sure that I am going to be Lord Aldeburgh—and a much better Peer than my predecessor,' said the young man.

'When you first came, I humoured you. Why, you amused me. You pretended to be impudent, yet you were afraid. You assumed the airs of a gentleman, with the manners of a twopenny schoolmaster; you tried to look at your ease, being mightily uneasy. You amused me. I thought I would fool you. Then I discovered that you could play—yes, you have a fine touch on the violin—you could manage a part in an opera, and so earn your living. I thought it would be pleasant to let you have a run. Of course, I knew that you could never become a gentleman, but you might make pretence and persuade yourself. How it was going to end I did not know. But it has ended. You can go.'

'The law, my Lord, give me permission to assure you, does not allow even a noble Lord to commit bigamy. If you are lying I am your heir. If you speak the truth you shall be prosecuted for bigamy.'

'Shall I?' His lordship laughed pleasantly. 'You are pleased to be facetious, sir.'

'Son or no son—heir or not.' Richard Archer stood over the helpless form sitting propped in the chair, form so helpless, and face so full of sneering purpose. 'You have pushed me on. You cannot now leave me in the lurch. If I cannot pay my debts of honour——'

'Honour? Debts of honour? Gentlemen—not such as you—may incur debts of honour. Your debts are nothing to me. I never promised you anything. I have given you money, it is true. You have been introduced to the society of gentlemen. You have

played at being a gentleman yourself. Well,
you can now go back to your gutter and
remember this time. The memory of the last
two years will console you, when you have to
stand again hat in hand and to bow low
before your betters. I shall do nothing more
for you.'

What answer was made by a man exas-
perated and enraged beyond all control may
be guessed. But by this time his lordship's
wrath had spent itself, and a relentless cold-
ness had taken its place. He listened without
interruption.

'But you have not done with me—no—
you have not done with me yet, my Lord,' the
.young man concluded.

'You are wrong, sir, you are wrong. I
have quite done with you. Be under no mis-
take upon that point. You will never be
admitted to my presence again, or to my
house.'

'I shall come back to it on the day when
you are carried out heels first. I shall be
your lordship's chief mourner. Ha! ha!
an inconsolable mourner—the new Lord

Aldeburgh. Happily, that event will not long be delayed,' he added, brutally. 'A month—a few weeks.'

Lord Aldeburgh rang his bell violently. Like most men of pleasure, the thought of death, though he was already so near his end, agitated and terrified him.

'Show this person to the door,' he shouted to his man.

'Yes, my Lord.'

'Give orders that he is never to be admitted again on any pretence.'

'Yes, my Lord.'

'I said that he was my son. I was mistaken: he is not my son. Do you hear?'

The man bowed low.

Richard Archer went out with a swagger and a laugh. But his face betrayed the despair of his soul; because, unless he could recover his losses by a fortunate run—a thing so rare that it cannot be hoped for—he was ruined indeed. He must leave the company in which he had lived, and he must go into hiding—where? Not, he reflected, for one day more, at least—one more trial of his luck. It would doubtless change. One more night at the green table.

He dined with some of his companions. His evil fortune caused one of them to propose repairing to Vauxhall before going to St. James's Street, where midnight is the choicest time for the gamester.

It was nearly nine o'clock, when the lamps were already lit in the gardens, and the place was full of people, that Richard Archer arrived with two or three more. They had all been drinking: they were talking and laughing noisily: they swaggered their shoulders, and took up the middle of the path, quiet visitors falling back to let them pass: and they looked into the faces of the girls with impudent eyes, which betokened a quarrel before long. At Vauxhall this kind of quarrel is not uncommon.

Outside the crowd gathered in front of the orchestra, on the gravel walk of the broad path leading from the gates, stood a little group, consisting of a middle-aged man, in appearance a sober shopkeeper, his wife matching her husband in looks and dress, his

daughter, a well-shaped, very pretty girl,
dressed neatly, as became her station. The
last of the group was a young man, tall, with
a small head, a shrill voice, a quick and eager
manner, and in appearance studious or
scholarly. This was none other than my late
companion of Newgate and the Press Yard—
the man who had been expelled from Oxford,
the Atheist and Republican and Poet. He had
retained his convictions ; and, as he was all
for the abolition of rank, he had already reduced himself to the station of printer's reader ;
and he was about to carry his ideas still
farther into practice by marrying the daughter
of a worthy seller of second-hand books, who
had a shop at Westminster. Alas ! the events
of this evening at once put an end to this
project, and showed him (one hopes for pardon
in the end, even for an Atheist) the folly and
wickedness of his unbelief.

When the swaggering, half-drunken band
drew near, this party stepped aside to let them
pass.

I suppose that the girl looked up as they
went by. I suppose that the light of the lamps

fell upon her pretty face and made it look still prettier. I suppose that Richard Archer was half drunk, and that he was strongly and suddenly tempted to his own destruction ; for he stepped out from the company and laid his arm round the girl's neck, and kissed her twice upon the cheek. She shrieked, and tore herself from his grasp. Then her lover rushed upon the assailant, and with a single blow from his fist hurled him headlong on the ground, and kicked him where he lay.

Archer sprang to his feet.

Then a very curious thing happened. When a man has been knocked down—a young man and vigorous—he returns the blow when he is able to get up, unless, which is of rare occurrence, he is a coward. If he is a gentleman, he not only fights his assailant then and there, in the true British manner, with his fists, but he meets him next morning with pistols. So that when Archer rose his companions, as a matter of course, formed a kind of circle for fair play.

The other man stood opposite ready for the encounter, his eyes flaring, his cheeks hot.

Well, Archer stood still. He gazed at his
assailant. He stared at him; his cheeks
turned pale; his jaw dropped; he saw, in
fact, the avenger. It was no longer a fight
over an insult offered to a girl; it was the
last and heaviest blow. His face showed con-
sternation and amazement.

'What the devil is the matter, Archer?'
asked one of his friends.

What was it, indeed? Why did he stand
there? Had he nothing even to say?

'Come,' said the girl, catching her lover
by the arm; 'let us go away quickly, before
worse happens.'

'Go away? Why, why go away, my
dear? Not yet. Oh! I have found the man
at last. Archer—villain! I have found
thee.'

'What does all this mean?' asked the
same man again. 'Man, you have been
knocked down, and you have not even—what
does it mean? Shall I take a message from
you? It seems the gentleman recognises
you. There has been an old quarrel. Sir,
will you give me the name of your second?'

'No, sir, I will not. We fight duels with gentlemen—with men of honour; not with Informers, Spies, and King's evidence.'

'Again, Archer,' said his friend, 'what does this mean? Words like these require explanation. Speak up man. Tell him that he lies.'

'Gentlemen,' my fellow-prisoner replied, 'I congratulate you on the company you keep. Or, perhaps, you are of the same profession or calling. Yet, I should think there can hardly be so many reptiles in the world. If so, informing is indeed a prosperous profession.'

'Sir,' said the same man, 'if you cannot make good your charges, give me leave to tell you that your quarrel will be with me and with my friends here, as well as with Mr. Archer—who may, I believe, be called the Honourable Richard Archer—son of the Right Honourable the Viscount Aldeburgh.'

'This person is certainly Richard Archer. As for you, and your friends, sir, give me leave to remind you that we commonly judge a man by the company he keeps. There is no safer rule. Richard Archer may be the son of a Viscount, or an Earl or a Duke, or even a Royal Prince. He is, none the less, Richard Archer. That is to say, he is the man who, when certain former associates of his were accused of High Treason, turned King's evidence, and bore witness against them, not only giving the Government information which nearly tied the hangman's rope round the necks of four unfortunate gentlemen, of whom I was one, but also, by his malignity, converted a club, where harmless discussions had been held, into a great revolutionary centre, and its members into traitors and conspirators. Nay, two of his victims are even now languishing on the shores of Botany Bay, on the great Australian Island.'

' Is this true, Archer?'

He made no reply at all. He still stood motionless, bent forward, his eyes staring, his mouth open, his cheek pale, but for a little blood caused by a scratch on the gravel when he fell.

' You would like to hear more about him, perhaps. He was a parish boy, brought up

and educated by the charity of the Society
of St. Katherine's Hospital. His mother supported herself by honest work, washing,
sewing, and the like. He showed parts, and
was promoted to be master of the Charity
School of the Hospital ; and, afterwards,
because he could make music, he was
appointed organist to the church, and so
remained until his villainy, when he was
turned out by the Chapter. Then, I know
not what he did, or what became of him.
Now I find him, dressed like a gentleman,
flaunting in Vauxhall, and insulting virtuous
girls with the insolence of a young lord.'

' Archer, are these things true ? '

He still made no reply ; his companions
drew away from him ; he was left standing
alone ; I think that he must have been
drinking very deep to be thus overwhelmed
and able to say nothing. You have heard
how he behaved when he met the Marquis
who knew as much.

' Enough,' said the bookseller, hastily ;
' let us leave him and get away from the place.
Come.'

Well, things might have ended there. A brawl in Vauxhall Gardens generally ends in the marching off of both parties in opposite directions. No harm would have been done except to Richard Archer himself, who could no longer show his face among his former companions.

'Come,' said his friends; 'we have had enough of this. Let us go.'

The altercation, though on the outskirts of the crowd, had already brought together a few of the people who love nothing so much as to watch the conduct of a quarrel, and are as critical of the behaviour of the combatants as some men are of a bottle of wine. Among them was one of the waiters of the place; this man had in his hand a tray, on which were the materials for a supper which he was serving in an alcove hard by; he stood looking on, mouth and eyes wide open. His guests must wait till the fight was finished.

Suddenly Archer recovered from the stupor in which he had been plunged; he stood upright; he looked around him. Right and left his friends shrank back. He was

thrust out from among them ; he was expelled
the society of gentlemen—he changed colour ;
he saw his enemy pointing at him with out-
stretched finger.   He gasped for breath, his
eyes flashed fire, he saw the waiter and his
tray ; he grasped a supper knife from the
tray, and rushed upon the man who had
revealed his past.

It was by two of his own friends that
Richard Archer was seized and held when the
unhappy gentleman—the Oxford scholar,
Atheist, Republican, and Poet—lay dying on
the ground, the knife plunged up to the
handle in his heart.

CHAPTER XXIX

THE VENGEANCE OF THE LORD

NEXT morning, about eleven o'clock, Lord Aldeburgh sat alone in his bow window looking at the people in the street below. This had been his sole amusement before Richard Archer came to him, and it seemed likely to be all that was left to him, now that he had driven the young man out of the house. I know not whether he repented of his wrath, and would have recalled him. After the events of the previous night it was too late for repentance or regrets. Even if he felt any, he was not the man to betray by his face any emotion so weak as self-reproach. His face was as hard and as calm as if nothing had happened. When a young fellow drove along the street in his curricle, he looked after

him with a sigh : such as that young man, so
had he been. If a pretty woman passed, his
eyes went after her till she was out of sight,
and his memory carried him back to former
conquests.

His table stood beside him, provided with
books, paper, pens, and cards ; but so long as
the weather was fine, and the people thronged
the street, he cared for nothing else.

His man opened the door noiselessly, and
stood before him.

'I beg your lordship's pardon. A woman
is below—an old woman—who prays for a
few words with your lordship. She says she
is the wife of one who formerly sailed under
your lordship's command.'

'I dare say some malingering, mutinous,
murmuring scoundrel. I hope he got his
deserts. If he sailed under me he probably
did. I cannot, at least, reproach myself
with any foolish clemency in the past. Well,
give her a guinea and let her go.'

'She wishes only to see your lordship.'

'Give her two guineas, then.'

'With submission, my lord, she says that

she has a thing of the greatest importance to communicate.'

'Let her come up, then. Once there were many old women who had things of importance to tell me, and it was always about the young ones. Such an old woman has not been to see me for long. Let her come up; though, if that is her errand, she is too late. Bring her up.'

The old woman was none other than the Wise Woman of the Precinct. She came in, courtesied, folded her hands, and looked at the sick man in his chair with curious eyes.

'Well, dame,' my lord asked her, 'what have you got to say?'

'You are Lord Aldeburgh—formerly the Honourable Stephen Archer, and once Captain of the *Enterprise*?'

'Certainly. At your service, my good woman. You are, perhaps, of the respectable calling of "go between."'

'My husband was on your ship, my lord.'

'That is very likely. There were eight hundred of the ship's company.'

'His name—but, perhaps, you will

remember his story better than his name.
He had the misfortune to incur your lordship's
displeasure. You ordered him, without considering whether he was guilty or innocent,
to be tied up at once for six dozen.'

'Very likely. Most of the eight hundred
got their six dozen in the course of the
voyage. We did not stop the navigation of
the ship in order to argue with the fellows.
Well, he got his six dozen. What then? It
is thirty years since I was Captain of the
Enterprise. Does he still remember such a
trifle ?'

'This man did not get his six dozen,
because he seized a marline-spike, and
knocked his Captain senseless on the deck.'

'Ha! I remember. So—you are his widow
—his name was—— I have it—Habbijam—
John Habbijam—able seaman. He was tried
by court-martial, and sentenced to be hanged.
Yes; I remember well. The fellow escaped.
It was very extraordinary—he escaped—
and no one could ever discover how, though
I have always suspected—— So you are
his widow. Well, old woman, if you will

tell me how he escaped I will give you a guinea—five guineas.'

'God forbid that I should take your money. He escaped because the sentries suffered him to go. All the ship's crew were ready to help—ay, all the petty officers—so much they commiserated the man. I will tell you how he escaped. He was let out of his prison, and taken to the lower deck, where, before the eyes of many—but none told the secret—he dropped out of a port, and swam ashore. He reached in safety the Isle of Wight. There he kept snug, and under cover ; but, sending me word of his whereabouts, and, after the Fleet had sailed, I brought him away.'

'He was a fortunate man. I wish I had known the cause of his escape. Such an example should have been made as—— Perhaps 'tis not yet too late. But, after thirty years—— Did you come here to tell me this ? '

'This and some more, my lord. I suppose you never thought, when you ordered this man and that man, for no offence at all, or a trifling fault, to be tied up and lashed—three dozen, six dozen, a hundred, five hundred lashes, till they were cut down more dead than alive—how the ship's company grew to hate you as no captain ever yet was hated?'

'No such thought ever entered my head, I do assure you. What would it matter how much the whole crew hated me?'

'Nor how they lamented that my Jack's blow wasn't a little harder. No, the sufferings of the men are of no account to the captain. Why should they be? Well, my lord, there's One above. And the thought has always been with my man and me that the Lord would let us see His Vengeance upon you before we died.'

'You can,' said his lordship, not in the least angry, 'look about you. I am still young enough to enjoy—I am not yet sixty —yet you see me a cripple. Is that enough for you? Call it the Lord's Vengeance and be happy. The Lord is always, of course, on the side of mutinous scoundrels. But the man—is he yet living? The man who escaped his hanging—doth he live?'

'He is yet living.'

'Still unhanged. Still under sentence. He has had a long rope. Well, we shall see to it. Go on—the Lord's Vengeance, I think you said.'

'Your lordship has a son.'

'Perhaps.'

'His name is Richard Archer. I found out years ago whose son he was. I told him, when the time came, and when he had shown what manner of man he is, why he must be your son—because he is a devil.'

'It may be so. Go on.' His attention was aroused, and, though he spoke lazily, his face quickened, and showed his interest.

'I told him who and what his father was; it was I who caused him to have no peace or rest until he came to you ; and I read your son's fortune ; no fortune ever came out more certain or more horrible. And now the cards have proved true, as they always do. You received him and allowed him to call himself, openly, your son—everybody knows him for your son. Oh ! I have seen him in his fine clothes and his curricle—who would recognise

the humble charity-boy of St. Katherine's?
I hope he has done credit to his noble father.
A proper man he is. Your lordship should
be proud of such an heir.'

'You have still something more to tell
me.'

'The Vengeance of the Lord has fallen at
last. Oh! it has fallen—it has fallen. Thank
God for it!' She clasped her hands and
grinned—the horrid grin of toothless jaws.

'More Vengeance?'

'Your son is in prison. He is in prison
charged with murder. He murdered a man
in Vauxhall Gardens last night. It was one
of the young gentlemen against whom he
gave evidence two years ago when he turned
King's evidence and Informer. He stabbed
him to the heart with a supper knife. And
now he will be hanged.'

His lordship changed colour. He closed
his eyes as one in pain, and lay back in his
chair. Presently he recovered and sat up
again.

'Go on,' he said, quietly. 'You were telling me——'

'He will be hanged. Your son will be hanged.'

'It seems to me that the Vengeance of the Lord has fallen upon a certain Richard Archer, and upon the man who was stabbed. Have you anything else to say?'

'That is all.'

'You say you knew this man—who calls himself my son,' his lordship said, slowly, 'when he was a child.'

'I have watched him growing up. I remember his mother bringing him a babe in arms.'

'That was in the place called St. Katherine's Precinct. Yes. That is where his mother lives—a place near the town, I believe, inhabited by the riverside gentry, where the press-gangs sometimes go to find their men.'

'That is the place, my lord.'

'And you rejoice over the misfortunes of this young man—who appears to have done you no injury—because you think they also fall upon me.'

'I do rejoice. Your Honour looked to

see my man hung up at the yard-arm. You did not see him. Now my man and I will go and see your son hung up outside Newgate Gaol.'

'You look forward, doubtless, to a great pleasure. The Lord is good, as has often been set forth, to His inferior creatures—in giving them such pleasures and so many of them. I hope you will not be disappointed. Meantime, good woman, remember that there is many a slip between the cup and the lip. You have said all you wished? Thank you. Good morning, Mrs. Habbijam. I trust that no disappointment——' He stopped again, with an expression of pain on his face—his cheeks twitched, his eyes rolled. The old woman with a low curtsey retired. His lordship lay back on his pillows, and rolled his head in pain. He recovered in a few moments. 'Ah!' he sighed. ''Twas a pinch—some day it will last a little too long. Then——' He pulled the table nearer, and took pen and paper. 'We shall, I believe, my good woman,' he murmured, 'take a step which will render this great pleasure impossible for your worthy husband.' Then he wrote as follows :

' To Messrs. Singleton and Sons, Solicitors and Attorneys-at-Law, Lincoln's Inn Fields.

' SIRS,—I have made the discovery that a certain sailor, who thirty years ago was condemned to be hanged for striking his Captain, myself, and escaped before his sentence was carried out, is still living, having eluded the most strenuous search. I can lay hands upon him at any moment. On receipt of this letter you will immediately repair to the Admiralty and communicate this fact. The man must be arrested, and at once lodged in gaol until the sentence can be carried out. The case was flagrant, the man evidently intending to murder his Captain. He expressed on his trial regret that his attempt had been unsuccessful. I have learned that the man now lives with his wife, or near her, in the place called——'

Here the letter remained unfinished. When Lord Aldeburgh's man, an hour later, entered the room, he found his master lying with his head on the table. And he was dead. He died hard and impenitent, desirous only of seeing this old man hanged. And he learned before his death that his son was a murderer, who would be hanged for murder.

'Vengeance of the Lord!' said the old woman.

CHAPTER XXX

EVIL HEART AND EVIL EYE

The end of the wretched man Archer and the condition to which he was now reduced were far worse than the misfortunes he had succeeded in bringing upon his victims. No single circumstance, indeed, was wanting in the horror of his fate. He was suddenly hurled down from the place where he stood among gentlemen of fortune, himself regarded as an acknowledged son, if not the heir, of a noble lord, to a prison cell. One day he ruffled and flaunted in Hyde Park among the best, he dined sumptuously, he was dressed in splendid raiment, he gambled and dined with half the House of Lords; the next day he was plunged into a common gaol. From St. James's Street to Newgate is a great and terrible drop. Nor was this all; for in the crowd which gathered round the group before the constables came to take him in custody were some of the light-fingered gentry, who eased him of handkerchief, his watch and seals, and his purse, and, even under the pretence of preventing his escape, stripped his fingers of the rings upon them and took the gold buckles from his shoes. They left him nothing. Nay, as they hustled and dragged him from the garden the crowd followed, and threw dust and gravel at him ; they tore his coat to rags ; they would have torn him to pieces but for the constables who protected him. When he was brought at last to the prison he presented a sad and sorry spectacle indeed—his fine coat bedabbled with dirt and blood, his hat gone, and his head covered with mud.

Now when his man-servant heard, an hour or two later, what had happened, he behaved with uncommon prudence and forethought ; for he immediately put together the whole of his master's effects, namely, a large sum of money in gold, a great quantity of valuable clothes, his rings, jewels, swords, fencing-foils, pistols—

everything that he possessed; he called a hack-
ney coach, told the landlord that his master
was called suddenly out of town and would
return shortly, and drove away. Whither he
went was never ascertained ; but then nobody
inquired. At break of day the same excellent servant repaired to the stables where
his master kept his horses, rode off upon one
and led the other, returned in a half an hour
and drove away his master's curricle and pair.
What the servant did with this splendid spoil
I know not, for, as I said above, nobody ever
inquired.

So he lost his freedom and all the wealth
that was left to him. He had nothing left
even to conduct his defence withal. The
impudent little attorney who pretended to
defend us would do nothing for him without
money.

One more loss awaited him. He borrowed
some paper and wrote to Lord Aldeburgh,
despatching the letter by one of the prison
messengers. The man returned with the
doleful news that his lordship was dead. He
had been found dead in his chair that very

morning at eleven o'clock. Had he lived, it is only reasonable to suppose that the prisoner's case would have been properly handled and defended.

He had, therefore, nothing left; not a sixpence in his pocket; not a friend in the world; not even a change of clothes.

Having nothing to give for garnish, he was treated with the utmost harshness, loaded with the heaviest irons, thrust into the common felons' side, where he raged at first like a wild beast, insomuch that his fellow prisoners, rough and rude though they were, fell back before him as he dragged his fetters up and down the yard, until weariness and hunger compelled him to rest. Again, as he had no money, there was nothing for him to eat except the rations of bread doled out daily among the poorest prisoners. Nay, there was no prisoner in the place but had some friend, mistress, or wife who brought him every day something—however small and poor—to eke out his bread-and-water diet. But for him, who had made so brave and gallant a show, there was no one. As

for his mother, who would have come to him
had she known of his evil case, she was lying
ill of some fever, and like to die ; therefore
they could not tell her—nor did the poor
woman ever learn the dreadful end that had
befallen her son, for when she recovered, she
was found to have lost some of her wits, and
though she still contrived to work with her
needle for the ladies, she chose to believe that
her son was now a great lord, and spoke of
him as his lordship.

I love not to linger over the sufferings of
this unhappy man, though he deserved them
all and more.

A fortnight later, the Grand Jury having,
without the least hesitation, found a true bill
against Richard Archer for wilful murder, he
was brought out and placed at the bar of the
Sessions House to stand his trial.

At the aspect of the prisoner the whole
Court shuddered. He was gaunt and pale,
because, since his imprisonment, he had lived
upon nothing but bread and water. This
fare, for one who came to it from the feast-
ings of Belteshazzar, was little short of sheer

starvation. He looked like a man more than
starved. His clothes were the same as those
in which he had been brought to the prison;
they were dirty and ragged; his silken waistcoat was discoloured, and still showed the
horrid stains of blood; his silk stockings were
in holes, and his coat hung upon him in rags.
But these were nothing compared with his
face, on which misery and despair were
stamped. One who was present told me that
he should never forget the face of the man—
strange, wild, covered with a black beard, the
forehead high and pale, the black eyes fierce
and wrathful, the black hair lying loose upon
his shoulders. 'So,' said my informant,
'might have stood some ancient British
savage brought to hear his doom, but knowing full well that he must die. Not afraid
to die, but anxious to get the business de-
spatched, glaring upon his captors like a wild
beast.'

He seemed to take little interest in the
progress of his case, about which there could
be no doubt whatever from the beginning.
The bookseller and his daughter appeared to

give evidence; they described the circumstances of the quarrel, and the fatal stab ; the
waiter from whom he had snatched the knife ;
the surgeon who had attended the dying
man ; one of the constables who had arrested
him—in turn gave their evidence.   The prisoner heard, or seemed not to hear—with
a proud carelessness—looking from time to
time fiercely round the Court as if he sought
some means of escape, and then relapsing into
an indifference which was as wonderful as it
was uncommon.   Finally, however, when the
Judge called upon him to say what he had to
say in his own defence, he spoke up and
spoke well, though not persuasively.

'It is true,' he said, his words and the
manner of his delivery—which were those of
a person well educated—strangely contrasting
with his appearance.   'It is most unhappily
true that I stabbed this man, and I suppose it
is also true that the wound inflicted by my
hand caused his death.   Everything stated
by the witnesses is true.   I did not ask them
any questions because I had no desire to
waste the time of the Court in even sug-

gesting that their evidence was not true. I
wish, however, to recall to the jury a certain
part of the evidence which will, I am convinced, cause them to acquit me of any desire
to kill this man. I had been drinking; being,
as they say, flushed with the fumes of wine,
I kissed a girl who was in the gardens with
her friends; that was the beginning of the
accident. Her lover—I did not blame him
therefor—resented this insult and knocked
me down, a thing not difficult for a powerful
man who is also sober, in dealing with one
who is not so strong and is also in liquor. He
did this in the rage and fury of the moment,
incensed by the outrage upon his mistress—I
do not blame him—I only speak the truth.
He assailed me without distinguishing or per-
ceiving who I was. Gentlemen of the jury, when
I sprang to my feet I discovered—and at the
same time he also discovered the fact—that I
had before me a man who regarded me as his
most bitter enemy, the most deadly enemy
that he had in the world. Observe that I regarded him, for my part, with no such
feeling. Why did he look upon me with so

much hostility? You have heard the Counsel
for the Crown give the reason. Because, on a
certain occasion, two years ago, I was the fortunate instrument of saving His Majesty's Government—nay—this whole country, and especially
the City of London, and the property of you its
citizens—from a great and imminent danger.
Without my evidence—my patriotism—my
sense of duty—the City would have been
seized by a Revolutionary mob, and such
things would have happened here as have
happened in France. Alone I saved you—I
nipped the conspiracy in the bud—I gave
information which caused the failure of one
seditious rising, and prevented five others in
different parts of the town from coming to a
head. In the trial which followed, this man
who died by my hand was one of the prisoners. In consequence of my evidence, he was
convicted of High Treason, and, with three
other conspirators, condemned to death. The
King's clemency changed their sentence in his
case into a short term of imprisonment.
Gentlemen, that man had been my friend.
Why did I denounce him? To save my

country. What pay did I receive for my
services? None. Are you satisfied that he
thought he had good reasons for hating me?

'This man, I say, was my enemy. Remember, he was wholly devoid of piety,
religion, or principles. He had been expelled
from Oxford University: he was an Atheist, a
revolutionary, an upholder of the theory that
all men are equal: he was also a desperate
man. Since his disgrace his parents had
turned him off, and would see no more of
him. I believe he had entered the service of
the worthy man whose evidence you have
heard, and persuaded him to allow some form
of engagement with his daughter, whose evidence you have also heard. Well, when this
man recognised me, he began by pouring out
a volley of blasphemous abuse; then he made
as if he would again rush upon me. I was
by this time partly sobered, yet not quite myself. With the instinct, common to us all, of
self-preservation, I snatched the knife from
the waiter's tray. You have heard the man
give his evidence. When we were separated,
the knife had pierced his ribs: he was dying.

Accident, accident, gentlemen of the jury : homicide by chance medley. Why should I wish to kill him ? I had everything to live for : he had nothing. Desperate as he was, and out of himself with rage, he would have murdered me if I had not, by this accident, slain him. Unfortunate accident, I call it, since it has overwhelmed me with the odium of murder, plunged me into the society of the greatest villains in the world, and deprived me of all my friends and all my means, so that I cannot appear before you now in decent attire. Better for me had this desperate villain choked the life out of me on the spot.'

More he said—much more ; but it was all said coldly, and convinced no one.

The Judge, in summing up, pointed out that the whole of the evidence showed that the prisoner was the assailant when he had gained possession of the knife. He it was who began the fatal assault. The facts of the case, he said, were plain according to the law of the land. One man had been killed by another ; that was certain. He then pointed out the distinction between homicide and murder; and he concluded by charging the jury that, by the law of the land and the evidence before them, this case was murder, and not homicide.

So the Wise Woman's prediction came true. All that this man had designed for others was recoiled upon himself; he had ruined George Bayssallance; he had robbed him of father, mistress, friends, and wealth; he had brought him to the condemned cell; but for his own change of fortunes he would have brought him to the gallows.

All this happened to himself, all this and more; he lost his father, his mistress, and his friends; he lost his worldly goods; he was brought to the condemned cell. And here the resemblance ends, because he was brought to the gallows.

They hanged him three days afterwards outside Newgate. It is a custom that condemned murderers are kept in their cells between the time of sentence and that of execution, guarded by warders, for fear they shall commit suicide, and so rob the gallows;

that they are fed on bread and water, and
only taken out for the service in the chapel
on Sunday morning, and the sermon addressed
to those who are about to die. Richard
Archer remained hard and impenitent to the
end, showing not the least sign of terror
or anxiety. He talked, however, freely to
those who guarded him.

'The day before I killed the fellow,' he
said not once, but many times, in substance,
'I was rich and fortunate; I had a noble
patron; I had horses and curricles; I had a
loving mistress; I had many friends; everything went at once—money, patron, love,
and friends. All were taken from me at once.
Job himself was not more evil-treated. All
were taken at once. Why, there is no life
worth having but the life of wealth and
luxury. Since that is gone, let me go too. I
care nothing. I have nothing to repent.
Since all that has been done is due to the
circumstances of my birth, which we call an
accident, the blame may fall upon those
circumstances, not upon me. I did not create
or cause those circumstances. Had I been

asked I should have chosen rank and wealth. Since I cannot have these I may as well die at once as live in misery. And if I must die a rope is as good a way as the surgeon's knife or the torture of a sick chamber. After death, the surgeons are welcome to my body.'

And so he died.

At any hanging, whether at Tyburn—where hangings are no longer held—or outside the prison, there is always congregated a great mob of people, who take pleasure in the spectacle; all the windows, and even the roofs, of the houses which command a view of the gallows, are filled with spectators. The mob are attracted by the spectacle of death, pain, and suffering. They throng the pillory as eagerly as the gallows; and in countries where until lately they tortured criminals in public, the mob would gather round the miserable wretch, trampling each other down to get a nearer view of his agonies. Thus, on the morning of Richard Archer's execution, the open place opposite Newgate and St. Sepulchre's Church was crowded with a dense throng of people to see

the brave show. Eight others were to suffer
with him. A rare hanging! Some of them had
stood there all night long, waiting patiently,
in order to get near the gallows, and to catch
sight of the faces of the poor wretches;
others had risen at early morning and hurried
to the spot in hope of being in time.

They were crying the Last Dying Speech
and Confession, and hawking the ballads with
which murders are always celebrated; they
were selling early purl, saloop, and beer, from
booths in Newgate Street! There was nothing
but laughing, merriment, and horseplay. Of
seriousness there was none. High up in a
garret window, exactly opposite the gallows,
and commanding a complete view of the
whole ceremony, might have been seen the
faces of two very old people. One of them
was an old man, his face soft and white; his
long hair silky; his eyes dull; his hands soft
and white, though the skin was wrinkled with
age. He was dropping fast into senile decay.
The other was an old woman, keen, and
eager; her eyes bright; her actions full of
life. They leaned their heads out of the

window, and looked down upon the crowd, and upon the gallows below.

The great bell of St. Sepulchre's began to toll the knell for the parting souls. The crowd heard it and were hushed : but, only for a moment. Then they began again to shout and laugh. Boom! Boom! The bell is for the dying men. Yet they continue to bawl these ballads and their Last Dying Speech and Confession. Boom! Boom! Yet they continue to fight, and push, and drink, and sing. Hush! The clock strikes eight. The crowd are hushed again, for the little door opens, and the procession appears. Boom! Boom! Those who are to die are brought out. Count them. One, two, three, four, five, six, seven. Boom! Boom! The seventh is the gentleman who stabbed the man in Vauxhall Gardens. They say he is the son of a great nobleman. They say the blood is still to be seen in the Broad Walk. It is daily covered up with fresh gravel, but daily reappears! Boom! Boom! He walks with courage, this fellow; he is game. It is a pleasure to see so resolute a man. The two

who are carried are women condemned for
shoplifting; they are senseless with terror,
and have fainted. Best for them if they
wake not till they find themselves—where?

'Look!' cried the old woman in the
garret. 'Look, Jack. There is one poor
wretch laughing. I suppose he hath gone
mad; often they go mad; and there is
another staggering about like a drunken
man; I suspect his fear hath 'made him
drunk. And there is one who moves his lips
continually; the Ordinary's prayers are not
enough for him; he must be a very great
criminal indeed. There is another who
weeps; his eyes run down with tears; he is
very contrite. I wish they would respite
him, poor creature. I love not to see a man
cry just because he is going to be hanged.
Look at the two women; they are like sacks;
can't the hussies have the decency to stand
up at their own hanging? And look at
Richard Archer. Ha!' she drew a deep
breath, 'I told his lordship you and me would
jump at his son's hanging. Why it does one
good only to see him. His father's son,

proud and hard. Look at him! a proper young man he is; look at him, Jack, and remember thirty years ago and more.'

Richard Archer neither wept nor staggered, nor fainted away, nor did he laugh. He walked firm, composed, and resolute; he looked calmly around upon the sea of up-turned faces below; he had even made some decent preparations for death, having dressed his long hair, and tied it behind in a white ribbon; by the kindness of his warders he had been shaved and his face washed; he had put off his ragged coat, and stood in his old silk waistcoat; his cheeks were pale, but his eyes were full of courage.

'That is where the good blood shows,' said the old woman. 'Such an one would scorn to cry and moan even if you cut him in pieces with a blunt knife. I wonder if he sees us; I should like him to catch sight of me. He might remember what I told him when I read his fortune by the cards. They always come true.' She waved a handker-chief from the window. 'I have caught his eye,' she cried. 'He sees me.' Whether he

did or not the old woman nodded her head
and shook her fingers to admonish the dying
man of her presence.

The old man began to grumble and to
growl, in a deep bass voice, things strange
and incoherent, but his wife took little heed.
Though every other word was an oath, these
need not be set down here. They may be
inferred by the reader if he pleases.

'See,' he said, 'here comes the captain.'
He remembered his face. 'Now we shall
begin. Pipe all hands, bo's'n. Hang him!
Why didn't I hit him harder? Why didn't
I kill him? As well be hanged for killing as
for mutiny, and so one more tyrant out of the
world.'

'Jack,' said his wife, 'it is his son. Your
old captain is dead; that is his son—as like
his father as one pea is like another. Your
old man died a fortnight ago. Who killed
him? I killed him, Jack, I killed him; but
you've forgotten. You forget everything. I
told him about his son. I told him that the
man he thought to hang was living still, and
resolved to see his lordship's own son hanged

outside Newgate Gaol. Ho! Since you and
me are one, Jack, you did kill him after all.
That should be a comfort to you.'

'A noble crowd of boats,' said the old
man, his eyes wandering like his thoughts.
'All the wherries of Portsmouth Harbour,
and all the girls of Gosport Town and Point,
come out to see a sailor hung at the yardarm.
A brave sight, isn't it? A fine morning, too—
just such a morning as one would choose.
Fresh breeze, and blue sky, and dancing
water; and here we are, in the middle of the
fleet—the great fleet of the King's ships, and
all the crowd to see. A good example, lads.
You must follow a good example. But do it
better—kill the tyrant! Kill him! Don't let
him live to see you hanged. A fine morning
indeed. Spithead, with a fleet riding at
anchor, is a lovely spot. There's Southsea
Castle on the beach, and the Isle of Wight
on the other side, and the Solent filled with
merchantmen waiting for convoy. Look at
his cruel white face and his black eyes.
Why'—with a horrid imprecation—'why—
why didn't I kill him? I shall never forgive

myself. Never—no, never. Who'd have thought,' he went on again, more cheerfully, ' so many would turn out to see me die—me? Why, I looked to die down below, among the wounded men, with a surgeon chopping at my legs! Look at his cruel black eyes, I say, and the sneer on his lips. Ah !——'

He saw nothing but, as he thought, the cruel face of his captain: he was no longer looking at the gibbet outside Newgate: he was back again on board his last ship, brought forth for execution: he was taking his last look at Spithead and the Solent: he was in the middle of the fleet, and the sea was crowded with boats come out to see him die.

His wife made no reply. Her lips quivered, and the tears stood in her eyes at the sight of the poor wretches standing all in a row while the hangman proceeded with his task. But at sight of the last of the row—at Richard Archer—she hardened. She felt no pity for the son of the man by whose cruelty her husband was so nearly brought to death.

'Ready,' said the sailor. 'Why, this is better than to be tied up for five hundred. Good-bye, lads, all. Under the left ear, mate —so. Turn me off quick. Where's the captain? I don't see the captain——'

At this moment the hangman drew the cap over Archer's head. He was the last of the nine. There then fell upon the crowd an awful hush : you could hear the catching of the breath : you could see the shudder that ran through all : and the voice of the Ordinary was heard plain and clear :

'Man that is born of a woman hath but a short time to live, and is full of misery. He cometh up, and is cut down like a flower.'

Then the ropes tightened, and the mob roared and howled, yet once more stillness fell upon them, and the Ordinary's voice was heard again.

'Blessed are the dead which die in the Lord ; even so, saith the Spirit ; for they rest from their labours.'

Then the riot began again, and no more was heard.

Thus died Richard Archer. Whether he truly had the fatal gift of the Evil Eye I know not, nor can we ever find out. Whether by his malignity, or by his passion for Sylvia, the disasters of which you have now heard a complete account fell upon us, or whether they were sent in the wisdom of Providence, I do not attempt to decide. Permitted by Providence they certainly must have been. Thus he died, a criminal, and by a shameful death, who might have lived long and done an honest life's work in a respectable position, but for the unfortunate circumstances of his birth, and for his own evil temper and inordinate ambitions. He went to meet his Judge in such a frame of mind as causes one to tremble. Perhaps the Lord is more merciful than men imagine.

'Come, Jack,' said the old woman presently. ' It is all over. The captain's son has gone to join his father. You've waited for your revenge for thirty years and more. But it's come at last. It's come at last, old man. Why, Jack, what's the matter? What's the matter, I say?'

For the old man sat bolt upright; his eyes closed; his face white with the pallor of death; his jaw dropped. He had died in his dream of Spithead and the fleet, and the morning when he was to have been taken out and hanged at the yardarm.

CHAPTER XXXI

CONCLUSION

My history is almost finished.

Most of those who took part in these scenes have passed away.

As for me, I occupy my father's place, and am now High Bailiff of St. Katherine's. I live, as he did, in the Master's house, and have the use of his garden and his orchard: daily I hear the service of morning prayer in the church.

Since I took my trial for High Treason—a thing now clean forgotten and gone out of mind, so that I believe there is not one person in the Precinct knows anything about it, or suspects that the High Bailiff of St. Katherine's was once condemned to death for High Treason—many great events have happened. The war which began that year continued, as all the world knows, to rage almost without intermission for twenty years and more. Every monarchy in Europe, save alone Russia and the United Kingdom of Great Britain and Ireland, was overthrown, and for the time subjugated. A man without family, without wealth, influence, or friends, succeeded in mounting the proudest Throne of the world, in placing his brothers—men of no ability—on other Thrones, and in deposing or humiliating Kings and Emperors. What good did these things for Liberty? Nothing. The very name of Liberty was lost: it was eclipsed and forgotten by the name of Glory. Who can estimate the number of those slaughtered for the glory of this one man? Who can enumerate —nay, the brain is unable to comprehend— all the ruined towns, all the children made orphans, all the women made widows, all the families reduced to starvation during these years of continual war? Now that Peace has come back again, and we can sit down and count the cost, we perceive that the cause of Liberty, for the sake of which these wars began, seems lost for ever. All the things for which the French people rose in insurrection, for which our own Corresponding Societies, our Constitutional Associations, and our Friends of the People were founded, have been forgotten and lost. Yet must I still believe that they will revive : not, perhaps, in my lifetime, but in the next generation.

When a true word has been once spoken, it lives : you cannot kill it. You may stifle its voice, but you cannot kill it. We have declared for the true Representation of the People : well, for the time that cry has been drowned and forgotten. But let us wait.

I no longer (because I am no longer young) think that the Kingdom of Heaven will begin when all men have acquired the equal rights to which they are born—a thing which I still advocate, in spite of the sufferings and rude lessons which I have endured. The advancement of humanity, I also truly believe, will become possible only when there are no more slaves, no more privileged classes, no longer an hereditary nobility, when all the offices in the country, highest and lowest, are thrown open to those destined for them by Heaven in the possession of the nobler gifts. In short, my imprisonment, my exile, my sufferings have not been able to extinguish in my soul the Republican principle. All the old things continue—and those worse than ever. The nobility, of whom I know nothing, never having so much as spoken to one of them, are reported to have become more insolent, more overbearing, than ever, because the long war and the increased value of the land have made them far richer than ever they were before ; the people seem, though this cannot really be so, more ignorant and more brutish, if possible, than they were formerly ; they lie for the most part in silence ; they have no hope ; they see no chance of making their voice to be heard ; only from the North of England, where the men who work in the factories think and reason, come murmurs—I believe they are growing murmurs—in the old strain ; the Republicans of the United States, who might be an example to us, are utterly unknown to our people ; we never go to them, and they never come to us ; it is rumoured that they continue in an unmeaning animosity towards us ; nay, this is proved by their conduct a few years since, when, in the midst of our struggle for life or death against the tyrant of the Continent and against the mightiest despotism that ever was arrayed in arms since the world began, they chose to declare a wanton and unjust war against us. Everything is dark and menacing ; black clouds overhead ; gloom and the silence of despair around.

Let us have patience; the old spirit will revive; the century is young; some yet remain of the old advocates for freedom. As I said above, the true word has been pronounced ; I myself may yet live to see the first great step in the restoration to the people of their own Parliament. That once achieved, the rest may follow if only the people are true to themselves.

In this humble corner, this quiet Precinct, I now sit and watch mankind, looking for the revival of the old generous thoughts. Around me during my fifty years of life there has grown up a new town filled with the rudest and roughest population, working men, tradesmen, sailors, and those who live by

sailors. I think of the prophecy uttered by
the Prebendary when he foresaw in the future
such a work for St. Katherine's Hospital
among the ignorant people of this great new
town as had never been contemplated by its
founders. The Church, he said, shall win
back the hearts of these poor folk so long
neglected ; St. Katherine's is the Westminster
Abbey of the East ; she is rich, and she grows
richer daily ; she belongs, with her wealth
and her noble church to our people, and to
none but them ; she shall become their proud
possession ; she shall lead them Heavenwards.

Let us return to Paramatta.

Our letters gone, we sat down, thinking
we should have a year and a half, at least, to
wait before we could receive a reply.

Well, I was no longer a Royal Marine.
I had no more drill or sentry-go. I went
about no longer in that terror of sergeant or
lieutenant which constantly fills the soul of
the private soldier. For, mark you, though
the man be so far gone in brutality as not to
feel disgraced by flogging, his shoulders are

as sensitive to the pain of the lash as those of
any fine gentleman. It is a shame to the
nation, which is in this respect no better than
the Muscovite, that an officer should have the
power to order any man to be flogged as long
as he chooses. Let mutineers be shot, not
torn to pieces; since men must be flogged, let
the power of the officers be restricted.

Being, therefore, now free to live as I
pleased, I lived with George, and became, with
him, a farmer, in a climate which rewards the
toil of the ploughman by rich and noble crops,
where the winter has neither frost nor snow,
and the summer is only too hot for a week or
two, when the wind blows from the interior.
But one should be born in the place in order
to be contented to dwell therein. For myself,
I listened daily for some voice across the
ocean—the great silent, empty ocean—where
there are no ships save here and there one
sailing slowly across its desolate face, with its
cargo of convicts coming to mock, with their
misery and their vice, the blue Australian
skies and the sweet Australian calm. George,
if he felt this longing, kept it within his own

breast. In the evenings, when work was done, we sat for the most part in silence. Why should we chatter when each knew what was in the other's soul?

Paramatta is about fifteen miles from Sydney. We were too far to hear the salute on the arrival or the departure of a ship; but when one came the news it brought, or the letters, reached us commonly in two or three days, because you may imagine that His Majesty's mails between Sydney and Paramatta are not carried to and fro with the regularity of the London post. Yet the fact of a ship's arrival reaches the people of the smaller settlements on the same day. The birds of the air carry the news; the breezes spread it abroad; there is no semaphore, and there is no mail coach; yet the tidings spread like lightning throughout the colony.

It was growing towards sunset on a lovely day in October, which is the month of spring in Australia. Work was done, and I was preparing a supper of pork fried in slices, with cabbage and potatoes and onions—what the housewife calls bubble-and-squeak—a toothsome dish. George was cleaning up the room.

'Shall we have a letter to-morrow?' I said, handling the frying-pan.

'No time for an answer yet. We must wait another year, lad,' he replied. 'There, things are ship-shape, now. The house is not so bad. When she comes I shall build another room, so that we may have two ; the gardens look well, now. When—or if—she comes, I say.'

He sat down on a box which did service for a chair.

'If she comes,' he repeated. 'If she comes. I say the same words all day long. Why should she come? It is too much to expect. We must not look for it. Yet she wrote that she wished to come. Well—it is as I said long ago, when the poor child was bewitched—I have had my share of love. Sylvia is too good for me.'

'If I know my sister,' I replied, 'she will come. If the ship is not wrecked by storm or cast away upon some rock, she will come. Cheer up, George. Here is your supper.'

With that I tossed the bubble-and-squeak into the dish and served it up, hot and hot. We had biscuit from the stores, but sometimes we made our own bread just as we brewed our own beer—and very good beer too—cut out and sewed our own clothes, built our own house, made our own furniture, and, in fact, did everything for ourselves.

George sighed, but cheerfully. He was grown grave in those days, it must be confessed that his trials were many ; but he was not melancholy, and he preserved an excellent appetite for supper.

The sun was getting low ; it was already half-past six, or thereabouts. Now as we sat I was facing the door, and George was sitting with his back to it. The only window of the cabin was one on the right hand of the door provided with a shutter to keep out the night-air, but of course there was no glass, not even of the old-fashioned kind, to say nothing of the modern sash.

We had finished supper ; we had drunk our mugs of beer ; there was nothing left but to sit outside for an hour or two while George smoked a pipe of tobacco—a sailor very easily falls into this habit—and so to bed.

Then I suddenly saw a ghost. I heard no footstep, I saw a face—the face of Sylvia looking in at the window. I started—I should have jumped up and run out, but she lifted her finger. I understood. It was no ghost, then. It was Sylvia herself come out to us.

She came in at the open door. George heard nothing. She stepped within, she laid her hand upon his shoulder. He turned quickly, and caught her in his arms.

'SYLVIA!'

THE END.

PRINTED BY
SPOTTISWOODE AND CO., NEW-STREET SQUARE
LONDON

U

April, 1891.

𝔄 𝔏𝔦𝔰𝔱 𝔬𝔣 𝔅𝔬𝔬𝔨𝔰

PUBLISHED BY

CHATTO & WINDUS,

214, Piccadilly, London, W.

Sold by all Booksellers, or sent post-free for the published price by the Publishers.

ABOUT.—THE FELLAH: An Egyptian Novel. By EDMOND ABOUT. Translated by Sir RANDAL ROBERTS. Post 8vo, illustrated boards, **2s.**

ADAMS (W. DAVENPORT), WORKS BY.
A DICTIONARY OF THE DRAMA. Being a comprehensive Guide to the Plays, Playwrights, Players, and Playhouses of the United Kingdom and America. Crown 8vo, half-bound, **12s. 6d.** [*Preparing.*
QUIPS AND QUIDDITIES. Selected by W. D. ADAMS. Post 8vo, cloth limp, **2s. 6d.**

ADAMS (W. H. D.).—WITCH, WARLOCK, AND MAGICIAN: Historical Sketches of Magic and Witchcraft in England and Scotland. By W. H. DAVENPORT ADAMS. Demy 8vo, cloth extra, **12s.**

AGONY COLUMN (THE) OF "THE TIMES," from 1800 to 1870. Edited, with an Introduction, by ALICE CLAY. Post 8vo, cloth limp, **2s. 6d.**

AIDE (HAMILTON), WORKS BY. Post 8vo, illustrated boards, **2s.** each.
CARR OF CARRLYON. | CONFIDENCES.

ALEXANDER (MRS.), NOVELS BY. Post 8vo, illustrated boards, **2s.** each.
MAID, WIFE, OR WIDOW? | VALERIE'S FATE.

ALLEN (GRANT), WORKS BY. Crown 8vo, cloth extra, **6s.** each.
THE EVOLUTIONIST AT LARGE. | COLIN CLOUT'S CALENDAR.
VIGNETTES FROM NATURE.

Crown 8vo, cloth extra, **6s.** each; post 8vo, illustrated boards, **2s.** each.
STRANGE STORIES. With a Frontispiece by GEORGE DU MAURIER.
THE BECKONING HAND. With a Frontispiece by TOWNLEY GREEN.

Crown 8vo, cloth extra, **3s. 6d.** each; post 8vo, illustrated boards, **2s.** each.
PHILISTIA. | FOR MAIMIE'S SAKE. | THIS MORTAL COIL.
BABYLON. | IN ALL SHADES. | THE TENTS OF SHEM.
| THE DEVIL'S DIE. |

THE GREAT TABOO. Crown 8vo, cloth extra, **3s. 6d.**

AMERICAN LITERATURE, A LIBRARY OF, from the Earliest Settlement to the Present Time. Compiled and Edited by EDMUND CLARENCE STEDMAN and ELLEN MACKAY HUTCHINSON. Eleven Vols., royal 8vo, cloth extra. A few copies are for sale by Messrs. CHATTO & WINDUS (published in New York by C. L. WEBSTER & Co.), price **£6 12s.** the set.

ARCHITECTURAL STYLES, A HANDBOOK OF. By A. ROSENGARTEN. Translated by W. COLLETT-SANDARS. With 630 Illusts. Cr. 8vo, cl. ex., **7s. 6d.**

ART (THE) OF AMUSING: A Collection of Graceful Arts, GAMES, Tricks, Puzzles, and Charades. By FRANK BELLEW. 300 Illusts. Cr. 8vo, cl. ex., **4s. 6d.**

ARNOLD (EDWIN LESTER), WORKS BY.
THE WONDERFUL ADVENTURES OF PHRA THE PHŒNICIAN. With Introduction by Sir EDWIN ARNOLD, K.C.I.E., and 12 Illusts. by H. M. PAGET. Three Vols.
BIRD LIFE IN ENGLAND. Crown 8vo, cloth extra, **6s.**

ARTEMUS WARD'S WORKS: The Works of CHARLES FARRER BROWNE, better known as ARTEMUS WARD. With Portrait and Facsimile. Crown 8vo, cloth extra, **7s. 6d.**—Also a POPULAR EDITION, post 8vo, picture boards, **2s.**
THE GENIAL SHOWMAN: Life and Adventures of ARTEMUS WARD. By EDWARD P. HINGSTON. With a Frontispiece. Crown 8vo, cloth extra. **3s. 6d.**

ASHTON (JOHN), WORKS BY. Crown 8vo, cloth extra, **7s. 6d.** each.
HISTORY OF THE CHAP-BOOKS OF THE 18th CENTURY. With 334 Illusts.
SOCIAL LIFE IN THE REIGN OF QUEEN ANNE. With 85 Illustrations.
HUMOUR, WIT, AND SATIRE OF SEVENTEENTH CENTURY. With 82 Illusts.
ENGLISH CARICATURE AND SATIRE ON NAPOLEON THE FIRST. 115 Illusts.
MODERN STREET BALLADS. With 57 Illustrations.

BACTERIA.— A SYNOPSIS OF THE BACTERIA AND YEAST FUNGI AND ALLIED SPECIES. By W. B. GROVE, B.A. With 87 Illustrations.
Crown 8vo, cloth extra, **3s. 6d.**

BARDSLEY (REV. C. W.), WORKS BY.
ENGLISH SURNAMES: Their Sources and Significations. Cr. 8vo, cloth, **7s. 6d.**
CURIOSITIES OF PURITAN NOMENCLATURE. Crown 8vo, cloth extra. **6s.**

BARING GOULD (S., Author of "John Herring," &c.), NOVELS BY.
Crown 8vo, cloth extra, **3s. 6d.** each; post 8vo, illustrated boards, **2s.** each.
RED SPIDER. | EVE.

BARRETT (FRANK, Author of "Lady Biddy Fane,") NOVELS BY.
FETTERED FOR LIFE. Post 8vo, illustrated boards, **2s.**; cloth, **2s. 6d.**
BETWEEN LIFE AND DEATH. Three Vols., crown 8vo.

BEACONSFIELD, LORD: A Biography. By T. P. O'CONNOR, M.P.
Sixth Edition, with an Introduction. Crown 8vo, cloth extra, **5s.**

BEAUCHAMP.—GRANTLEY GRANGE: A Novel. By SHELSLEY BEAUCHAMP. Post 8vo, illustrated boards, **2s.**

BEAUTIFUL PICTURES BY BRITISH ARTISTS: A Gathering of Favourites from our Picture Galleries, beautifully engraved on Steel. With Notices of the Artists by SYDNEY ARMYTAGE, M.A. Imperial 4to, cloth extra, gilt edges, **21s.**

BECHSTEIN.—AS PRETTY AS SEVEN, and other German Stories. Collected by LUDWIG BECHSTEIN. With Additional Tales by the Brothers GRIMM, and 98 Illustrations by RICHTER. Square 8vo, cloth extra, **6s. 6d.**; gilt edges, **7s. 6d.**

BEERBOHM.—WANDERINGS IN PATAGONIA; or, Life among the Ostrich Hunters. By JULIUS BEERBOHM. With Illusts. Cr. 8vo, cl. extra, **3s. 6d.**

BESANT (WALTER), NOVELS BY.
Cr. 8vo, cl. ex., **3s. 6d.** each; post 8vo, illust. bds., **2s.** each; cl. limp, **2s. 6d.** each.
ALL SORTS AND CONDITIONS OF MEN. With Illustrations by FRED. BARNARD.
THE CAPTAINS' ROOM, &c. With Frontispiece by E. J. WHEELER.
ALL IN A GARDEN FAIR. With 6 Illustrations by HARRY FURNISS.
DOROTHY FORSTER. With Frontispiece by CHARLES GREEN.
UNCLE JACK, and other Stories. | CHILDREN OF GIBEON.
THE WORLD WENT VERY WELL THEN. With 12 Illustrations by A. FORESTIER.
HERR PAULUS: His Rise, his Greatness, and his Fall.
FOR FAITH AND FREEDOM. With Illustrations by A. FORESTIER and F. WADDY.

Crown 8vo, cloth extra, **3s. 6d.** each.
TO CALL HER MINE, &c. With 9 Illustrations by A. FORESTIER.
THE BELL OF ST. PAUL'S.

THE HOLY ROSE, &c. With Frontispiece by F. BARNARD. Cr. 8vo, cloth extra, **6s.**
ARMOREL OF LYONESSE: A Romance of To-day. Three Vols., crown 8vo.
ST. KATHERINE'S BY THE TOWER. With 12 full-page Illustrations by C. GREEN. Three Vols., crown 8vo. *[May.*
FIFTY YEARS AGO. With 137 Plates and Woodcuts. Demy 8vo, cloth extra, **16s.**
THE EULOGY OF RICHARD JEFFERIES. With Portrait. Cr. 8vo, cl. extra, **6s.**
THE ART OF FICTION. Demy 8vo, **1s.**

BESANT (WALTER) AND JAMES RICE, NOVELS BY.
Cr. 8vo, cl. ex., **3s. 6d.** each; post 8vo, illust. bds., **2s.** each; cl. limp, **2s. 6d.** each.

READY-MONEY MORTIBOY.	BY CELIA'S ARBOUR.
MY LITTLE GIRL.	THE CHAPLAIN OF THE FLEET.
WITH HARP AND CROWN.	THE SEAMY SIDE.
THIS SON OF VULCAN.	THE CASE OF MR. LUCRAFT, &c.
THE GOLDEN BUTTERFLY.	'TWAS IN TRAFALGAR'S BAY, &c.
THE MONKS OF THELEMA.	THE TEN YEARS' TENANT, &c.

. There is also a LIBRARY EDITION of the above Twelve Volumes, handsomely set in new type, on a large crown 8vo page, and bound in cloth extra. **6s.** each.

BENNETT (W. C., LL.D.), WORKS BY. Post 8vo, cloth limp, **2s.** each.
A BALLAD HISTORY OF ENGLAND. | SONGS FOR SAILORS.

BEWICK (THOMAS) AND HIS PUPILS. By AUSTIN DOBSON. With
95 Illustrations. Square 8vo, cloth extra, **6s.**

BLACKBURN'S (HENRY) ART HANDBOOKS.
ACADEMY NOTES, separate years, from 1875-1887, 1889, and 1890, each **1s.**
ACADEMY NOTES, 1891. With Illustrations. **1s.** [May.
ACADEMY NOTES, 1875-79. Complete in One Vol., with 600 Illusts. Cloth limp, **6s.**
ACADEMY NOTES, 1880-84. Complete in One Vol., with 700 Illusts. Cloth limp, **6s.**
GROSVENOR NOTES, 1877. **6d.**
GROSVENOR NOTES, separate years, from 1878 to 1890, each **1s.**
GROSVENOR NOTES, Vol. I., 1877-82. With 300 Illusts. Demy 8vo, cloth limp, **6s.**
GROSVENOR NOTES, Vol. II., 1883-87. With 300 Illusts. Demy 8vo, cloth limp, **6s.**
THE NEW GALLERY, 1888-1890. With numerous Illustrations, each **1s.**
THE NEW GALLERY, 1891. With Illustrations. **1s.** [May
ENGLISH PICTURES AT THE NATIONAL GALLERY. 114 Illustrations. **1s.**
OLD MASTERS AT THE NATIONAL GALLERY. 128 Illustrations. **1s. 6d.**
ILLUSTRATED CATALOGUE TO THE NATIONAL GALLERY. 242 Illusts. cl., **3s.**

THE PARIS SALON, 1891. With Facsimile Sketches. **3s.** [May.
THE PARIS SOCIETY OF FINE ARTS, 1891. With Sketches. **3s. 6d.** [May.

BLAKE (WILLIAM): India-proof Etchings from his Works by WILLIAM
BELL SCOTT. With descriptive Text. Folio, half-bound boards. **21s.**

BLIND.—THE ASCENT OF MAN: A Poem. By MATHILDE BLIND.
Crown 8vo, printed on hand-made paper, cloth extra, **5s.**

BOURNE (H. R. FOX), WORKS BY.
ENGLISH MERCHANTS: Memoirs in Illustration of the Progress of British Commerce. With numerous Illustrations. Crown 8vo, cloth extra, **7s. 6d.**
ENGLISH NEWSPAPERS: The History of Journalism. Two Vols., demy 8vo, cl., **25s.**
THE OTHER SIDE OF THE EMIN PASHA RELIEF EXPEDITION. Crown 8vo, cloth extra, **6s.**

BOWERS' (G.) HUNTING SKETCHES. Oblong 4to, hf.-bd. bds., **21s.** each.
CANTERS IN CRAMPSHIRE. | LEAVES FROM A HUNTING JOURNAL.

BOYLE (FREDERICK), WORKS BY. Post 8vo, illustrated boards, **2s.** each.
CHRONICLES OF NO-MAN'S LAND. | CAMP NOTES.
SAVAGE LIFE. Crown 8vo, cloth extra, **3s. 6d.**; post 8vo, picture boards, **2s.**

BRAND'S OBSERVATIONS ON POPULAR ANTIQUITIES; chiefly
illustrating the Origin of our Vulgar Customs, Ceremonies, and Superstitions. With the Additions of Sir HENRY ELLIS, and Illustrations. Cr. 8vo, cloth extra, **7s. 6d.**

BREWER (REV. DR.), WORKS BY.
THE READER'S HANDBOOK OF ALLUSIONS, REFERENCES, PLOTS, AND STORIES. Fifteenth Thousand. crown 8vo, cloth extra, **7s. 6d.**
AUTHORS AND THEIR WORKS, WITH THE DATES: Being the Appendices to "The Reader's Handbook,' separately printed. Crown 8vo, cloth limp, **2s.**
A DICTIONARY OF MIRACLES. Crown 8vo, cloth extra, **7s. 6d.**

BREWSTER (SIR DAVID), WORKS BY. Post 8vo, cl. ex., **4s. 6d.** each.
MORE WORLDS THAN ONE: Creed of Philosopher and Hope of Christian. Plates.
THE MARTYRS OF SCIENCE: GALILEO, TYCHO BRAHE, and KEPLER. With Portraits.
LETTERS ON NATURAL MAGIC. With numerous Illustrations.

BRET HARTE, WORKS BY.

LIBRARY EDITION, Complete in Six Volumes, crown 8vo, cloth extra, **6s.** each.
BRET HARTE'S COLLECTED WORKS. Arranged and Revised by the Author.
Vol. I. COMPLETE POETICAL AND DRAMATIC WORKS. With Steel Portrait.
Vol. II. LUCK OF ROARING CAMP—BOHEMIAN PAPERS—AMERICAN LEGENDS.
Vol. III. TALES OF THE ARGONAUTS—EASTERN SKETCHES.
Vol. IV. GABRIEL CONROY.
Vol. V. STORIES—CONDENSED NOVELS, &c.
Vol. VI. TALES OF THE PACIFIC SLOPE.

THE SELECT WORKS OF BRET HARTE, in Prose and Poetry. With Introductory Essay by J. M. BELLEW, Portrait of Author, and 50 Illusts. Cr. 8vo, cl. ex., **7s. 6d.**
BRET HARTE'S POETICAL WORKS. Hand-made paper & buckram. Cr.8vo, **4s.6d.**
THE QUEEN OF THE PIRATE ISLE. With 28 original Drawings by KATE GREENAWAY, reproduced in Colours by EDMUND EVANS. Small 4to, cloth, **5s.**

Crown 8vo, cloth extra, **3s. 6d.** each.
A WAIF OF THE PLAINS. With 60 Illustrations by STANLEY L. WOOD.
A WARD OF THE GOLDEN GATE. With 59 Illustrations by STANLEY L. WOOD.
A SAPPHO OF GREEN SPRINGS, &c. With Two Illustrations by HUME NISBET.

Post 8vo, illustrated boards, **2s.** each.

GABRIEL CONROY.	**THE LUCK OF ROARING CAMP, &c.**
AN HEIRESS OF RED DOG, &c.	**CALIFORNIAN STORIES.**

Post 8vo, illustrated boards, **2s.** each; cloth limp, **2s. 6d.** each.

FLIP.	**MARUJA.**	**A PHYLLIS OF THE SIERRAS.**

Fcap. 8vo picture cover. **1s.** each.

THE TWINS OF TABLE MOUNTAIN.	**JEFF BRIGGS'S LOVE STORY.**

BRILLAT-SAVARIN.—GASTRONOMY AS A FINE ART. By BRILLAT-SAVARIN. Translated by R. E. ANDERSON, M.A. Post 8vo, half-bound, **2s.**

BRYDGES.—UNCLE SAM AT HOME. By HAROLD BRYDGES. Post 8vo, illustrated boards, **2s.**; cloth limp, **2s. 6d.**

BUCHANAN'S (ROBERT) WORKS. Crown 8vo, cloth extra, **6s.** each.

SELECTED POEMS OF ROBERT BUCHANAN. With Frontispiece by T. DALZIEL.
THE EARTHQUAKE; or, Six Days and a Sabbath.
THE CITY OF DREAM: An Epic Poem. With Two Illustrations by P. MACNAB.
THE OUTCAST: A Rhyme for the Time. With 12 Full-page Illustrations and numerous Vignettes. Crown 8vo, cloth extra, **8s.**

ROBERT BUCHANAN'S COMPLETE POETICAL WORKS. With Steel-plate Portrait. Crown 8vo, cloth extra, **7s. 6d.**

Crown 8vo, cloth extra, **3s. 6d.** each; post 8vo, illustrated boards, **2s.** each.

THE SHADOW OF THE SWORD.	**LOVE ME FOR EVER.** Frontispiece.
A CHILD OF NATURE. Frontispiece.	**ANNAN WATER.** | **FOXGLOVE MANOR.**
GOD AND THE MAN. With 11 Illustrations by FRED. BARNARD.	**THE NEW ABELARD.**
	MATT: A Story of a Caravan. Front.
THE MARTYRDOM OF MADELINE.	**THE MASTER OF THE MINE.** Front.
With Frontispiece by A. W. COOPER.	**THE HEIR OF LINNE.**

BURTON (CAPTAIN). — THE BOOK OF THE SWORD: Being a History of the Sword and its Use in all Countries, from the Earliest Times. By RICHARD F. BURTON. With over 400 Illustrations. Square 8vo, cloth extra. **32s.**

BURTON (ROBERT).

THE ANATOMY OF MELANCHOLY: A New Edition, with translations of the Classical Extracts. Demy 8vo, cloth extra, **7s. 6d.**
MELANCHOLY ANATOMISED: Being an Abridgment, for popular use, of BURTON'S ANATOMY OF MELANCHOLY. Post 8vo, cloth limp, **2s. 6d.**

CAINE (T. HALL), NOVELS BY. Crown 8vo, cloth extra, **3s. 6d.** each; post 8vo, illustrated boards, **2s.** each; cloth limp, **2s. 6d.** each.

SHADOW OF A CRIME.	**A SON OF HAGAR.**	**THE DEEMSTER.**

CAMERON (COMMANDER). — THE CRUISE OF THE "BLACK PRINCE" PRIVATEER. By V. LOVETT CAMERON, R.N., C.B. With Two Illustrations by P. MACNAB. Crown 8vo, cloth extra, **5s.**; post 8vo, illustrated boards, **2s.**

CAMERON (MRS. H. LOVETT), NOVELS BY.

Crown 8vo, cloth extra, **3s. 6d.** each; post 8vo, illustrated boards, **2s.** each.

JULIET'S GUARDIAN,	**DECEIVERS EVER.**

CARLYLE (THOMAS) ON THE CHOICE OF BOOKS. With Life
by R. H. SHEPHERD, and Three Illustrations. Post 8vo, cloth extra, **1s. 6d.**
THE CORRESPONDENCE OF THOMAS CARLYLE AND RALPH WALDO
EMERSON, 1834 to 1872. Edited by CHARLES ELIOT NORTON. With Portraits.
Two Vols., crown 8vo cloth extra, **24s.**

CARLYLE (JANE WELSH), LIFE OF. By Mrs. ALEXANDER IRELAND.
With Portrait and Facsimile Letter. Small demy 8vo, cloth extra, **7s. 6d.**

CHAPMAN'S (GEORGE) WORKS. Vol. I. contains the Plays complete,
including the doubtful ones. Vol. II., the Poems and Minor Translations, with an
Introductory Essay by ALGERNON CHARLES SWINBURNE. Vol. III., the Translations
of the Iliad and Odyssey. Three Vols., crown 8vo, cloth extra, **6s.** each.

CHATTO AND JACKSON.—A TREATISE ON WOOD ENGRAVING,
Historical and Practical. By WILLIAM ANDREW CHATTO and JOHN JACKSON. With
an Additional Chapter by HENRY G. BOHN, and 450 fine Illusts. Large 4to, hf.-bd., **28s.**

CHAUCER FOR CHILDREN: A Golden Key. By Mrs. H. R. HAWEIS.
With 8 Coloured Plates and 30 Woodcuts. Small 4to, cloth extra, **6s.**
CHAUCER FOR SCHOOLS. By Mrs. H. R. HAWEIS. Demy 8vo, cloth limp, **2s. 6d.**

CLARE.—FOR THE LOVE OF A LASS: A Tale of Tynedale. By
AUSTIN CLARE. Post 8vo, picture boards, **2s.**; cloth limp, **2s. 6d.**

CLIVE (MRS. ARCHER), NOVELS BY. Post 8vo, illust. boards, **2s.** each.
PAUL FERROLL. | WHY PAUL FERROLL KILLED HIS WIFE.

CLODD (EDW., F.R.A.S.).—MYTHS AND DREAMS. Cr. 8vo, cl. ex., 5s.

COBBAN.—THE CURE OF SOULS: A Story. By J. MACLAREN
COBBAN. Post 8vo, illustrated boards, **2s.**

COLEMAN (JOHN), WORKS BY.
PLAYERS AND PLAYWRIGHTS I HAVE KNOWN. Two Vols., 8vo, cloth, **21s.**
CURLY: An Actor's Story. With 21 Illusts. by J. C. DOLLMAN. Cr. 8vo, cl., **1s. 6d.**

COLLINS (C. ALLSTON).—THE BAR SINISTER. Post 8vo, 2s.

COLLINS (MORTIMER AND FRANCES), NOVELS BY.
Crown 8vo, cloth extra, **3s. 6d.** each; post 8vo, illustrated boards, **2s.** each.
SWEET ANNE PAGE. | FROM MIDNIGHT TO MIDNIGHT. | TRANSMIGRATION.
BLACKSMITH AND SCHOLAR. | YOU PLAY ME FALSE. | VILLAGE COMEDY.

Post 8vo, illustrated boards, **2s.** each.
A FIGHT WITH FORTUNE. | SWEET AND TWENTY. | FRANCES.

COLLINS (WILKIE), NOVELS BY.
Cr. 8vo, cl. ex., **3s. 6d.** each; post 8vo, illust. bds., **2s.** each; cl. limp, **2s. 6d.** each.
ANTONINA. With a Frontispiece by Sir JOHN GILBERT, R.A.
BASIL. Illustrated by Sir JOHN GILBERT, R.A., and J. MAHONEY.
HIDE AND SEEK. Illustrated by Sir JOHN GILBERT, R.A., and J. MAHONEY.
AFTER DARK. With Illustrations by A. B. HOUGHTON.
THE DEAD SECRET. With a Frontispiece by Sir JOHN GILBERT, R.A.
QUEEN OF HEARTS. With a Frontispiece by Sir JOHN GILBERT, R.A.
THE WOMAN IN WHITE. With Illusts. by Sir J. GILBERT, R.A., and F. A. FRASER.
NO NAME. With Illustrations by Sir J. E. MILLAIS, R.A., and A. W. COOPER.
MY MISCELLANIES. With a Steel-plate Portrait of WILKIE COLLINS.
ARMADALE. With Illustrations by G. H. THOMAS.
THE MOONSTONE. With Illustrations by G. DU MAURIER and F. A. FRASER.
MAN AND WIFE. With Illustrations by WILLIAM SMALL.
POOR MISS FINCH. Illustrated by G. DU MAURIER and EDWARD HUGHES.
MISS OR MRS.? With Illusts. by S. L. FILDES, R.A., and HENRY WOODS, A.R.A.
THE NEW MAGDALEN. Illustrated by G. DU MAURIER and C. S. REINHARDT.
THE FROZEN DEEP. Illustrated by G. DU MAURIER and J. MAHONEY.
THE LAW AND THE LADY. Illusts. by S. L. FILDES, R.A., and SYDNEY HALL.
THE TWO DESTINIES.
THE HAUNTED HOTEL. Illustrated by ARTHUR HOPKINS.
THE FALLEN LEAVES. | HEART AND SCIENCE. | THE EVIL GENIUS.
JEZEBEL'S DAUGHTER. | "I SAY NO." | LITTLE NOVELS.
THE BLACK ROBE. | A ROGUE'S LIFE. | THE LEGACY OF CAIN.

BLIND LOVE. With a Preface by WALTER BESANT, and 36 Illustrations by
A. FORESTIER. Crown 8vo, cloth extra, **3s. 6d.**

COLLINS (CHURTON).—A MONOGRAPH ON DEAN SWIFT. By
J. CHURTON COLLINS. Crown 8vo, cloth extra. **8s.**   [*Shortly.*

COLMAN'S HUMOROUS WORKS: "Broad Grins," "My Nightgown
and Slippers," and other Humorous Works of GEORGE COLMAN. With Life by
G. B. BUCKSTONE, and Frontispiece by HOGARTH. Crown 8vo. cloth extra, **7s. 6d.**

COLQUHOUN.—EVERY INCH A SOLDIER: A Novel. By M. J.
COLQUHOUN. Post 8vo. illustrated boards, **2s.**

CONVALESCENT COOKERY: A Family Handbook. By CATHERINE
RYAN Crown 8vo, **1s.;** cloth limp. **1s. 6d.**

CONWAY (MONCURE D.), WORKS BY.
DEMONOLOGY AND DEVIL-LORE. With 65 Illustrations. Third Edition. Two
   Vols., demy 8vo, cloth extra, **28s.**
A NECKLACE OF STORIES. 25 Illusts. by W. J. HENNESSY. Sq. 8vo, cloth, **6s.**
PINE AND PALM: A Novel. Two Vols.. crown 8vo, cloth extra. **21s.**
GEORGE WASHINGTON'S RULES OF CIVILITY Traced to their Sources and
   Restored. Fcap. 8vo, Japanese vellum, **2s. 6d.**

COOK (DUTTON), NOVELS BY.
PAUL FOSTER'S DAUGHTER. Cr. 8vo, cl. ex., **3s. 6d.**; post 8vo, illust. boards, **2s.**
LEO. Post 8vo, illustrated boards, **2s.**

CORNWALL.—POPULAR ROMANCES OF THE WEST OF ENG-
LAND; or, The Drolls, Traditions, and Superstitions of Old Cornwall. Collected
by ROBERT HUNT. F.R.S. Two Steel-plates by GEO.CRUIKSHANK. Cr. 8vo, cl., **7s. 6d.**

CRADDOCK.—THE PROPHET OF THE GREAT SMOKY MOUN-
TAINS. By CHARLES EGBERT CRADDOCK. Post 8vo, illust bds., **2s.**; cl. limp. **2s. 6d.**

CRUIKSHANK'S COMIC ALMANACK. Complete in Two SERIES:
The FIRST from 1835 to 1843; the SECOND from 1844 to 1853. A Gathering of
the BEST HUMOUR of THACKERAY, HOOD, MAYHEW, ALBERT SMITH, A'BECKETT,
ROBERT BROUGH, &c. With numerous Steel Engravings and Woodcuts by CRUIK-
SHANK, HINE, LANDELLS, &c. Two Vols, crown 8vo, cloth gilt, **7s. 6d.** each.
THE LIFE OF GEORGE CRUIKSHANK. By BLANCHARD JERROLD. With 84
Illustrations and a Bibliography Crown 8vo, cloth extra, **7s. 6d.**

CUMMING (C. F. GORDON), WORKS BY. Demy 8vo, cl. ex., **8s. 6d.** each.
IN THE HEBRIDES. With Autotype Facsimile and 23 Illustrations.
IN THE HIMALAYAS AND ON THE INDIAN PLAINS. With 42 Illustrations.

VIA CORNWALL TO EGYPT. With Photogravure Frontis. Demy 8vo, cl., **7s. 6d.**

CUSSANS.—A HANDBOOK OF HERALDRY; with Instructions for
Tracing Pedigrees and Deciphering Ancient MSS., &c. By JOHN E. CUSSANS. With
408 Woodcuts, Two Coloured and Two Plain Plates. Crown 8vo, cloth extra, **7s. 6d.**

CYPLES(W.)—HEARTS of GOLD. Cr.8vo, cl.,**3s.6d.**; post 8vo,bds.,**2s.**

DANIEL.—MERRIE ENGLAND IN THE OLDEN TIME. By GEORGE
DANIEL. With Illustrations by ROBERT CRUIKSHANK. Crown 8vo, cloth extra, **3s. 6d.**

DAUDET.—THE EVANGELIST; or, Port Salvation. By ALPHONSE
DAUDET. Crown 8vo, cloth extra. **3s. 6d.**; post 8vo, illustrated boards, **2s.**

DAVENANT.—HINTS FOR PARENTS ON THE CHOICE OF A PRO-
FESSION FOR THEIR SONS. By F. DAVENANT, M.A. Post 8vo. **1s.;** cl., **1s. 6d.**

DAVIES (DR. N. E. YORKE-), WORKS BY.
Crown 8vo, **1s.** each; cloth limp, **1s. 6d.** each.
ONE THOUSAND MEDICAL MAXIMS AND SURGICAL HINTS.
NURSERY HINTS: A Mother's Guide in Health and Disease.
FOODS FOR THE FAT: A Treatise on Corpulency, and a Dietary for its Cure.

AIDS TO LONG LIFE. Crown 8vo, **2s.;** cloth limp. **2s. 6d.**

DAVIES' (SIR JOHN) COMPLETE POETICAL WORKS, including
Psalms I. to L. in Verse, and other hitherto Unpublished MSS., for the first time
Collected and Edited, with Memorial-Introduction and Notes, by the REV. A. B.
GROSART, D.D. Two Vols., crown 8vo, cloth boards, **12s.**

DE MAISTRE.—A JOURNEY ROUND MY ROOM. By XAVIER DE
MAISTRE. Translated by HENRY ATTWELL. Post 8vo, cloth limp, **2s. 6d.**

DE MILLE.—A CASTLE IN SPAIN. By JAMES DE MILLE. With a
Frontispiece. Crown 8vo, cloth extra, **3s. 6d.**; post 8vo. illustrated boards, **2s.**

DERBY (THE).—THE BLUE RIBBON OF THE TURF: A Chronicle
of the RACE FOR THE DERBY, from Diomed to Donovan. With Notes on the Winning Horses, the Men who trained them, Jockeys who rode them, and Gentlemen to
whom they belonged ; also Notices of the Betting and Betting Men of the period, and
Brief Accounts of THE OAKS. By LOUIS HENRY CURZON. Cr. 8vo, cloth extra, **6s.**

DERWENT (LEITH), NOVELS BY. Cr.8vo,cl., **3s.6d.** ea.; post 8vo,bds.,**2s.**ea.
OUR LADY OF TEARS. | CIRCE'S LOVERS.

DICKENS (CHARLES), NOVELS BY. Post 8vo, illustrated boards, **2s.** each.
SKETCHES BY BOZ. | NICHOLAS NICKLEBY.
THE PICKWICK PAPERS. | OLIVER TWIST.
THE SPEECHES OF CHARLES DICKENS, 1841-1870. With a New Bibliography.
Edited by RICHARD HERNE SHEPHERD. Crown 8vo, cloth extra, **6s.**—Also a
SMALLER EDITION, in the Mayfair Library, post 8vo, cloth limp, **2s. 6d.**
ABOUT ENGLAND WITH DICKENS. By ALFRED RIMMER. With 57 Illustrations
by C. A. VANDERHOOF, ALFRED RIMMER, and others. Sq. 8vo, cloth extra. **7s. 6d.**

DICTIONARIES.
A DICTIONARY OF MIRACLES: Imitative, Realistic, and Dogmatic. By the Rev.
E. C. BREWER, LL.D. Crown 8vo, cloth extra, **7s. 6d.**
THE READER'S HANDBOOK OF ALLUSIONS, REFERENCES, PLOTS, AND
STORIES. By the Rev. E. C. BREWER, LL.D. With an ENGLISH BIBLIOGRAPHY.
Fifteenth Thousand. Crown 8vo. cloth extra. **7s. 6d.**
AUTHORS AND THEIR WORKS, WITH THE DATES. Cr. 8vo, cloth limp, **2s.**
FAMILIAR SHORT SAYINGS OF GREAT MEN. With Historical and Explana-
tory Notes. By SAMUEL A. BENT, A.M. Crown 8vo, cloth extra, **7s. 6d.**
SLANG DICTIONARY: Etymological, Historical, and Anecdotal. Cr. 8vo, cl., **6s. 6d.**
WOMEN OF THE DAY: A Biographical Dictionary. By F. HAYS. Cr. 8vo, cl., **5s.**
WORDS, FACTS, AND PHRASES: A Dictionary of Curious, Quaint, and Out-of-
the-Way Matters. By ELIEZER EDWARDS. Crown 8vo, cloth extra, **7s. 6d.**

DIDEROT.—THE PARADOX OF ACTING. Translated, with Annotations, from Diderot's "Le Paradoxe sur le Comédien," by WALTER HERRIES POLLOCK.
With a Preface by HENRY IRVING. Crown 8vo, parchment, **4s. 6d.**

DOBSON (AUSTIN), WORKS BY.
THOMAS BEWICK & HIS PUPILS. With 95 Illustrations. Square 8vo, cloth, **6s.**
FOUR FRENCHWOMEN: MADEMOISELLE DE CORDAY; MADAME ROLAND; THE
PRINCESS DE LAMBALLE ; MADAME DE GENLIS. Fcap. 8vo, hf.-roxburghe, **2s. 6d.**

DOBSON (W. T.), WORKS BY. Post 8vo, cloth limp, **2s. 6d.** each.
LITERARY FRIVOLITIES, FANCIES, FOLLIES, AND FROLICS.
POETICAL INGENUITIES AND ECCENTRICITIES.

DONOVAN (DICK), DETECTIVE STORIES BY.
Post 8vo. illustrated boards, **2s.** each; cloth limp, **2s. 6d.** each.
THE MAN-HUNTER. | TRACKED AND TAKEN.
CAUGHT AT LAST! | WHO POISONED HETTY DUNCAN?
A DETECTIVE'S TRIUMPHS. [Preparing.
THE MAN FROM MANCHESTER. With 23 Illustrations. Crown 8vo, cloth, **6s.** ;
post 8vo, illustrated boards, **2s.**

DOYLE (A. CONAN, Author of "Micah Clarke"), **NOVELS BY.**
THE FIRM OF GIRDLESTONE. Crown 8vo, cloth extra, **6s.**
STRANGE SECRETS. Told by CONAN DOYLE, PERCY FITZGERALD, FLORENCE
MARRYAT, &c. Cr. 8vo, cl. ex., Eight Illusts.. **6s.**; post 8vo, illust. bds , **2s.**

DRAMATISTS, THE OLD. With Vignette Portraits. Cr. 8vo, cl. ex., **6s.** per Vol.
BEN JONSON'S WORKS. With Notes Critical and Explanatory, and a Bio-
graphical Memoir by WM. GIFFORD. Edited by Col. CUNNINGHAM. Three Vols.
CHAPMAN'S WORKS. Complete in Three Vols. Vol. I. contains the Plays
complete; Vol. II., Poems and Minor Translations, with an Introductory Essay
by A. C. SWINBURNE ; Vol. III., Translations of the Iliad and Odyssey.
MARLOWE'S WORKS. Edited, with Notes, by Col. CUNNINGHAM. One Vol.
MASSINGER'S PLAYS. From GIFFORD'S Text. Edit. by Col. CUNNINGHAM. One Vol.

DUNCAN (SARA JEANNETTE), WORKS BY.
A SOCIAL DEPARTURE: How Orthodocia and I Went round the World by Ourselves. With 111 Illustrations by F. H. TOWNSEND. Crown 8vo, cloth, **7s. 6d.**
AN AMERICAN GIRL IN LONDON. With 80 Illustrations by F. H. TOWNSEND. Crown 8vo. cloth extra, **7s. 6d.** [*Preparing.*

DYER.—THE FOLK-LORE OF PLANTS. By Rev. T. F. THISELTON DYER, M.A. Crown 8vo, cloth extra, **6s.**

EARLY ENGLISH POETS. Edited, with Introductions and Annotations, by Rev. A. B. GROSART, D.D. Crown 8vo, cloth boards, **6s.** per Volume.
FLETCHER'S (GILES) COMPLETE POEMS. One Vol.
DAVIES' (SIR JOHN) COMPLETE POETICAL WORKS. Two Vols.
HERRICK'S (ROBERT) COMPLETE COLLECTED POEMS. Three Vols.
SIDNEY'S (SIR PHILIP) COMPLETE POETICAL WORKS. Three Vols.

EDGCUMBE.—ZEPHYRUS: A Holiday in Brazil and on the River Plate. By E. R. PEARCE EDGCUMBE. With 41 Illustrations. Crown 8vo, cloth extra, **5s.**

EDWARDES (MRS. ANNIE), NOVELS BY:
A POINT OF HONOUR. Post 8vo, illustrated boards, **2s.**
ARCHIE LOVELL. Crown 8vo, cloth extra, **3s. 6d.**; post 8vo, illust. boards, **2s.**

EDWARDS (ELIEZER).—WORDS, FACTS, AND PHRASES: A Dictionary of Curious, Quaint, and Out-of-the-Way Matters. By ELIEZER EDWARDS. Crown 8vo, cloth extra, **7s. 6d.**

EDWARDS (M. BETHAM-), NOVELS BY.
KITTY. Post 8vo, illustrated boards, **2s.**; cloth limp, **2s. 6d.**
FELICIA. Post 8vo, illustrated boards, **2s.**

EGGLESTON (EDWARD).—ROXY: A Novel. Post 8vo, illust. bds., 2s.

EMANUEL.—ON DIAMONDS AND PRECIOUS STONES: Their History, Value, and Properties; with Simple Tests for ascertaining their Reality. By HARRY EMANUEL, F.R.G.S. With Illustrations, tinted and plain. Cr. 8vo, cl. ex., **6s.**

ENGLISHMAN'S HOUSE, THE: A Practical Guide to all interested in Selecting or Building a House; with Estimates of Cost, Quantities, &c. By C. J. RICHARDSON. With Coloured Frontispiece and 600 Illusts. Crown 8vo, cloth, **7s. 6d.**

EWALD (ALEX. CHARLES, F.S.A.), WORKS BY.
THE LIFE AND TIMES OF PRINCE CHARLES STUART, Count of Albany (THE YOUNG PRETENDER). With a Portrait. Crown 8vo, cloth extra, **7s. 6d.**
STORIES FROM THE STATE PAPERS. With an Autotype. Crown 8vo, cloth, **6s.**

EYES, OUR: How to Preserve Them from Infancy to Old Age. By JOHN BROWNING, F.R.A.S. With 70 Illusts. Eleventh Edition. Crown 8vo, cl., **1s.**

FAMILIAR SHORT SAYINGS OF GREAT MEN. By SAMUEL ARTHUR BENT, A.M. Fifth Edition, Revised and Enlarged. Crown 8vo, cloth extra, **7s. 6d.**

FARADAY (MICHAEL), WORKS BY. Post 8vo, cloth extra, **4s. 6d.** each.
THE CHEMICAL HISTORY OF A CANDLE: Lectures delivered before a Juvenile Audience. Edited by WILLIAM CROOKES, F.C.S. With numerous Illustrations.
ON THE VARIOUS FORCES OF NATURE, AND THEIR RELATIONS TO EACH OTHER. Edited by WILLIAM CROOKES, F.C.S. With Illustrations.

FARRER (J. ANSON), WORKS BY.
MILITARY MANNERS AND CUSTOMS. Crown 8vo, cloth extra, **6s.**
WAR: Three Essays, reprinted from "Military Manners." Cr. 8vo, **1s.**; cl., **1s. 6d.**

FELLOW (A) OF TRINITY: A Novel. By ALAN ST. AUBYN. With a "Note" by OLIVER WENDELL HOLMES, and a Frontispiece. Crown 8vo, cloth extra, **3s. 6d.**; post 8vo, illustrated boards, **2s.**

FICTION.—A CATALOGUE OF NEARLY SIX HUNDRED WORKS OF FICTION published by CHATTO & WINDUS, with a Short Critical Notice of each (40 pages, demy 8vo), will be sent *free* upon application.

FIN-BEC.—THE CUPBOARD PAPERS: Observations on the Art of Living and Dining. By FIN-BEC. Post 8vo, cloth limp, **2s. 6d.**

FIREWORKS, THE COMPLETE ART OF MAKING; or, The Pyrotechnist's Treasury. By THOMAS KENTISH. With 267 Illustrations. Cr. 8vo, cl., **5s.**

FITZGERALD (PERCY, M.A., F.S.A.), WORKS BY.
THE WORLD BEHIND THE SCENES. Crown 8vo, cloth extra, 3s. 6d.
LITTLE ESSAYS: Passages from Letters of CHARLES LAMB. Post 8vo, cl., 2s. 6d.
A DAY'S TOUR: Journey through France and Belgium. With Sketches. Cr. 4to, 1s.
FATAL ZERO. Crown 8vo, cloth extra, 3s. 6d.; post 8vo, illustrated boards, 2s.

Post 8vo, illustrated boards, 2s. each.
BELLA DONNA. | LADY OF BRANTOME. | THE SECOND MRS. TILLOTSON.
POLLY. | NEVER FORGOTTEN. | SEVENTY-FIVE BROOKE STREET.

LIFE OF JAMES BOSWELL (of Auchinleck). With an Account of his Sayings,
Doings, and Writings. Two Vols., demy 8vo, cloth extra, with Illustrations,
24s. [Preparing.

FLETCHER'S (GILES, B.D.) COMPLETE POEMS: Christ's Victorie
in Heaven, Christ's Victorie on Earth, Christ's Triumph over Death, and Minor
Poems. With Notes by Rev. A. B. GROSART, D.D. Crown 8vo, cloth boards, 6s.

FLUDYER (HARRY) AT CAMBRIDGE: A Series of Family Letters.
Post 8vo, picture cover, 1s.; cloth limp, 1s. 6d.

FONBLANQUE (ALBANY).—FILTHY LUCRE. Post 8vo, illust. bds., 2s.

FRANCILLON (R. E.), NOVELS BY.
Crown 8vo, cloth extra, 3s. 6d. each; post 8vo, illustrated boards, 2s. each.
ONE BY ONE. | QUEEN COPHETUA. | A REAL QUEEN. | KING OR KNAVE?
OLYMPIA. Post 8vo, illust. bds., 2s. | ESTHER'S GLOVE. Fcap. 8vo, pict. cover, 1s.
ROMANCES OF THE LAW. Crown 8vo, cloth, 6s.; post 8vo, illust. boards, 2s.

FREDERIC (HAROLD), NOVELS BY.
SETH'S BROTHER'S WIFE. Post 8vo, illustrated boards, 2s.
THE LAWTON GIRL. With Frontispiece by F. BARNARD. Cr. 8vo, cloth ex., 6s.;
post 8vo, illustrated boards, 2s.

FRENCH LITERATURE, A HISTORY OF. By HENRY VAN LAUN.
Three Vols., demy 8vo, cloth boards, 7s. 6d. each.

FRENZENY.—FIFTY YEARS ON THE TRAIL: Adventures of JOHN
Y. NELSON, Scout, Guide, and Interpreter. By HARINGTON O'REILLY. With 100
Illustrations by PAUL FRENZENY. Crown 8vo, 3s. 6d.; cloth extra, 4s. 6d.

FRERE.—PANDURANG HARI; or, Memoirs of a Hindoo. With a
Preface by Sir H. BARTLE FRERE, G.C.S.I., &c. Crown 8vo, cloth extra, 3s. 6d.

FRISWELL (HAIN).—ONE OF TWO: A Novel. Post 8vo, illust. bds., 2s.

FROST (THOMAS), WORKS BY. Crown 8vo, cloth extra, 3s. 6d. each.
CIRCUS LIFE AND CIRCUS CELEBRITIES. | LIVES OF THE CONJURERS.
THE OLD SHOWMEN AND THE OLD LONDON FAIRS.

FRY'S (HERBERT) ROYAL GUIDE TO THE LONDON CHARITIES.
Showing their Name, Date of Foundation, Objects, Income, Officials, &c. Edited
by JOHN LANE. Published Annually. Crown 8vo, cloth, 1s. 6d.

GARDENING BOOKS. Post 8vo, 1s. each; cloth limp, 1s. 6d. each.
A YEAR'S WORK IN GARDEN AND GREENHOUSE: Practical Advice as to the
Management of the Flower, Fruit, and Frame Garden. By GEORGE GLENNY.
OUR KITCHEN GARDEN: Plants, and How we Cook Them. By TOM JERROLD.
HOUSEHOLD HORTICULTURE. By TOM and JANE JERROLD. Illustrated.
THE GARDEN THAT PAID THE RENT. By TOM JERROLD.

MY GARDEN WILD, AND WHAT I GREW THERE. By FRANCIS G. HEATH.
Crown 8vo, cloth extra, gilt edges, 6s.

GARRETT.—THE CAPEL GIRLS: A Novel. By EDWARD GARRETT.
Crown 8vo, cloth extra, 3s. 6d.; post 8vo, illustrated boards, 2s.

GENTLEMAN'S MAGAZINE, THE. 1s. Monthly. In addition to the
Articles upon subjects in Literature, Science, and Art, for which this Magazine has
so high a reputation, "TABLE TALK" by SYLVANUS URBAN appears monthly.
⁎ Bound Volumes for recent years kept in stock, 8s. 6d. each. Cases for binding, 2s.

GENTLEMAN'S ANNUAL, THE. Published Annually in November. 1s.

GERMAN POPULAR STORIES. Collected by the Brothers GRIMM and Translated by EDGAR TAYLOR. With Introduction by JOHN RUSKIN, and 22 Steel Plates by GEORGE CRUIKSHANK. Square 8vo. cloth, **6s. 6d.**; gilt edges, **7s. 6d.**

GIBBON (CHARLES), NOVELS BY. Crown 8vo, cloth extra, **3s. 6d.** each ; post 8vo, illustrated boards, **2s.** each.

ROBIN GRAY. | LOVING A DREAM. | THE GOLDEN SHAFT.
QUEEN OF THE MEADOW. | OF HIGH DEGREE.
THE FLOWER OF THE FOREST. | IN HONOUR BOUND.

Post 8vo, illustrated boards, **2s.** each.

THE DEAD HEART. | A HEART'S PROBLEM.
FOR LACK OF GOLD. | BY MEAD AND STREAM.
WHAT WILL THE WORLD SAY? | THE BRAES OF YARROW.
FOR THE KING. | BLOOD-MONEY. | FANCY FREE.
IN PASTURES GREEN. | A HARD KNOT.
IN LOVE AND WAR. | HEART'S DELIGHT.

GIBNEY (SOMERVILLE).—SENTENCED! Cr. 8vo, 1s. ; cl., 1s. 6d.

GILBERT (WILLIAM), NOVELS BY. Post 8vo, illustrated boards, **2s.** each.

DR. AUSTIN'S GUESTS. | JAMES DUKE, COSTERMONGER.
THE WIZARD OF THE MOUNTAIN. |

GILBERT (W. S.), ORIGINAL PLAYS BY. In Two Series, each complete in itself, price **2s. 6d.** each.

The FIRST SERIES contains: The Wicked World—Pygmalion and Galatea—Charity—The Princess—The Palace of Truth—Trial by Jury.
The SECOND SERIES: Broken Hearts—Engaged—Sweethearts—Gretchen—Dan'l Druce—Tom Cobb—H.M.S. " Pinafore "—The Sorcerer—Pirates of Penzance.

EIGHT ORIGINAL COMIC OPERAS written by W. S. GILBERT. Containing: The Sorcerer—H.M.S. " Pinafore "—Pirates of Penzance—Iolanthe—Patience—Princess Ida—The Mikado—Trial by Jury. Demy 8vo. cloth limp, **2s. 6d.**
THE "GILBERT AND SULLIVAN" BIRTHDAY BOOK: Quotations for Every Day in the Year, Selected from Plays by W. S. GILBERT set to Music by Sir A. SULLIVAN. Compiled by ALEX. WATSON. Royal 16mo. Jap. leather, **2s. 6d.**

GLANVILLE.—THE LOST HEIRESS: A Tale of Love and Battle. By ERNEST GLANVILLE. 2 Illusts. by HUME NISBET. Cr. 8vo, cloth extra. **3s. 6d.**

GLENNY.—A YEAR'S WORK IN GARDEN AND GREENHOUSE: Practical Advice to Amateur Gardeners as to the Management of the Flower, Fruit, and Frame Garden. By GEORGE GLENNY. Post 8vo, **1s.**; cloth limp, **1s. 6d.**

GODWIN.—LIVES OF THE NECROMANCERS. By WILLIAM GODWIN. Post 8vo, cloth limp, **2s.**

GOLDEN TREASURY OF THOUGHT, THE: An Encyclopædia of QUOTATIONS. Edited by THEODORE TAYLOR. Crown 8vo, cloth gilt, **7s. 6d.**

GOWING.—FIVE THOUSAND MILES IN A SLEDGE: A Midwinter Journey Across Siberia. By LIONEL F. GOWING. With 30 Illustrations by C. J. UREN, and a Map by E. WELLER. Large crown 8vo. cloth extra. **8s.**

GRAHAM. — THE PROFESSOR'S WIFE: A Story. By LEONARD GRAHAM. Fcap. 8vo, picture cover, **1s.**

GREEKS AND ROMANS, THE LIFE OF THE, described from Antique Monuments. By ERNST GUHL and W. KONER. Edited by Dr. F. HUEFFER. With 545 Illustrations. Large crown 8vo. cloth extra, **7s. 6d.**

GREENWOOD (JAMES), WORKS BY Cr. 8vo, cloth extra, **3s. 6d.** each.

THE WILDS OF LONDON. | LOW-LIFE DEEPS.

GREVILLE (HENRY), NOVELS BY:

NIKANOR. Translated by ELIZA E. CHASE With 8 Illusts Cr. 8vo. cl. extra, **6s.**
A NOBLE WOMAN. Translated by ALBERT D VANDAM. Crown 8vo, clo.h extra **3s.**; post 8vo. illustrated boards, **2s.**

HABBERTON (JOHN, Author of " Helen's Babies "). NOVELS BY. Post 8vo, illustrated boards **2s.** each, cloth limp, **2s. 6d.** each.

BRUETON'S BAYOU. | COUNTRY LUCK.

HAIR, THE : Its Treatment in Health, Weakness, and Disease.   Translated from the German of Dr. J. PINCUS.   Crown 8vo, 1s.; cloth limp, 1s. 6d.

HAKE (DR. THOMAS GORDON), POEMS BY.   Cr. 8vo, cl. ex., 6s. each.
NEW SYMBOLS. | LEGENDS OF THE MORROW. | THE SERPENT PLAY.

MAIDEN ECSTASY.   Small 4to, cloth extra, 8s.

HALL.—SKETCHES OF IRISH CHARACTER.   By Mrs. S. C. HALL.
With numerous Illustrations on Steel and Wood by MACLISE, GILBERT, HARVEY, and
GEORGE CRUIKSHANK.   Medium 8vo. cloth extra, 7s. 6d.

HALLIDAY (ANDR.).—EVERY-DAY PAPERS.   Post 8vo, bds., 2s.

HANDWRITING, THE PHILOSOPHY OF.   With over 100 Facsimiles
and Explanatory Text.   By DON FELIX DE SALAMANCA.   Post 8vo. cloth limp. 2s. 6d.

HANKY-PANKY : A Collection of Very Easy Tricks, Very Difficult
Tricks, White Magic, Sleight of Hand, &c.   Edited by W. H. CREMER.   With 200
Illustrations.   Crown 8vo. cloth extra, 4s. 6d.

HARDY (LADY DUFFUS). — PAUL WYNTER'S SACRIFICE.   By
Lady DUFFUS HARDY.   Post 8vo, illustrated boards, 2s.

HARDY (THOMAS). — UNDER THE GREENWOOD TREE.   By
THOMAS HARDY, Author of "Far from the Madding Crowd."   Post 8vo, illust. bds., 2s.

HARWOOD.—THE TENTH EARL.   By J. BERWICK HARWOOD.   Post
8vo, illustrated boards, 2s.

HAWEIS (MRS. H. R.), WORKS BY.   Square 8vo, cloth extra, 6s. each.
THE ART OF BEAUTY.   With Coloured Frontispiece and 91 Illustrations.
THE ART OF DECORATION.   With Coloured Frontispiece and 74 Illustrations.
CHAUCER FOR CHILDREN.   With 8 Coloured Plates and 30 Woodcuts.

THE ART OF DRESS.   With 32 Illustrations.   Post 8vo, 1s. ; cloth, 1s. 6d.
CHAUCER FOR SCHOOLS.   Demy 8vo cloth limp, 2s. 6d.

HAWEIS (Rev. H. R., M.A.). —AMERICAN HUMORISTS : WASHINGTON
IRVING, OLIVER WENDELL HOLMES, JAMES RUSSELL LOWELL, ARTEMUS WARD,
MARK TWAIN, and BRET HARTE.   Third Edition.   Crown 8vo. cloth extra. 6s.

HAWLEY SMART.—WITHOUT LOVE OR LICENCE : A Novel.   By
HAWLEY SMART.   Crown 8vo. cloth extra, 3s. 6d.

HAWTHORNE. —OUR OLD HOME.   By NATHANIEL HAWTHORNE.
Annotated with Passages from the Author's Note-book, and Illustrated with 31
Photogravures.   Two Vols., crown 8vo, buckram, gilt top, 15s.

HAWTHORNE (JULIAN), NOVELS BY.
Crown 8vo, cloth extra, 3s. 6d. each ; post 8vo, illustrated boards, 2s. each.
GARTH. | ELLICE QUENTIN. | BEATRIX RANDOLPH. | DUST.
SEBASTIAN STROME. | DAVID POINDEXTER.
FORTUNE'S FOOL. | THE SPECTRE OF THE CAMERA.

Post 8vo, illustrated boards, 2s. each.
MISS CADOGNA. | LOVE—OR A NAME.

MRS. GAINSBOROUGH'S DIAMONDS.   Fcap. 8vo, illustrated cover, 1s.
A DREAM AND A FORGETTING.   Post 8vo, cloth limp, 1s. 6d.

HAYS.—WOMEN OF THE DAY : A Biographical Dictionary of Notable
Contemporaries.   By FRANCES HAYS.   Cr w 8vo cloth extra, 5s.

HEATH.—MY GARDEN WILD, AND WHAT I GREW THERE.
By FRANCIS GEORGE HEATH.   Crown 8vo, cloth e tra, gilt edges, 6s.

HELPS (SIR ARTHUR), WORKS BY.   Post 8vo, cloth limp, 2s. 6d. each.
ANIMALS AND THEIR MASTERS. | SOCIAL PRESSURE.

IVAN DE BIRON : A Novel.   Cr. 8vo, cl. extra, 3s. 6d. ; post 8vo, illust. bds., 2s.

HENDERSON.—AGATHA PAGE : A Novel.   By ISAAC HENDERSON.
Crown 8vo, cloth extra, 3s. 6d.

HERRICK'S (ROBERT) HESPERIDES, NOBLE NUMBERS, AND COMPLETE COLLECTED POEMS. With Memorial-Introduction and Notes by the Rev. A. B. GROSART, D.D.; Steel Portrait, &c. Three Vols., crown 8vo, cl. bds., 18s.

HERTZKA.—FREELAND : A Social Anticipation. By Dr. THEODOR HERTZKA. Translated by ARTHUR RANSOM. Crown 8vo, cloth extra, 6s.

HESSE-WARTEGG.—TUNIS : The Land and the People. By Chevalier ERNST VON HESSE-WARTEGG. With 22 Illustrations. Cr. 8vo, cloth extra, 3s. 6d.

HINDLEY (CHARLES), WORKS BY.
TAVERN ANECDOTES AND SAYINGS: Including the Origin of Signs, and Reminiscences connected with Taverns, Coffee Houses, Clubs, &c. With Illustrations. Crown 8vo, cloth extra, 3s. 6d.
THE LIFE AND ADVENTURES OF A CHEAP JACK. By ONE OF THE FRATERNITY. Edited by CHARLES HINDLEY. Crown 8vo, cloth extra, 3s. 6d.

HOEY.—THE LOVER'S CREED. By Mrs. CASHEL HOEY. Post 8vo, illustrated boards, 2s.

HOLLINGSHEAD (JOHN).—NIAGARA SPRAY. Crown 8vo, 1s.

HOLMES.—THE SCIENCE OF VOICE PRODUCTION AND VOICE PRESERVATION: A Popular Manual for the Use of Speakers and Singers. By GORDON HOLMES, M.D. With Illustrations. Crown 8vo, 1s.; cloth, 1s. 6d.

HOLMES (OLIVER WENDELL), WORKS BY.
THE AUTOCRAT OF THE BREAKFAST-TABLE. Illustrated by J. GORDON THOMSON. Post 8vo, cloth limp, 2s. 6d.—Another Edition, in smaller type, with an Introduction by G. A. SALA. Post 8vo, cloth limp, 2s.
THE PROFESSOR AT THE BREAKFAST-TABLE. Post 8vo, cloth limp, 2s.

HOOD'S (THOMAS) CHOICE WORKS, in Prose and Verse. With Life of the Author, Portrait, and 200 Illustrations. Crown 8vo, cloth extra, 7s. 6d.
HOOD'S WHIMS AND ODDITIES. With 85 Illustrations. Post 8vo, printed on laid paper and half-bound, 2s.

HOOD (TOM).—FROM NOWHERE TO THE NORTH POLE: A Noah's Arkæological Narrative. By TOM HOOD. With 25 Illustrations by W. BRUNTON and E. C. BARNES. Square 8vo, cloth extra, gilt edges, 6s.

HOOK'S (THEODORE) CHOICE HUMOROUS WORKS; including his Ludicrous Adventures, Bons Mots, Puns, and Hoaxes. With Life of the Author, Portraits, Facsimiles, and Illustrations. Crown 8vo, cloth extra, 7s. 6d.

HOOPER.—THE HOUSE OF RABY: A Novel. By Mrs. GEORGE HOOPER. Post 8vo, illustrated boards, 2s.

HOPKINS.—"'TWIXT LOVE AND DUTY:" A Novel. By TIGHE HOPKINS. Post 8vo, illustrated boards, 2s.

HORNE. — ORION: An Epic Poem. By RICHARD HENGIST HORNE. With Photographic Portrait by SUMMERS. Tenth Edition. Cr. 8vo, cloth extra, 7s.

HORSE (THE) AND HIS RIDER: An Anecdotic Medley. By "THORMANBY." Crown 8vo, cloth extra, 6s.

HUNT.—ESSAYS BY LEIGH HUNT: A TALE FOR A CHIMNEY CORNER, and other Pieces. Edited, with an Introduction, by EDMUND OLLIER. Post 8vo, printed on laid paper and half-bd., 2s. Also in sm. sq. 8vo, cl. extra, at same price.

HUNT (MRS. ALFRED), NOVELS BY.
Crown 8vo, cloth extra, 3s. 6d. each; post 8vo, illustrated boards, 2s. each.
THE LEADEN CASKET. | SELF-CONDEMNED. | THAT OTHER PERSON.
THORNICROFT'S MODEL. Post 8vo, illustrated boards, 2s.

HYDROPHOBIA: An Account of M. PASTEUR's System. Containing a Translation of all his Communications on the Subject, the Technique of his Method, and Statistics. By RENAUD SUZOR, M.B. Crown 8vo, cloth extra, 6s.

INGELOW (JEAN).—FATED TO BE FREE. With 24 Illustrations by G. J. PINWELL. Cr. 8vo, cloth extra, 3s. 6d.; post 8vo, illustrated boards, 2s.

INDOOR PAUPERS. By ONE OF THEM. Crown 8vo, 1s.; cloth, 1s. 6d.

IRISH WIT AND HUMOUR, SONGS OF. Collected and Edited by A. Perceval Graves. Post 8vo, cloth limp, **2s. 6d.**

JAMES.—A ROMANCE OF THE QUEEN'S HOUNDS. By Charles James. Post 8vo, picture cover, **1s.**; cloth limp, **1s. 6d.**

JANVIER.—PRACTICAL KERAMICS FOR STUDENTS. By Catherine A. Janvier. Crown 8vo, cloth extra, **6s.**

JAY (HARRIETT), NOVELS BY. Post 8vo, illustrated boards, **2s.** each.
THE DARK COLLEEN. | THE QUEEN OF CONNAUGHT.

JEFFERIES (RICHARD), WORKS BY. Post 8vo, cloth limp, **2s. 6d.** each.
NATURE NEAR LONDON. | THE LIFE OF THE FIELDS. | THE OPEN AIR.
THE EULOGY OF RICHARD JEFFERIES. By Walter Besant. Second Edition. With a Photograph Portrait. Crown 8vo, cloth extra, **6s.**

JENNINGS (H. J.), WORKS BY.
CURIOSITIES OF CRITICISM. Post 8vo, cloth limp, **2s. 6d.**
LORD TENNYSON: A Biographical Sketch. With a Photograph. Cr. 8vo, cl., **6s.**

JEROME.—STAGELAND: Curious Habits and Customs of its Inhabitants. By Jerome K. Jerome. With 64 Illustrations by J. Bernard Partridge. Sixteenth Thousand. Fcap. 4to, cloth extra, **3s. 6d.**

JERROLD.—THE BARBER'S CHAIR; & THE HEDGEHOG LETTERS. By Douglas Jerrold. Post 8vo, printed on laid paper and half-bound, **2s.**

JERROLD (TOM), WORKS BY. Post 8vo, **1s.** each; cloth limp, **1s. 6d.** each.
THE GARDEN THAT PAID THE RENT.
HOUSEHOLD HORTICULTURE: A Gossip about Flowers. Illustrated.
OUR KITCHEN GARDEN: The Plants we Grow, and How we Cook Them.

JESSE.—SCENES AND OCCUPATIONS OF A COUNTRY LIFE. By Edward Jesse. Post 8vo, cloth limp, **2s.**

JONES (WILLIAM, F.S.A.), WORKS BY. Cr. 8vo, cl. extra, **7s. 6d.** each.
FINGER-RING LORE: Historical, Legendary, and Anecdotal. With nearly 300 Illustrations. Second Edition, Revised and Enlarged.
CREDULITIES, PAST AND PRESENT. Including the Sea and Seamen, Miners, Talismans, Word and Letter Divination, Exorcising and Blessing of Animals, Birds, Eggs, Luck, &c. With an Etched Frontispiece.
CROWNS AND CORONATIONS: A History of Regalia. With 100 Illustrations.

JONSON'S (BEN) WORKS. With Notes Critical and Explanatory, and a Biographical Memoir by William Gifford. Edited by Colonel Cunningham. Three Vols., crown 8vo, cloth extra, **6s.** each.

JOSEPHUS, THE COMPLETE WORKS OF. Translated by Whiston. Containing "The Antiquities of the Jews" and "The Wars of the Jews." With 52 Illustrations and Maps. Two Vols., demy 8vo, half-bound, **12s. 6d.**

KEMPT.—PENCIL AND PALETTE: Chapters on Art and Artists. By Robert Kempt. Post 8vo, cloth limp, **2s. 6d.**

KERSHAW.—COLONIAL FACTS AND FICTIONS: Humorous Sketches. By Mark Kershaw. Post 8vo, illustrated boards, **2s.**; cloth, **2s. 6d.**

KEYSER.—CUT BY THE MESS: A Novel. By Arthur Keyser. Crown 8vo, picture cover, **1s.**; cloth limp, **1s. 6d.**

KING (R. ASHE), NOVELS BY. Cr. 8vo, cl., **3s. 6d.** ea.; post 8vo, bds., **2s.** ea.
A DRAWN GAME. | "THE WEARING OF THE GREEN."
PASSION'S SLAVE. Post 8vo, illustrated boards, **2s.**
BELL BARRY. 2 vols., crown 8vo.

KINGSLEY (HENRY), NOVELS BY.
OAKSHOTT CASTLE. Post 8vo, illustrated boards, **2s.**
NUMBER SEVENTEEN. Crown 8vo, cloth extra, **3s. 6d.**

KNIGHTS (THE) OF THE LION: A Romance of the Thirteenth Century. Edited, with an Introduction, by the Marquess of Lorne, K.T. Cr. 8vo, cl. ex., **6s.**

KNIGHT.—THE PATIENT'S VADE MECUM: How to Get Most Benefit from Medical Advice. By WILLIAM KNIGHT, M.R.C.S., and EDWARD KNIGHT, L.R.C.P. Crown 8vo, 1s.; cloth limp, 1s. 6d.

LAMB'S (CHARLES) COMPLETE WORKS, in Prose and Verse. Edited, with Notes and Introduction, by R. H. SHEPHERD. With Two Portraits and Facsimile of a page of the "Essay on Roast Pig." Cr. 8vo, cl. ex., 7s. 6d.
THE ESSAYS OF ELIA. Post 8vo, printed on laid paper and half-bound, 2s.
LITTLE ESSAYS: Sketches and Characters by CHARLES LAMB, selected from his Letters by PERCY FITZGERALD. Post 8vo, cloth limp, 2s. 6d.

LANDOR.—CITATION AND EXAMINATION OF WILLIAM SHAKS-PEARE, &c., before Sir THOMAS LUCY touching Deer-stealing. 19th September, 1582. To which is added, A CONFERENCE OF MASTER EDMUND SPENSER with the Earl of Essex, touching the State of Ireland, 1595. By WALTER SAVAGE LANDOR. Fcap 8vo, half-Roxburghe, 2s. 6d.

LANE.—THE THOUSAND AND ONE NIGHTS, commonly called in England THE ARABIAN NIGHTS' ENTERTAINMENTS. Translated from the Arabic, with Notes, by EDWARD WILLIAM LANE. Illustrated by many hundred Engravings from Designs by HARVEY. Edited by EDWARD STANLEY POOLE. With a Preface by STANLEY LANE-POOLE. Three Vols., demy 8vo, cloth extra, 7s. 6d. each.

LARWOOD (JACOB), WORKS BY.
THE STORY OF THE LONDON PARKS. With Illusts. Cr. 8vo, cl. extra, 3s. 6d.
ANECDOTES OF THE CLERGY: The Antiquities, Humours, and Eccentricities of the Cloth. Post 8vo, printed on laid paper and half-bound, 2s.

Post 8vo, cloth limp, 2s. 6d. each.
FORENSIC ANECDOTES. | THEATRICAL ANECDOTES.

LEIGH (HENRY S.), WORKS BY.
CAROLS OF COCKAYNE. Printed on hand-made paper, bound in buckram, 5s.
JEUX D'ESPRIT. Edited by HENRY S. LEIGH Post 8vo. cloth limp, 2s. 6d.

LEYS (JOHN). THE LINDSAYS: A Romance. Post 8vo, illust. bds., 2s.

LIFE IN LONDON; or, The History of JERRY HAWTHORN and CORINTHIAN TOM. With CRUIKSHANK's Coloured Illustrations. Crown 8vo, cloth extra, 7s. 6d. [New Edition preparing.

LINSKILL. IN EXCHANGE FOR A SOUL. By MARY LINSKILL. Post 8vo. illustrated boards, 2s.

LINTON (E. LYNN), WORKS BY. Post 8vo, cloth limp, 2s. 6d. each.
WITCH STORIES. | OURSELVES: ESSAYS ON WOMEN.

Crown 8vo, cloth extra, 3s. 6d. each; post 8vo, illustrated boards, 2s. each.
SOWING THE WIND.   UNDER WHICH LORD?
PATRICIA KEMBALL.   "MY LOVE!" | IONE.
ATONEMENT OF LEAM DUNDAS.   PASTON CAREW, Millionaire & Miser.
THE WORLD WELL LOST.

Post 8vo, illustrated boards, 2s. each.
THE REBEL OF THE FAMILY. | WITH A SILKEN THREAD.

LONGFELLOW'S POETICAL WORKS. With numerous Illustrations on Steel and Wood. Crown 8vo, cloth extra, 7s. 6d.

LUCY.—GIDEON FLEYCE: A Novel. By HENRY W. LUCY. Crown 8vo, cloth extra, 3s. 6d.; post 8vo, illustrated boards, 2s.

LUSIAD (THE) OF CAMOENS. Translated into English Spenserian Verse by ROBERT FFRENCH DUFF. With 11 Plates. Demy 8vo, cloth boards, 18s.

MACALPINE (AVERY), NOVELS BY.
TERESA ITASCA, and other Stories. Crown 8vo, bound in canvas, 2s. 6d.
BROKEN WINGS. With 6 Illusts. by W. J. HENNESSY. Crown 8vo, cloth extra, 6s.

MACCOLL (HUGH), NOVELS BY.
MR. STRANGER'S SEALED PACKET. Second Edition. Crown 8vo, cl. extra, 5s.
EDNOR WHITLOCK. Crown 8vo, cloth extra, 6s.

McCARTHY (JUSTIN, M.P.), WORKS BY.

A HISTORY OF OUR OWN TIMES, from the Accession of Queen Victoria to the General Election of 1880. Four Vols. demy 8vo, cloth extra, **12s.** each.—Also a POPULAR EDITION, in Four Vols., crown 8vo, cloth extra, **6s.** each.—And a JUBILEE EDITION, with an Appendix of Events to the end of 1886, in Two Vols., large crown 8vo, cloth extra, **7s. 6d.** each.

A SHORT HISTORY OF OUR OWN TIMES. One Vol., crown 8vo, cloth extra, **6s.** —Also a CHEAP POPULAR EDITION, post 8vo, cloth limp, **2s. 6d.**

A HISTORY OF THE FOUR GEORGES. Four Vols. demy 8vo, cloth extra, **12s.** each. [Vols. I. & II. *ready*.

Crown 8vo, cloth extra, **3s. 6d.** each; post 8vo, illustrated boards, **2s.** each.

THE WATERDALE NEIGHBOURS.	MISS MISANTHROPE.
MY ENEMY'S DAUGHTER.	DONNA QUIXOTE.
A FAIR SAXON.	THE COMET OF A SEASON.
LINLEY ROCHFORD.	MAID OF ATHENS.
DEAR LADY DISDAIN.	CAMIOLA: A Girl with a Fortune.

"THE RIGHT HONOURABLE." By JUSTIN McCARTHY, M.P., and Mrs. CAMPBELL-PRAED. Fourth Edition. Crown 8vo, cloth extra, **6s.**

McCARTHY (JUSTIN H., M.P.), WORKS BY.

THE FRENCH REVOLUTION. Four Vols. 8vo, **12s.** each. [Vols. I. & II. *ready*.
AN OUTLINE OF THE HISTORY OF IRELAND. Crown 8vo, **1s.**; cloth, **1s. 6d.**
IRELAND SINCE THE UNION: Irish History, 1798-1886. Crown 8vo, cloth, **6s.**
ENGLAND UNDER GLADSTONE, 1880-85. Crown 8vo, cloth extra, **6s.**

HAFIZ IN LONDON: Poems. Small 8vo, gold cloth, **3s. 6d.**
HARLEQUINADE: Poems. Small 4to, Japanese vellum, **8s.**

OUR SENSATION NOVEL. Crown 8vo, picture cover, **1s.**; cloth limp, **1s 6d.**
DOOM! An Atlantic Episode. Crown 8vo, picture cover, **1s.**
DOLLY: A Sketch. Crown 8vo, picture cover, **1s.**; cloth limp, **1s. 6d.**
LILY LASS: A Romance. Crown 8vo, picture cover, **1s.**; cloth limp, **1s. 6d.**

MACDONALD.—WORKS OF FANCY AND IMAGINATION. By

GEORGE MACDONALD, LL.D. Ten Vols., cloth extra, gilt edges, in cloth case, **21s.** Or the Vols. may be had separately, bound in grolier cloth, at **2s. 6d.** each.

Vol. I. WITHIN AND WITHOUT.—THE HIDDEN LIFE.
,, II. THE DISCIPLE.—THE GOSPEL WOMEN.—BOOK OF SONNETS.—ORGAN SONGS.
,, III. VIOLIN SONGS.—SONGS OF THE DAYS AND NIGHTS.—A BOOK OF DREAMS.—ROADSIDE POEMS.—POEMS FOR CHILDREN.
,, IV. PARABLES.—BALLADS.—SCOTCH SONGS.
,, V. & VI. PHANTASTES: A Faerie Romance. | Vol. VII. THE PORTENT.
VIII. THE LIGHT PRINCESS.—THE GIANT'S HEART.—SHADOWS.
,, IX. CROSS PURPOSES.—THE GOLDEN KEY.—THE CARASOYN.—LITTLE DAYLIGHT.
,, X. THE CRUEL PAINTER.—THE WOW O' RIVVEN.—THE CASTLE.—THE BROKEN SWORDS.—THE GRAY WOLF.—UNCLE CORNELIUS.

MACDONELL.—QUAKER COUSINS: A Novel. By AGNES MACDONELL.

Crown 8vo, cloth extra, **3s. 6d.**; post 8vo, illustrated boards, **2s.**

MACGREGOR. — PASTIMES AND PLAYERS: Notes on Popular

Games. By ROBERT MACGREGOR. Post 8vo, cloth limp, **2s. 6d.**

MACKAY.—INTERLUDES AND UNDERTONES; or, Music at Twilight.

By CHARLES MACKAY, LL.D. Crown 8vo, cloth extra, **6s.**

MACLISE PORTRAIT GALLERY (THE) OF ILLUSTRIOUS LITER-

ARY CHARACTERS: 85 PORTRAITS; with Memoirs — Biographical, Critical, Bibliographical, and Anecdotal—illustrative of the Literature of the former half of the Present Century, by WILLIAM BATES, B.A. Crown 8vo, cloth extra, **7s. 6d.**

MACQUOID (MRS.), WORKS BY. Square 8vo, cloth extra, **7s. 6d.** each.

IN THE ARDENNES. With 50 Illustrations by THOMAS R. MACQUOID.
PICTURES AND LEGENDS FROM NORMANDY AND BRITTANY. With 34 Illustrations by THOMAS R. MACQUOID.
THROUGH NORMANDY. With 92 Illustrations by T. R. MACQUOID, and a Map.
THROUGH BRITTANY. With 35 Illustrations by T. R. MACQUOID, and a Map.
ABOUT YORKSHIRE. With 67 Illustrations by T. R. MACQUOID.

Post 8vo, illustrated boards, **2s.** each.
THE EVIL EYE, and other Stories. | LOST ROSE,

MAGIC LANTERN, THE, and its Management: including full Practical Directions for producing the Limelight, making Oxygen Gas, and preparing Lantern Slides. By T. C. HEPWORTH. With 10 Illustrations. Cr. 8vo. **1s.**; cloth. **1s. 6d.**

MAGICIAN'S OWN BOOK, THE : Performances with Cups and Balls, Eggs, Hats, Handkerchiefs, &c. All from actual Experience. Edited by W. H. CREMER. With 200 Illustrations. Crown 8vo, cloth extra. **4s. 6d.**

MAGNA CHARTA : An Exact Facsimile of the Original in the British Museum, 3 feet by 2 feet, with Arms and Seals emblazoned in Gold and Colours, **5s.**

MALLOCK (W. H.), WORKS BY.
THE NEW REPUBLIC. Post 8vo, picture cover, **2s.**; cloth limp, **2s. 6d.**
THE NEW PAUL & VIRGINIA : Positivism on an Island. Post 8vo, cloth, **2s. 6d.**
POEMS. Small 4to, parchment, **8s.**
IS LIFE WORTH LIVING? Crown 8vo, cloth extra, **6s.**

MALLORY'S (SIR THOMAS) MORT D'ARTHUR : The Stories of King Arthur and of the Knights of the Round Table. (A Selection.) Edited by B. MONTGOMERIE RANKING. Post 8vo, cloth limp, **2s.**

MARK TWAIN, WORKS BY. Crown 8vo, cloth extra, **7s. 6d.** each.
THE CHOICE WORKS OF MARK TWAIN. Revised and Corrected throughout by the Author. With Life, Portrait, and numerous Illustrations.
ROUGHING IT, and INNOCENTS AT HOME. With 200 Illusts. by F. A. FRASER.
THE GILDED AGE. By MARK TWAIN and C. D. WARNER. With 212 Illustrations.
MARK TWAIN'S LIBRARY OF HUMOUR. With 197 Illustrations.
A YANKEE AT THE COURT OF KING ARTHUR. With 220 Illusts. by BEARD.

Crown 8vo, cloth extra (illustrated), **7s. 6d.** each; post 8vo, illust. boards, **2s.** each.
THE INNOCENTS ABROAD; or New Pilgrim's Progress. With 234 Illustrations. (The Two-Shilling Edition is entitled MARK TWAIN'S PLEASURE TRIP.)
THE ADVENTURES OF TOM SAWYER. With 111 Illustrations.
A TRAMP ABROAD. With 314 Illustrations.
THE PRINCE AND THE PAUPER. With 190 Illustrations.
LIFE ON THE MISSISSIPPI. With 300 Illustrations.
ADVENTURES OF HUCKLEBERRY FINN. With 174 Illusts. by E. W. KEMBLE.

THE STOLEN WHITE ELEPHANT, &c. Cr. 8vo, cl., **6s.**; post 8vo, illust. bds., **2s.**

MARLOWE'S WORKS. Including his Translations. Edited, with Notes and Introductions, by Col. CUNNINGHAM. Crown 8vo, cloth extra, **6s.**

MARRYAT (FLORENCE), NOVELS BY. Post 8vo, illust. boards, **2s.** each.
A HARVEST OF WILD OATS. | WRITTEN IN FIRE. | FIGHTING THE AIR.
OPEN ! SESAME ! Crown 8vo, cloth extra, **3s. 6d.**; post 8vo, picture boards. **2s.**

MASSINGER'S PLAYS. From the Text of WILLIAM GIFFORD. Edited by Col. CUNNINGHAM. Crown 8vo, cloth extra, **6s.**

MASTERMAN.—HALF-A-DOZEN DAUGHTERS : A Novel. By J. MASTERMAN. Post 8vo, illustrated boards, **2s.**

MATTHEWS.—A SECRET OF THE SEA, &c. By BRANDER MATTHEWS. Post 8vo, illustrated boards, **2s.**; cloth limp, **2s. 6d.**

MAYHEW.—LONDON CHARACTERS AND THE HUMOROUS SIDE OF LONDON LIFE. By HENRY MAYHEW. With Illusts. Crown 8vo, cloth, **3s. 6d.**

MENKEN.—INFELICIA : Poems by ADAH ISAACS MENKEN. With Biographical Preface, Illustrations by F. E. LUMMIS and F. O. C. DARLEY, and Facsimile of a Letter from CHARLES DICKENS. Small 4to, cloth extra, **7s. 6d.**

MEXICAN MUSTANG (ON A), through Texas to the Rio Grande. By A. E. SWEET and J. ARMOY KNOX. With 265 Illusts. Cr. 8vo, cloth extra, **7s. 6d.**

MIDDLEMASS (JEAN), NOVELS BY. Post 8vo, illust. boards, **2s.** each.
TOUCH AND GO. | MR. DORILLION.

MILLER.—PHYSIOLOGY FOR THE YOUNG; or, The House of Life : Human Physiology, with its application to the Preservation of Health. By Mrs. F. FENWICK MILLER. With numerous Illustrations. Post 8vo, cloth limp, **2s. 6d.**

MILTON (J. L.), WORKS BY. Post 8vo, 1s. each; cloth, 1s. 6d. each.
THE HYGIENE OF THE SKIN. With Directions for Diet, Soaps, Baths, &c.
THE BATH IN DISEASES OF THE SKIN.
THE LAWS OF LIFE, AND THEIR RELATION TO DISEASES OF THE SKIN.
THE SUCCESSFUL TREATMENT OF LEPROSY. Demy 8vo, 1s.

MINTO (WM.)—WAS SHE GOOD OR BAD? Cr. 8vo, 1s. ; cloth, 1s. 6d.

MOLESWORTH (MRS.), NOVELS BY.
HATHERCOURT RECTORY. Post 8vo, illustrated boards, 2s.
THAT GIRL IN BLACK. Crown 8vo, picture cover, 1s.; cloth, 1s. 6d.

MOORE (THOMAS), WORKS BY.
THE EPICUREAN; and ALCIPHRON. Post 8vo, half-bound, 2s.
PROSE AND VERSE, Humorous, Satirical, and Sentimental, by THOMAS MOORE ;
with Suppressed Passages from the MEMOIRS OF LORD BYRON. Edited by R.
HERNE SHEPHERD. With Portrait. Crown 8vo, cloth extra, 7s. 6d.

MUDDOCK (J. E.), STORIES BY.
STORIES WEIRD AND WONDERFUL. Post 8vo, illust. boards, 2s.; cloth, 2s. 6d.
THE DEAD MAN'S SECRET; or, The Valley of Gold: A Narrative of Strange
Adventure. With a Frontispiece by F. BARNARD. Crown 8vo, cloth extra, 5s.;
post 8vo, illustrated boards, 2s.

MURRAY (D. CHRISTIE), NOVELS BY.
Crown 8vo, cloth extra, 3s. 6d. each; post 8vo, illustrated boards, 2s. each.
A LIFE'S ATONEMENT. | A MODEL FATHER. | A BIT OF HUMAN NATURE.
JOSEPH'S COAT. | HEARTS. | FIRST PERSON SINGULAR.
COALS OF FIRE. | THE WAY OF THE | CYNIC FORTUNE.
VAL STRANGE. | WORLD. |
BY THE GATE OF THE SEA. Post 8vo, picture boards, 2s.
OLD BLAZER'S HERO. With Three Illustrations by A. McCORMICK. Crown 8vo,
cloth extra, 6s.; post 8vo, illustrated boards, 2s.

MURRAY (D. CHRISTIE) & HENRY HERMAN, WORKS BY.
Crown 8vo, cloth extra 6s. each; post 8vo, illustrated boards, 2s. each.
ONE TRAVELLER RETURNS.
PAUL JONES'S ALIAS. With 13 Illustrations by A. FORESTIER and G. NICOLET.
THE BISHOPS' BIBLE. Crown 8vo, cloth extra, 3s. 6d.

MURRAY.—A GAME OF BLUFF: A Novel. By HENRY MURRAY.
Post 8vo, picture boards, 2s.; cloth limp, 2s. 6d.

NISBET.—"BAIL UP!" A Romance of BUSHRANGERS AND BLACKS.
By HUME NISBET. With Frontispiece and Vignette. Crown 8vo, cloth extra, 3s. 6d.

NOVELISTS.—HALF-HOURS WITH THE BEST NOVELISTS OF
THE CENTURY. Edit. by H. T. MACKENZIE BELL. Cr. 8vo, cl., 3s. 6d. [Preparing.

O'CONNOR. — LORD BEACONSFIELD: A Biography. By T. P.
O'CONNOR, M.P. Sixth Edition, with an Introduction. Crown 8vo, cloth extra, 5s.

O'HANLON (ALICE), NOVELS BY. Post 8vo, illustrated boards, 2s. each.
THE UNFORESEEN. | CHANCE? OR FATE?

OHNET (GEORGES), NOVELS BY.
DOCTOR RAMEAU. Translated by Mrs. CASHEL HOEY. With 9 Illustrations by
E. BAYARD. Crown 8vo, cloth extra, 6s.; post 8vo, illustrated boards, 2s.
A LAST LOVE. Translated by ALBERT D. VANDAM. Crown 8vo, cloth extra, 5s.;
post 8vo, illustrated boards, 2s.
A WEIRD GIFT. Translated by ALBERT D. VANDAM. Crown 8vo, cloth, 3s. 6d.

OLIPHANT (MRS.), NOVELS BY. Post 8vo, illustrated boards, 2s. each.
THE PRIMROSE PATH. | THE GREATEST HEIRESS IN ENGLAND.
WHITELADIES. With Illustrations by ARTHUR HOPKINS and HENRY WOODS,
A.R.A. Crown 8vo, cloth extra, 3s. 6d.; post 8vo, illustrated boards, 2s.

O'REILLY (MRS.).—PHŒBE'S FORTUNES. Post 8vo, illust. bds., 2s.

O'SHAUGHNESSY (ARTHUR), POEMS BY.
LAYS OF FRANCE. Crown 8vo, cloth extra, 10s. 6d.
MUSIC AND MOONLIGHT. Fcap. 8vo, cloth extra. 7s. 6d.
SONGS OF A WORKER, Fcap. 8vo, cloth extra, 7s. 6d.

OUIDA, NOVELS BY. Cr. 8vo, cl., 3s. 6d. each; post 8vo, illust. bds., 2s. each.

HELD IN BONDAGE.
TRICOTRIN.
STRATHMORE.
CHANDOS.
CECIL CASTLEMAINE'S GAGE.
IDALIA.
UNDER TWO FLAGS.
PUCK.

FOLLE-FARINE.
A DOG OF FLANDERS.
PASCAREL.
TWO LITTLE WOODEN SHOES.
SIGNA.
IN A WINTER CITY.
ARIADNE.
FRIENDSHIP.

MOTHS.
PIPISTRELLO.
A VILLAGE COMMUNE.
IN MAREMMA.
BIMBI.
WANDA.
FRESCOES.
PRINCESS NAPRAXINE.
OTHMAR. | GUILDEROY.

Crown 8vo, cloth extra, 3s. 6d. each.

SYRLIN. | RUFFINO.

WISDOM, WIT, AND PATHOS, selected from the Works of OUIDA by F. SYDNEY MORRIS. Post 8vo, cloth extra, 5s.—CHEAP EDITION, illustrated boards, 2s.

PAGE (H. A.), WORKS BY.
THOREAU: His Life and Aims. With Portrait. Post 8vo, cloth limp, 2s. 6d.
ANIMAL ANECDOTES. Arranged on a New Principle. Crown 8vo, cloth extra, 5s.

PASCAL'S PROVINCIAL LETTERS. A New Translation, with Historical Introduction and Notes by T. M'CRIE, D.D. Post 8vo, cloth limp, 2s.

PAUL.—GENTLE AND SIMPLE. By MARGARET A. PAUL. With Frontispiece by HELEN PATERSON. Crown 8vo, cloth, 3s. 6d.; post 8vo, illust. boards, 2s.

PAYN (JAMES), NOVELS BY.
Crown 8vo, cloth extra, 3s. 6d. each; post 8vo, illustrated boards, 2s. each.

LOST SIR MASSINGBERD.
WALTER'S WORD.
LESS BLACK THAN WE'RE PAINTED.
BY PROXY.
HIGH SPIRITS.
UNDER ONE ROOF.
A CONFIDENTIAL AGENT.

A GRAPE FROM A THORN.
FROM EXILE.
SOME PRIVATE VIEWS.
THE CANON'S WARD.
THE TALK OF THE TOWN.
HOLIDAY TASKS.
GLOW-WORM TALES.
THE MYSTERY OF MIRBRIDGE.

Post 8vo, illustrated boards, 2s. each.

HUMOROUS STORIES.
THE FOSTER BROTHERS.
THE FAMILY SCAPEGRACE.
MARRIED BENEATH HIM.
BENTINCK'S TUTOR.
A PERFECT TREASURE.
A COUNTY FAMILY.
LIKE FATHER, LIKE SON.
A WOMAN'S VENGEANCE.
CARLYON'S YEAR. CECIL'S TRYST.
MURPHY'S MASTER.
AT HER MERCY.

THE CLYFFARDS OF CLYFFE.
FOUND DEAD.
GWENDOLINE'S HARVEST.
A MARINE RESIDENCE.
MIRK ABBEY.
NOT WOOED, BUT WON.
TWO HUNDRED POUNDS REWARD.
THE BEST OF HUSBANDS.
HALVES.
FALLEN FORTUNES.
WHAT HE COST HER.
KIT: A MEMORY. | FOR CASH ONLY.

IN PERIL AND PRIVATION: Stories of MARINE ADVENTURE Re-told. With 17 Illustrations. Crown 8vo, cloth extra, 3s. 6d.
NOTES FROM THE "NEWS." Crown 8vo, portrait cover, 1s.; cloth, 1s. 6d.
THE BURNT MILLION. Crown 8vo, cloth extra, 3s. 6d.
THE WORD AND THE WILL. Three Vols., crown 8vo.
SUNNY STORIES, and some SHADY ONES. With a Frontispiece by FRED. BARNARD. Crown 8vo cloth extra, 3s. 6d. [Shortly.

PENNELL (H. CHOLMONDELEY), WORKS BY. Post 8vo, cl., 2s. 6d. each.
PUCK ON PEGASUS. With Illustrations.
PEGASUS RE-SADDLED. With Ten full-page Illustrations by G. DU MAURIER.
THE MUSES OF MAYFAIR. Vers de Société. Selected by H. C. PENNELL.

PHELPS (E. STUART), WORKS BY. Post 8vo, 1s. each; cloth, 1s. 6d. each.
BEYOND THE GATES. By the Author of "The Gates Ajar."
JACK THE FISHERMAN. Illustrated by C. W. REED. Cr 8vo, 1s.; cloth, 1s. 6d.

AN OLD MAID'S PARADISE.
BURGLARS IN PARADISE.

PIRKIS (C. L.), NOVELS BY.
TROOPING WITH CROWS. Fcap. 8vo, picture cover 1s.
LADY LOVELACE. Post 8vo, illustrated boards, 2s.

PLANCHE (J. R.), WORKS BY.
THE PURSUIVANT OF ARMS; or, Heraldry Founded upon Facts. With
Coloured Frontispiece, Five Plates, and 209 Illusts. Crown 8vo, cloth, **7s. 6d.**
SONGS AND POEMS, 1819-1879. Introduction by Mrs. MACKARNESS. Cr. 8vo, cl., **6s.**

PLUTARCH'S LIVES OF ILLUSTRIOUS MEN. Translated from the
Greek, with Notes Critical and Historical, and a Life of Plutarch, by JOHN and
WILLIAM LANGHORNE. With Portraits. Two Vols., demy 8vo, half-bound, **10s. 6d.**

POE'S (EDGAR ALLAN) CHOICE WORKS, in Prose and Poetry. Introduction by CHAS. BAUDELAIRE, Portrait, and Facsimiles. Cr. 8vo, cloth, **7s. 6d.**
THE MYSTERY OF MARIE ROGET, &c. Post 8vo illustrated boards, **2s.**

POPE'S POETICAL WORKS. Post 8vo, cloth limp, 2s.

PRICE (E. C.), NOVELS BY.
Crown 8vo, cloth extra, **3s. 6d.** each ; post 8vo, illustrated boards, **2s.** each.
VALENTINA. | THE FOREIGNERS. | MRS. LANCASTER'S RIVAL.
GERALD. Post 8vo, illustrated boards, **2s.**

PRINCESS OLGA.—RADNA ; or, The Great Conspiracy of 1881. By
the Princess OLGA. Crown 8vo, cloth extra, **6s.**

PROCTOR (RICHARD A., B.A.), WORKS BY.
FLOWERS OF THE SKY. With 55 Illusts. Small crown 8vo, cloth extra, **3s. 6d.**
EASY STAR LESSONS. With Star Maps for Every Night in the Year, Drawings
of the Constellations, &c Crown 8vo, cloth extra, **6s.**
FAMILIAR SCIENCE STUDIES. Crown 8vo, cloth extra, **6s.**
SATURN AND ITS SYSTEM. With 13 Steel Plates. Demy 8vo, cloth ex., **10s. 6d.**
MYSTERIES OF TIME AND SPACE. With Illustrations. Cr. 8vo, cloth extra, **6s.**
THE UNIVERSE OF SUNS. With numerous Illustrations. Cr. 8vo, cloth ex., **6s.**
WAGES AND WANTS OF SCIENCE WORKERS. Crown 8vo, **1s. 6d.**

RAMBOSSON.—POPULAR ASTRONOMY. By J. RAMBOSSON, Laureate
of the Institute of France. With numerous Illusts. Crown 8vo, cloth extra, **7s. 6d.**

RANDOLPH.—AUNT ABIGAIL DYKES : A Novel. By Lt.-Colonel
GEORGE RANDOLPH, U.S.A. Crown 8vo, cloth extra, **7s. 6d.**

READE (CHARLES), NOVELS BY.
Crown 8vo, cloth extra, illustrated, **3s. 6d.** each ; post 8vo, illust. bds., **2s.** each.
PEG WOFFINGTON. Illustrated by S. L. FILDES, R.A.—Also a POCKET EDITION,
set in New Type, in Elzevir style, fcap. 8vo, half-leather, **2s. 6d.**
CHRISTIE JOHNSTONE. Illustrated by WILLIAM SMALL.—Also a POCKET EDITION,
set in New Type, in Elzevir style, fcap. 8vo, half-leather, **2s. 6d.**
IT IS NEVER TOO LATE TO MEND. Illustrated by G. J. PINWELL.
THE COURSE OF TRUE LOVE NEVER DID RUN SMOOTH. Illustrated by
HELEN PATERSON.
THE AUTOBIOGRAPHY OF A THIEF, &c. Illustrated by MATT STRETCH.
LOVE ME LITTLE, LOVE ME LONG. Illustrated by M. ELLEN EDWARDS.
THE DOUBLE MARRIAGE. Illusts. by Sir JOHN GILBERT, R.A., and C. KEENE
THE CLOISTER AND THE HEARTH. Illustrated by CHARLES KEENE.
HARD CASH. Illustrated by F. W. LAWSON.
GRIFFITH GAUNT. Illustrated by S. L. FILDES, R.A., and WILLIAM SMALL.
FOUL PLAY. Illustrated by GEORGE DU MAURIER.
PUT YOURSELF IN HIS PLACE. Illustrated by ROBERT BARNES.
A TERRIBLE TEMPTATION. Illustrated by EDWARD HUGHES and A. W. COOPER.
A SIMPLETON. Illustrated by KATE CRAUFURD.
THE WANDERING HEIR. Illustrated by HELEN PATERSON, S. L. FILDES, R.A.,
C. GREEN, and HENRY WOODS, A.R.A.
A WOMAN-HATER. Illustrated by THOMAS COULDERY.
SINGLEHEART AND DOUBLEFACE. Illustrated by P. MACNAB.
GOOD STORIES OF MEN AND OTHER ANIMALS. Illustrated by E. A.
ABBEY, PERCY MACQUOID, R.W.S., and JOSEPH NASH.
THE JILT, and other Stories. Illustrated by JOSEPH NASH.
READIANA. With a Steel-plate Portrait of CHARLES READE.

BIBLE CHARACTERS: Studies of David, Paul, &c. Fcap. 8vo, leatherette, **1s.**

SELECTIONS FROM THE WORKS OF CHARLES READE. With an Introduction
by Mrs. ALEX. IRELAND, and a Steel-Plate Portrait. Crown 8vo, buckram, gilt
top, **6s.** *[Preparing.*

RIDDELL (MRS. J. H.), NOVELS BY.
Crown 8vo, cloth extra, **3s. 6d.** each; post 8vo, illustrated boards, **2s.** each.
HER MOTHER'S DARLING. | WEIRD STORIES.
THE PRINCE OF WALES'S GARDEN PARTY.

Post 8vo, illustrated boards, **2s.** each.
UNINHABITED HOUSE. | FAIRY WATER. | MYSTERY IN PALACE GARDENS.

RIMMER (ALFRED), WORKS BY. Square 8vo, cloth gilt, **7s. 6d.** each.
OUR OLD COUNTRY TOWNS. With 55 Illustrations.
RAMBLES ROUND ETON AND HARROW. With 50 Illustrations.
ABOUT ENGLAND WITH DICKENS. With 58 Illusts. by C. A. VANDERHOOF, &c.

ROBINSON CRUSOE. By DANIEL DEFOE. (MAJOR'S EDITION.) With 37 Illustrations by GEORGE CRUIKSHANK. Post 8vo, half-bound, **2s.**

ROBINSON (F. W.), NOVELS BY.
Crown 8vo, cloth extra, **3s. 6d.** each; post 8vo, illustrated boards, **2s.** each.
WOMEN ARE STRANGE. | THE HANDS OF JUSTICE.

ROBINSON (PHIL), WORKS BY. Crown 8vo, cloth extra, **7s. 6d.** each.
THE POETS' BIRDS. | THE POETS' BEASTS.
THE POETS AND NATURE: REPTILES, FISHES, INSECTS. [Preparing.

ROCHEFOUCAULD'S MAXIMS AND MORAL REFLECTIONS. With Notes, and an Introductory Essay by SAINTE-BEUVE. Post 8vo, cloth limp, **2s.**

ROLL OF BATTLE ABBEY, THE : A List of the Principal Warriors who came from Normandy with William the Conqueror, and Settled in this Country, A.D. 1066-7. With Arms emblazoned in Gold and Colours. Handsomely printed, **5s.**

ROWLEY (HON. HUGH), WORKS BY. Post 8vo, cloth, **2s. 6d.** each.
PUNIANA: RIDDLES AND JOKES. With numerous Illustrations.
MORE PUNIANA. Profusely Illustrated.

RUNCIMAN (JAMES), STORIES BY.
Post 8vo, illustrated boards, **2s.** each; cloth limp, **2s. 6d.** each.
SKIPPERS AND SHELLBACKS. | GRACE BALMAIGN'S SWEETHEART.
SCHOOLS AND SCHOLARS. |

RUSSELL (W. CLARK), BOOKS AND NOVELS BY :
Crown 8vo, cloth extra, **6s.** each; post 8vo, illustrated boards, **2s.** each.
ROUND THE GALLEY-FIRE. | A BOOK FOR THE HAMMOCK.
IN THE MIDDLE WATCH. | MYSTERY OF THE "OCEAN STAR."
A VOYAGE TO THE CAPE. | THE ROMANCE OF JENNY HARLOWE.

ON THE FO'K'SLE HEAD. Post 8vo, illustrated boards, **2s.**
AN OCEAN TRAGEDY. Cr. 8vo, cloth extra, **3s. 6d.**; post 8vo, illust. bds., **2s.**
MY SHIPMATE LOUISE. Three Vols., crown 8vo.

SALA.—GASLIGHT AND DAYLIGHT. By GEORGE AUGUSTUS SALA. Post 8vo, illustrated boards. **2s.**

SANSON.—SEVEN GENERATIONS OF EXECUTIONERS : Memoirs of the Sanson Family (1688 to 1847). Crown 8vo, cloth extra, **3s. 6d.**

SAUNDERS (JOHN), NOVELS BY.
Crown 8vo, cloth extra, **3s. 6d.** each; post 8vo, illustrated boards, **2s.** each.
GUY WATERMAN. | THE LION IN THE PATH. | THE TWO DREAMERS.
BOUND TO THE WHEEL. Crown 8vo, cloth extra, **3s. 6d.**

SAUNDERS (KATHARINE), NOVELS BY.
Crown 8vo, cloth extra, **3s. 6d.** each; post 8vo, illustrated boards, **2s.** each.
MARGARET AND ELIZABETH. | HEART SALVAGE.
THE HIGH MILLS. | SEBASTIAN.

JOAN MERRYWEATHER. Post 8vo, illustrated boards, **2s.**
GIDEON'S ROCK. Crown 8vo, cloth extra, **3s. 6d.**

SCIENCE-GOSSIP : An Illustrated Medium of Interchange for Students and Lovers of Nature. Edited by Dr. J. E. TAYLOR, F.L.S., &c. Devoted to Geology, Botany, Physiology, Chemistry, Zoology, Microscopy, Telescopy, Physiography, Photography, &c. Price **4d.** Monthly; or **5s.** per year, post-free. Vols. I. to XIX. may be had, **7s. 6d.** each; Vols. XX. to date, **5s.** each. Cases for Binding, **1s. 6d.**

SECRET OUT, THE: One Thousand Tricks with Cards; with Entertaining Experiments in Drawing-room or "White Magic." By W. H. CREMER. With 300 Illustrations. Crown 8vo, cloth extra, 4s. 6d.

SEGUIN (L. G.), WORKS BY.
THE COUNTRY OF THE PASSION PLAY (OBERAMMERGAU) and the Highlands of Bavaria. With Map and 37 Illustrations. Crown 8vo, cloth extra, 3s. 6d.
WALKS IN ALGIERS. With 2 Maps and 16 Illusts. Crown 8vo, cloth extra. 6s.

SENIOR (WM.).—BY STREAM AND SEA. Post 8vo, cloth, 2s. 6d.

SHAKESPEARE, THE FIRST FOLIO.—MR WILLIAM SHAKESPEARE'S COMEDIES, HISTORIES, AND TRAGEDIES. Published according to the true Originall Copies. London, Printed by ISAAC IAGGARD and ED. BLOUNT. 1623.— A reduced Photographic Reproduction. Small 8vo, half-Roxburghe, 7s. 6d.
SHAKESPEARE FOR CHILDREN: LAMB'S TALES FROM SHAKESPEARE. With Illustrations, coloured and plain, by J MOYR SMITH. Crown 4to, cloth, 6s.

SHARP.—CHILDREN OF TO-MORROW: A Novel. By WILLIAM SHARP. Crown 8vo, cloth extra, 6s.

SHELLEY.—THE COMPLETE WORKS IN VERSE AND PROSE OF PERCY BYSSHE SHELLEY. Edited, Prefaced, and Annotated by R. HERNE SHEPHERD. Five Vols., crown 8vo, cloth boards, 3s. 6d. each.
POETICAL WORKS, in Three Vols.:
Vol. I. Introduction by the Editor; Posthumous Fragments of Margaret Nicholson; Shelley's Correspondence with Stockdale; The Wandering Jew; Queen Mab, with the Notes; Alastor, and other Poems; Rosalind and Helen; Prometheus Unbound; Adonais, &c.
Vol. II. Laon and Cythna; The Cenci; Julian and Maddalo; Swellfoot the Tyrant; The Witch of Atlas; Epipsychidion; Hellas.
Vol. III. Posthumous Poems; The Masque of Anarchy; and other Pieces.
PROSE WORKS, in Two Vols.:
Vol. I. The Two Romances of Zastrozzi and St. Irvyne; the Dublin and Marlow Pamphlets; A Refutation of Deism; Letters to Leigh Hunt, and some Minor Writings and Fragments.
Vol. II. The Essays; Letters from Abroad; Translations and Fragments, Edited by Mrs. SHELLEY. With a Bibliography of Shelley, and an Index of the Prose Works.

SHERARD.—ROGUES: A Novel. By R. H. SHERARD. Crown 8vo, picture cover, 1s.: cloth, 1s. 6d.

SHERIDAN (GENERAL). — PERSONAL MEMOIRS OF GENERAL P. H. SHERIDAN. With Portraits and Facsimiles. Two Vols., demy 8vo, cloth, 24s.

SHERIDAN'S (RICHARD BRINSLEY) COMPLETE WORKS. With Life and Anecdotes. Including his Dramatic Writings, his Works in Prose and Poetry, Translations, Speeches, Jokes, &c. With 10 Illusts. Cr. 8vo, cl, 7s. 6d.
THE RIVALS, THE SCHOOL FOR SCANDAL, and other Plays. Post 8vo, printed on laid paper and half-bound, 2s.
SHERIDAN'S COMEDIES: THE RIVALS and THE SCHOOL FOR SCANDAL. Edited, with an Introduction and Notes to each Play, and a Biographical Sketch, by BRANDER MATTHEWS. With Illustrations. Demy 8vo, half-parchment, 12s. 6d.

SIDNEY'S (SIR PHILIP) COMPLETE POETICAL WORKS, including all those in "Arcadia." With Portrait, Memorial-Introduction, Notes, &c. by the Rev. A. B. GROSART, D.D. Three Vols., crown 8vo, cloth boards, 18s.

SIGNBOARDS: Their History. With Anecdotes of Famous Taverns and Remarkable Characters. By JACOB LARWOOD and JOHN CAMDEN HOTTEN. With Coloured Frontispiece and 94 Illustrations. Crown 8vo, cloth extra. 7s. 6d.

SIMS (GEORGE R.), WORKS BY.
Post 8vo, illustrated boards, 2s. each; cloth limp, 2s. 6d. each.
ROGUES AND VAGABONDS. | MARY JANE MARRIED.
THE RING O' BELLS. | TALES OF TO-DAY.
MARY JANE'S MEMOIRS. | DRAMAS OF LIFE. With 60 Illustrations.
TINKLETOP'S CRIME. With a Frontispiece by MAURICE GREIFFENHAGEN.

Crown 8vo, picture cover, 1s. each; cloth, 1s. 6d. each.
HOW THE POOR LIVE; and HORRIBLE LONDON.
THE DAGONET RECITER AND READER: being Readings and Recitations in Prose and Verse, selected from his own Works by GEORGE R. SIMS.
THE CASE OF GEORGE CANDLEMAS.

SISTER DORA: A Biography. By MARGARET LONSDALE. With Four Illustrations. Demy 8vo, picture cover, 4d.; cloth, 6d.

SKETCHLEY.—A MATCH IN THE DARK. By ARTHUR SKETCHLEY.
Post 8vo, illustrated boards, **2s.**

SLANG DICTIONARY (THE): Etymological, Historical, and Anecdotal. Crown 8vo, cloth extra, **6s. 6d.**

SMITH (J. MOYR), WORKS BY.
THE PRINCE OF ARGOLIS. With 130 Illusts. Post 8vo, cloth extra. **3s. 6d.**
TALES OF OLD THULE. With numerous Illustrations. Crown 8vo, cloth gilt, **6s.**
THE WOOING OF THE WATER WITCH. Illustrated. Post 8vo, cloth. **6s.**

SOCIETY IN LONDON. By A FOREIGN RESIDENT. Crown 8vo,
1s.; cloth, **1s. 6d.**

SOCIETY IN PARIS: The Upper Ten Thousand. A Series of Letters from Count PAUL VASILI to a Young French Diplomat. Crown 8vo, cloth, **6s.**

SOMERSET. — SONGS OF ADIEU. By Lord HENRY SOMERSET.
Small 4to, Japanese vellum, **6s.**

SPALDING.—ELIZABETHAN DEMONOLOGY: An Essay on the Belief in the Existence of Devils. By T. A. SPALDING, LL.B. Crown 8vo, cloth extra, **5s.**

SPEIGHT (T. W.), NOVELS BY.
Post 8vo, illustrated boards, **2s.** each.

THE MYSTERIES OF HERON DYKE. | THE GOLDEN HOOP.
BY DEVIOUS WAYS, and A BARREN | HOODWINKED; and THE SANDY-
    TITLE. | CROFT MYSTERY.

Post 8vo, cloth limp, **1s. 6d.** each.
A BARREN TITLE. | WIFE OR NO WIFE?

THE SANDYCROFT MYSTERY. Crown 8vo, picture cover, **1s.**

SPENSER FOR CHILDREN. By M. H. TOWRY. With Illustrations by WALTER J. MORGAN. Crown 4to, cloth gilt, **6s.**

STARRY HEAVENS (THE): A POETICAL BIRTHDAY BOOK. Royal 16mo, cloth extra, **2s. 6d.**

STAUNTON.—THE LAWS AND PRACTICE OF CHESS. With an Analysis of the Openings. By HOWARD STAUNTON. Edited by ROBERT B. WORMALD. Crown 8vo, cloth extra, **5s.**

STEDMAN (E. C.), WORKS BY.
VICTORIAN POETS. Thirteenth Edition. Crown 8vo. cloth extra, **9s.**
THE POETS OF AMERICA. Crown 8vo, cloth extra, **9s.**

STERNDALE. — THE AFGHAN KNIFE: A Novel. By ROBERT ARMITAGE STERNDALE. Cr. 8vo, cloth extra, **3s. 6d.**; post 8vo, illust. boards, **2s.**

STEVENSON (R. LOUIS), WORKS BY. Post 8vo, cl. limp, **2s. 6d.** each.
TRAVELS WITH A DONKEY. Eighth Edit. With a Frontis. by WALTER CRANE.
AN INLAND VOYAGE. Fourth Edition. With a Frontispiece by WALTER CRANE.

Crown 8vo, buckram, gilt top, **6s.** each.
FAMILIAR STUDIES OF MEN AND BOOKS. Fifth Edition.
THE SILVERADO SQUATTERS. With a Frontispiece. Third Edition.
THE MERRY MEN. Second Edition. | UNDERWOODS: Poems. Fifth Edition.
MEMORIES AND PORTRAITS. Third Edition.
VIRGINIBUS PUERISQUE, and other Papers. Fifth Edition. | BALLADS.

Crown 8vo, buckram, gilt top, **6s.** each; post 8vo, illustrated boards, **2s.** each.
NEW ARABIAN NIGHTS. Eleventh Edition. | PRINCE OTTO. Sixth Edition.

FATHER DAMIEN: An Open Letter to the Rev. Dr. Hyde. Second Edition.
Crown 8vo, hand-made and brown paper, **1s.**

STODDARD. — SUMMER CRUISING IN THE SOUTH SEAS. By C. WARREN STODDARD. Illustrated by WALLIS MACKAY. Cr. 8vo. cl. extra, **3s. 6d.**

STORIES FROM FOREIGN NOVELISTS. With Notices by HELEN and ALICE ZIMMERN. Crown 8vo, cloth extra, **3s. 6d.**; post 8vo, illustrated boards, **2s.**

STRANGE MANUSCRIPT (A) FOUND IN A COPPER CYLINDER.
With 19 Illustrations by GILBERT GAUL. Third Edition. Crown 8vo, cloth extra, 5s.

STRUTT'S SPORTS AND PASTIMES OF THE PEOPLE OF ENGLAND; including the Rural and Domestic Recreations, May Games, Mummeries, Shows, &c., from the Earliest Period to the Present Time. Edited by WILLIAM HONE. With 140 Illustrations. Crown 8vo, cloth extra, 7s. 6d.

SUBURBAN HOMES (THE) OF LONDON: A Residential Guide. With a Map, and Notes on Rental, Rates, and Accommodation Crown 8vo, cloth, 7s. 6d.

SWIFT'S (DEAN) CHOICE WORKS, in Prose and Verse. With Memoir, Portrait, and Facsimiles of the Maps in "Gulliver's Travels." Cr. 8vo, cl., 7s. 6d.

GULLIVER'S TRAVELS, and **A TALE OF A TUB.** Post 8vo, printed on laid paper and half-bound, 2s.

A MONOGRAPH ON SWIFT. By J. CHURTON COLLINS. Cr. 8vo, cloth, 8s. [Shortly.

SWINBURNE (ALGERNON C.), WORKS BY.

SELECTIONS FROM POETICAL WORKS OF A. C. SWINBURNE. Fcap. 8vo, 6s.	**GEORGE CHAPMAN.** (See Vol. II. of G. CHAPMAN's Works.) Crown 8vo, 6s.
ATALANTA IN CALYDON. Cr. 8vo, 6s.	**ESSAYS AND STUDIES.** Cr. 8vo, 12s.
CHASTELARD: A Tragedy. Cr. 8vo, 7s.	**ERECHTHEUS:** A Tragedy. Cr. 8vo, 6s.
NOTES ON POEMS AND REVIEWS. Demy 8vo, 1s.	**SONGS OF THE SPRINGTIDES.** Crown 8vo, 6s.
POEMS AND BALLADS. FIRST SERIES. Crown 8vo or fcap. 8vo, 9s.	**STUDIES IN SONG.** Crown 8vo, 7s.
POEMS AND BALLADS. SECOND SERIES. Crown 8vo or fcap. 8vo, 9s.	**MARY STUART:** A Tragedy. Cr. 8vo 8s.
	TRISTRAM OF LYONESSE. Cr. 8vo, 9s.
	A CENTURY OF ROUNDELS. Sm. 4to, 8s.
POEMS AND BALLADS. THIRD SERIES. Crown 8vo, 7s.	**A MIDSUMMER HOLIDAY.** Cr. 8vo, 7s.
SONGS BEFORE SUNRISE. Crown 8vo, 10s. 6d.	**MARINO FALIERO:** A Tragedy. Crown 8vo, 6s.
BOTHWELL: A Tragedy. Crown 8vo, 12s. 6d.	**A STUDY OF VICTOR HUGO.** Cr. 8vo, 6s.
	MISCELLANIES. Crown 8vo, 12s.
SONGS OF TWO NATIONS. Cr. 8vo, 6s.	**LOCRINE:** A Tragedy. Cr. 8vo, 6s.
	A STUDY OF BEN JONSON. Cr. 8vo. 7s.

SYMONDS.—WINE, WOMEN, AND SONG: Mediæval Latin Students' Songs. With Essay and Trans. by J. ADDINGTON SYMONDS. Fcap. 8vo, parchment, 6s.

SYNTAX'S (DR.) THREE TOURS: In Search of the Picturesque, in Search of Consolation, and in Search of a Wife. With ROWLANDSON'S Coloured Illustrations, and Life of the Author by J. C. HOTTEN. Crown 8vo, cloth extra, 7s. 6d.

TAINE'S HISTORY OF ENGLISH LITERATURE. Translated by HENRY VAN LAUN. Four Vols., medium 8vo, cloth boards, 30s.—POPULAR EDITION, Two Vols., large crown 8vo, cloth extra, 15s.

TAYLOR'S (BAYARD) DIVERSIONS OF THE ECHO CLUB: Burlesques of Modern Writers. Post 8vo, cloth limp, 2s.

TAYLOR (DR. J. E., F.L.S.), WORKS BY. Cr. 8vo, cl. ex., 7s. 6d. each.
THE SAGACITY AND MORALITY OF PLANTS: A Sketch of the Life and Conduct of the Vegetable Kingdom. With a Coloured Frontispiece and 100 Illustrations.
OUR COMMON BRITISH FOSSILS, and Where to Find Them. 331 Illustrations.

THE PLAYTIME NATURALIST. With 366 Illustrations. Crown 8vo, cloth, 5s.

TAYLOR'S (TOM) HISTORICAL DRAMAS. Containing "Clancarty," "Jeanne Darc," "'Twixt Axe and Crown," "The Fool's Revenge," "Arkwright's Wife," "Anne Boleyn," "Plot and Passion." Crown 8vo, cloth extra, 7s. 6d.
⁎ The Plays may also be had separately, at 1s. each.

TENNYSON (LORD): A Biographical Sketch. By H. J. JENNINGS. With a Photograph-Portrait. Crown 8vo, cloth extra, 6s.

THACKERAYANA: Notes and Anecdotes. Illustrated by Hundreds of Sketches by WILLIAM MAKEPEACE THACKERAY, depicting Humorous Incidents in his School-life, and Favourite Characters in the Books of his Every-day Reading. With a Coloured Frontispiece. Crown 8vo, cloth extra, 7s. 6d.

THAMES.—A NEW PICTORIAL HISTORY OF THE THAMES. By A. S. KRAUSSE. With 340 Illustrations. Post 8vo, 1s.; cloth, 1s. 6d.

THOMAS (BERTHA), NOVELS BY. Cr. 8vo, cl., 3s. 6d. ea.; post 8vo, 2s. ea.

| CRESSIDA. | THE VIOLIN-PLAYER. | PROUD MAISIE. |

THOMSON'S SEASONS, and CASTLE OF INDOLENCE. Introduction by Allan Cunningham, and Illustrations on Steel and Wood. Cr. 8vo, cl., 7s. 6d.

THORNBURY (WALTER), WORKS BY. Cr. 8vo, cl. extra, 7s. 6d. each.
THE LIFE AND CORRESPONDENCE OF J. M. W. TURNER. Founded upon Letters and Papers furnished by his Friends. With Illustrations in Colours.
HAUNTED LONDON. Edit. by E. Walford, M.A. Illusts. by F. W. Fairholt, F.S.A.

Post 8vo, illustrated boards. 2s. each.

| OLD STORIES RE-TOLD. | TALES FOR THE MARINES. |

TIMBS (JOHN), WORKS BY. Crown 8vo, cloth extra, 7s. 6d. each.
THE HISTORY OF CLUBS AND CLUB LIFE IN LONDON: Anecdotes of its Famous Coffee-houses, Hostelries, and Taverns. With 42 Illustrations.
ENGLISH ECCENTRICS AND ECCENTRICITIES: Stories of Wealth and Fashion, Delusions, Impostures, and Fanatic Missions, Sporting Scenes, Eccentric Artists, Theatrical Folk, Men of Letters, &c. With 48 Illustrations.

TROLLOPE (ANTHONY), NOVELS BY.
Crown 8vo, cloth extra, 3s. 6d. each; post 8vo, illustrated boards, 2s. each.

THE WAY WE LIVE NOW.	MARION FAY.
KEPT IN THE DARK.	MR. SCARBOROUGH'S FAMILY.
FRAU FROHMANN.	THE LAND-LEAGUERS.

Post 8vo, illustrated boards, 2s. each.

| GOLDEN LION OF GRANPERE. | JOHN CALDIGATE. | AMERICAN SENATOR. |

TROLLOPE (FRANCES E.), NOVELS BY.
Crown 8vo, cloth extra, 3s. 6d. each; post 8vo, illustrated boards, 2s. each.

| LIKE SHIPS UPON THE SEA. | MABEL'S PROGRESS. | ANNE FURNESS. |

TROLLOPE (T. A.).—DIAMOND CUT DIAMOND. Post 8vo, illust. bds., 2s.

TROWBRIDGE.—FARNELL'S FOLLY: A Novel. By J. T. Trowbridge. Post 8vo, illustrated boards, 2s.

TYTLER (C. C. FRASER-).—MISTRESS JUDITH: A Novel. By C. C. Fraser-Tytler. Crown 8vo, cloth extra, 3s. 6d.; post 8vo, illust. boards. 2s.

TYTLER (SARAH), NOVELS BY.
Crown 8vo, cloth extra, 3s. 6d. each; post 8vo, illustrated boards, 2s. each.

WHAT SHE CAME THROUGH.	LADY BELL.
THE BRIDE'S PASS.	BURIED DIAMONDS.
NOBLESSE OBLIGE.	THE BLACKHALL GHOSTS.

Post 8vo, illustrated boards, 2s. each.

SAINT MUNGO'S CITY.	DISAPPEARED.
BEAUTY AND THE BEAST.	THE HUGUENOT FAMILY.
CITOYENNE JACQUELINE.	

VILLARI.—A DOUBLE BOND. By Linda Villari. Fcap. 8vo, picture cover 1s.

WALT WHITMAN, POEMS BY. Edited, with Introduction, by William M. Rossetti. With Portrait. Cr. 8vo, hand-made paper and buckram, 6s.

WALTON AND COTTON'S COMPLETE ANGLER; or, The Contemplative Man's Recreation, by Izaak Walton; and Instructions how to Angle for a Trout or Grayling in a clear Stream, by Charles Cotton. With Memoirs and Notes by Sir Harris Nicolas, and 61 Illustrations. Crown 8vo, cloth antique, 7s. 6d.

WARD (HERBERT), WORKS BY.
FIVE YEARS WITH THE CONGO CANNIBALS. With 92 Illustrations by the Author, Victor Perard, and W. B. Davis. Third ed. Roy. 8vo, cloth ex., 14s.
MY LIFE WITH STANLEY'S REAR GUARD. With a Map by F. S. Weller, F.R.G.S. Post 8vo, 1s.; cloth, 1s. 6d.

WARNER.—A ROUNDABOUT JOURNEY, By Charles Dudley Warner. Crown 8vo, cloth extra, 6s.

WALFORD (EDWARD, M.A.), WORKS BY.

WALFORD'S COUNTY FAMILIES OF THE UNITED KINGDOM (1891). Containing the Descent, Birth, Marriage, Education, &c., of 12,000 Heads of Families, their Heirs, Offices, Addresses, Clubs, &c. Royal 8vo, cloth gilt, **50s.**

WALFORD'S SHILLING PEERAGE (1891). Containing a List of the House of Lords, Scotch and Irish Peers, &c. 32mo, cloth, **1s.**

WALFORD'S SHILLING BARONETAGE (1891). Containing a List of the Baronets of the United Kingdom, Biographical Notices, Addresses, &c. 32mo, cloth, **1s.**

WALFORD'S SHILLING KNIGHTAGE (1891). Containing a List of the Knights of the United Kingdom, Biographical Notices, Addresses, &c. 32mo, cloth, **1s.**

WALFORD'S SHILLING HOUSE OF COMMONS (1891). Containing a List of all Members of Parliament, their Addresses, Clubs, &c. 32mo, cloth, **1s.**

WALFORD'S COMPLETE PEERAGE, BARONETAGE, KNIGHTAGE, AND HOUSE OF COMMONS (1891). Royal 32mo, cloth extra, gilt edges **5s.**

WALFORD'S WINDSOR PEERAGE, BARONETAGE, AND KNIGHTAGE (1891). Crown 8vo, cloth extra, **12s. 6d.**

TALES OF OUR GREAT FAMILIES. Crown 8vo, cloth extra, **3s. 6d.**

WILLIAM PITT: A Biography. Post 8vo, cloth extra, **5s.**

WARRANT TO EXECUTE CHARLES I. A Facsimile, with the 59
Signatures and Seals. Printed on paper 22 in. by 14 in. **2s.**

WARRANT TO EXECUTE MARY QUEEN OF SCOTS. A Facsimile, including Queen Elizabeth's Signature and the Great Seal. **2s.**

WEATHER, HOW TO FORETELL THE, WITH POCKET SPEC-
TROSCOPE. By F. W. Cory. With 10 Illustrations Cr. 8vo **1s.;** cloth, **1s. 6d.**

WESTROPP.—HANDBOOK OF POTTERY AND PORCELAIN. By
Hodder M. Westropp. With Illusts. and List of Marks. Cr. 8vo, cloth, **4s. 6d.**

WHIST.—HOW TO PLAY SOLO WHIST. By Abraham S. Wilks
and Charles F. Pardon. Crown 8vo, cloth extra, **3s. 6d.**

WHISTLER'S (MR.) TEN O'CLOCK. Cr. 8vo, hand-made paper, 1s.

WHITE.—THE NATURAL HISTORY OF SELBORNE. By Gilbert
White, M.A. Post 8vo, printed on laid paper and half-bound, **2s.**

WILLIAMS (W. MATTIEU, F.R.A.S.), WORKS BY.

SCIENCE IN SHORT CHAPTERS. Crown 8vo, cloth extra, **7s. 6d.**

A SIMPLE TREATISE ON HEAT. With Illusts. Cr. 8vo, cloth limp, **2s. 6d.**

THE CHEMISTRY OF COOKERY. Crown 8vo, cloth extra, **6s.**

THE CHEMISTRY OF IRON AND STEEL MAKING. Crown 8vo, cloth extra, **9s.**

WILSON (DR. ANDREW, F.R.S.E.), WORKS BY.

CHAPTERS ON EVOLUTION. With 259 Illustrations. Cr. 8vo, cloth extra, **7s. 6d.**

LEAVES FROM A NATURALIST'S NOTE-BOOK. Post 8vo, cloth limp, **2s. 6d.**

LEISURE-TIME STUDIES. With Illustrations. Crown 8vo, cloth extra, **6s.**

STUDIES IN LIFE AND SENSE. With numerous Illusts. Cr. 8vo, cl. ex., **6s.**

COMMON ACCIDENTS: HOW TO TREAT THEM. Illusts. Cr. 8vo. **1s.;** cl., **1s. 6d.**

GLIMPSES OF LIFE AND NATURE. Crown 8vo, cloth extra, **3s. 6d.** [Shortly.

WINTER (J. S.), STORIES BY. Post 8vo, illustrated boards, **2s.** each.
CAVALRY LIFE. | REGIMENTAL LEGENDS.

WOOD.—SABINA: A Novel. By Lady Wood. Post 8vo, boards, 2s.

WOOD (H. F.), DETECTIVE STORIES BY.
Crown 8vo, cloth extra, **6s.** each; post 8vo, illustrated boards, **2s.** each.
PASSENGER FROM SCOTLAND YARD. | **ENGLISHMAN OF THE RUE CAIN.**

WOOLLEY.—RACHEL ARMSTRONG; or, Love and Theology. By
Celia Parker Woolley. Post 8vo, illustrated boards, **2s.;** cloth, **2s. 6d.**

WRIGHT (THOMAS), WORKS BY. Crown 8vo, cloth extra, **7s. 6d.** each.

CARICATURE HISTORY OF THE GEORGES. With 400 Pictures, Caricatures, Squibs, Broadsides, Window Pictures, &c.

HISTORY OF CARICATURE AND OF THE GROTESQUE IN ART, LITERA-TURE, SCULPTURE, AND PAINTING. Illustrated by F. W. Fairholt, F.S.A.

YATES (EDMUND), NOVELS BY. Post 8vo, illustrated boards, **2s.** each.
LAND AT LAST. | THE FORLORN HOPE. | CASTAWAY.

LISTS OF BOOKS CLASSIFIED IN SERIES.

. *For full cataloguing, see alphabetical arrangement, pp. 1-25.*

THE MAYFAIR LIBRARY. Post 8vo, cloth limp, 2s. 6d. per Volume.

A Journey Round My Room. By XAVIER DE MAISTRE
Quips and Quiddities. By W. D. ADAMS.
The Agony Column of "The Times."
Melancholy Anatomised: Abridgment of "Burton's Anatomy of Melancholy."
The Speeches of Charles Dickens.
Literary Frivolities, Fancies, Follies, and Frolics. By W. T. DOBSON.
Poetical Ingenuities. By W. T. DOBSON.
The Cupboard Papers. By FIN-BEC
W. S. Gilbert's Plays. FIRST SERIES.
W. S. Gilbert's Plays. SECOND SERIES.
Songs of Irish Wit and Humour.
Animals and Masters. By Sir A. HELPS.
Social Pressure. By Sir A. HELPS.
Curiosities of Criticism. H. J. JENNINGS.
Holmes's Autocrat of Breakfast-Table.
Pencil and Palette. By R. KEMPT.

Little Essays: from LAMB'S Letters.
Forensic Anecdotes. By JACOB LARWOOD
Theatrical Anecdotes. JACOB LARWOOD.
Jeux d'Esprit. Edited by HENRY S. LEIGH.
Witch Stories. By E. LYNN LINTON.
Ourselves. By E. LYNN LINTON.
Pastimes & Players. By R. MACGREGOR.
New Paul and Virginia. W.H.MALLOCK.
New Republic. By WM. H. MALLOCK.
Puck on Pegasus. By H. C. PENNELL.
Pegasus Re-Saddled. By H. C. PENNELL.
Muses of Mayfair. Ed. H. C. PENNELL.
Thoreau: His Life & Aims. By H. A. PAGE.
Puniana. By Hon. HUGH ROWLEY.
More Puniana. By Hon. HUGH ROWLEY.
The Philosophy of Handwriting.
By Stream and Sea. By WM. SENIOR.
Leaves from a Naturalist's Note-Book. By Dr. ANDREW WILSON.

THE GOLDEN LIBRARY. Post 8vo, cloth limp, 2s. per Volume.

Bayard Taylor's Diversions of the Echo Club.
Bennett's Ballad History of England.
Bennett's Songs for Sailors.
Godwin's Lives of the Necromancers.
Pope's Poetical Works.
Holmes's Autocrat of Breakfast Table.

Holmes's Professor at Breakfast Table.
Jesse's Scenes of Country Life.
Leigh Hunt's Tale for a Chimney Corner.
Mallory's Mort d'Arthur: Selections.
Pascal's Provincial Letters.
Rochefoucauld's Maxims & Reflections.

THE WANDERER'S LIBRARY. Crown 8vo, cloth extra, 3s. 6d. each.

Wanderings in Patagonia. By JULIUS BEERBOHM. Illustrated.
Camp Notes. By FREDERICK BOYLE.
Savage Life. By FREDERICK BOYLE.
Merrie England in the Olden Time. By G. DANIEL. Illustrated by CRUIKSHANK.
Circus Life. By THOMAS FROST.
Lives of the Conjurers. THOMAS FROST.
The Old Showmen and the Old London Fairs. By THOMAS FROST.
Low-Life Deeps. By JAMES GREENWOOD.

Wilds of London. JAMES GREENWOOD.
Tunis. Chev. HESSE-WARTEGG. 22 Illusts.
Life and Adventures of a Cheap Jack.
World Behind the Scenes. P. FITZGERALD.
Tavern Anecdotes and Sayings.
The Genial Showman. By E. P. HINGSTON
Story of London Parks. JACOB LARWOOD.
London Characters. By HENRY MAYHEW.
Seven Generations of Executioners.
Summer Cruising in the South Seas. By C. WARREN STODDARD. Illustrated.

POPULAR SHILLING BOOKS.

Harry Fludyer at Cambridge.
Jeff Briggs's Love Story. BRET HARTE.
Twins of Table Mountain. BRET HARTE.
A Day's Tour. By PERCY FITZGERALD.
Esther's Glove. By R. E. FRANCILLON.
Sentenced! By SOMERVILLE GIBNEY.
The Professor's Wife. By L. GRAHAM.
Mrs. Gainsborough's Diamonds. By JULIAN HAWTHORNE.
Niagara Spray. By J. HOLLINGSHEAD.
A Romance of the Queen's Hounds. By CHARLES JAMES.
The Garden that Paid the Rent. By TOM JERROLD.
Cut by the Mess. By ARTHUR KEYSER.
Our Sensation Novel. J. H. McCARTHY.
Doom! By JUSTIN H. McCARTHY, M.P.
Dolly. By JUSTIN H. McCARTHY, M.P.
Lily Lass. JUSTIN H. McCARTHY, M.P.

Was She Good or Bad? By W. MINTO.
That Girl in Black. Mrs. MOLESWORTH.
Notes from the "News." By JAS. PAYN.
Beyond the Gates. By E. S. PHELPS.
Old Maid's Paradise. By E. S. PHELPS.
Burglars in Paradise. By E. S. PHELPS.
Jack the Fisherman. By E. S. PHELPS.
Trooping with Crows. By C. L. PIRKIS.
Bible Characters. By CHARLES READE.
Rogues. By R. H. SHERARD.
The Dagonet Reciter. By G. R. SIMS.
How the Poor Live. By G. R. SIMS.
Case of George Candlemas. G. R. SIMS.
Sandycroft Mystery. T. W. SPEIGHT.
Hoodwinked. By T. W. SPEIGHT.
Father Damien. By R. L. STEVENSON.
A Double Bond. By LINDA VILLARI.
My Life with Stanley's Rear Guard. By HERBERT WARD.

MY LIBRARY.

Choice Works, printed on laid paper, bound half-Roxburghe, 2s. 6d. each.

Four Frenchwomen. By AUSTIN DOBSON.
Citation and Examination of William Shakspeare. By W. S. LANDOR.

Christie Johnstone. By CHARLES READE. With a Photogravure Frontispiece.
Peg Woffington. By CHARLES READE.

THE POCKET LIBRARY. Post 8vo, printed on laid paper and hf.-bd., 2s. each.

The Essays of Elia. By CHARLES LAMB.
Robinson Crusoe. Edited by JOHN MAJOR. With 37 Illusts. by GEORGE CRUIKSHANK.
Whims and Oddities. By THOMAS HOOD. With 85 Illustrations.
The Barber's Chair, and The Hedgehog Letters. By DOUGLAS JERROLD.
Gastronomy as a Fine Art. By BRILLAT-SAVARIN. Trans. R. E. ANDERSON, M.A.

The Epicurean, &c. By THOMAS MOORE.
Leigh Hunt's Essays. Ed. E. OLLIER.
The Natural History of Selborne. By GILBERT WHITE.
Gulliver's Travels, and The Tale of a Tub. By Dean SWIFT.
The Rivals, School for Scandal, and other Plays by RICHARD BRINSLEY SHERIDAN.
Anecdotes of the Clergy. J. LARWOOD

THE PICCADILLY NOVELS.

LIBRARY EDITIONS OF NOVELS BY THE BEST AUTHORS, many Illustrated, crown 8vo, cloth extra, 3s. 6d. each.

By GRANT ALLEN.
Philistia.
Babylon
In all Shades.
The Tents of Shem.
For Maimie's Sake.
The Devil's Die.
This Mortal Coil.
The Great Taboo.

By ALAN ST. AUBYN.
A Fellow of Trinity.

By Rev. S. BARING GOULD.
Red Spider. | Eve.

By W. BESANT & J. RICE.
My Little Girl.
Case of Mr.Lucraft.
This Son of Vulcan.
Golden Butterfly.
Ready-Money Mortiboy.
With Harp and Crown.
'Twas in Trafalgar's Bay.
The Chaplain of the Fleet.
By Celia's Arbour.
Monks of Thelema.
The Seamy Side.
Ten Years' Tenant.

By WALTER BESANT.
All Sorts and Conditions of Men.
The Captains' Room.
All in a Garden Fair
The World Went Very Well Then.
For Faith and Freedom.
Dorothy Forster. | Herr Paulus.
Uncle Jack. | Bell of St. Paul's.
Children of Gibeon. | To Call Her Mine.

By ROBERT BUCHANAN.
The Shadow of the Sword.
A Child of Nature.
The Martyrdom of Madeline.
God and the Man. | The New Abelard.
Love Me for Ever. | Foxglove Manor.
Annan Water. | Master of the Mine.
Matt. | Heir of Linne.

By HALL CAINE.
The Shadow of a Crime.
A Son of Hagar. | The Deemster.

MORT. & FRANCES COLLINS.
Sweet Anne Page. | Transmigration.
From Midnight to Midnight.
Blacksmith and Scholar.
Village Comedy. | You Play Me False

By Mrs. H. LOVETT CAMERON.
Juliet's Guardian. | Deceivers Ever.

By WILKIE COLLINS.
Armadale.
After Dark.
No Name.
Antonina. | Basil.
Hide and Seek.
The Dead Secret.
Queen of Hearts.
My Miscellanies.
Woman in White.
The Moonstone.
Man and Wife.
Poor Miss Finch.
Miss or Mrs?
New Magdalen.
The Frozen Deep.
The Two Destinies.
Law and the Lady.
Haunted Hotel.
The Fallen Leaves.
Jezebel's Daughter.
The Black Robe.
Heart and Science.
"I Say No."
Little Novels.
The Evil Genius.
The Legacy of Cain
A Rogue's Life.
Blind Love.

By DUTTON COOK.
Paul Foster's Daughter.

By WILLIAM CYPLES.
Hearts of Gold.

By ALPHONSE DAUDET.
The Evangelist; or, Port Salvation.

By JAMES DE MILLE.
A Castle in Spain.

By J. LEITH DERWENT.
Our Lady of Tears. | Circe's Lovers.

By Mrs. ANNIE EDWARDES.
Archie Lovell.

By PERCY FITZGERALD.
Fatal Zero.

By R. E. FRANCILLON.
Queen Cophetua. | A Real Queen.
One by One. | King or Knave?

Pref. by Sir BARTLE FRERE.
Pandurang Hari.

By EDWARD GARRETT.
The Capel Girls.

THE PICCADILLY (3/6) NOVELS—*continued.*

By CHARLES GIBBON.
Robin Gray. | The Golden Shaft.
In Honour Bound. | Of High Degree.
Loving a Dream.
Queen of the Meadow.
The Flower of the Forest.

By JULIAN HAWTHORNE.
Garth. | Dust.
Ellice Quentin. | Fortune's Fool.
Sebastian Strome. | Beatrix Randolph.
David Poindexter's Disappearance.
The Spectre of the Camera.

By Sir A. HELPS.
Ivan de Biron.

By ISAAC HENDERSON.
Agatha Page.

By Mrs. ALFRED HUNT.
The Leaden Casket. | Self-Condemned.
That other Person.

By JEAN INGELOW.
Fated to be Free.

By R. ASHE KING.
A Drawn Game.
"The Wearing of the Green."

By HENRY KINGSLEY.
Number Seventeen.

By E. LYNN LINTON.
Patricia Kemball. | Ione.
Under which Lord? | Paston Carew.
"My Love!" | Sowing the Wind.
The Atonement of Leam Dundas.
The World Well Lost.

By HENRY W. LUCY.
Gideon Fleyce.

By JUSTIN McCARTHY.
A Fair Saxon. | Donna Quixote.
Linley Rochford. | Maid of Athens.
Miss Misanthrope. | Camiola.
The Waterdale Neighbours.
My Enemy's Daughter.
Dear Lady Disdain.
The Comet of a Season.

By AGNES MACDONELL.
Quaker Cousins.

By FLORENCE MARRYAT.
Open! Sesame!

By D. CHRISTIE MURRAY.
Life's Atonement. | Coals of Fire.
Joseph's Coat. | Val Strange.
A Model Father. | Hearts.
A Bit of Human Nature.
First Person Singular.
Cynic Fortune.
The Way of the World.

By MURRAY & HERMAN.
The Bishops' Bible.

By GEORGES OHNET.
A Weird Gift.

THE PICCADILLY (3 6) NOVELS—*continued.*

By Mrs. OLIPHANT.
Whiteladies.

By OUIDA.
Held in Bondage. | Two Little Wooden
Strathmore. | Shoes.
Chandos. | In a Winter City.
Under Two Flags. | Ariadne.
Idalia. | Friendship.
CecilCastlemaine's | Moths. | Ruffino.
Gage. | Pipistrello.
Tricotrin. | Puck. | A Village Commune
Folle Farine. | Bimbi. | Wanda.
A Dog of Flanders. | Frescoes.
Pascarel. Signa. | In Maremma.
Princess Naprax- | Othmar. | Syrlin.
ine. | Guilderoy.

By MARGARET A. PAUL.
Gentle and Simple.

By JAMES PAYN.
Lost Sir Massingberd.
Less Black than We're Painted.
A Confidential Agent.
A Grape from a Thorn.
Some Private Views.
In Peril and Privation.
The Mystery of Mirbridge.
The Canon's Ward.
Walter's Word. | Glow-worm Tales.
By Proxy. | Talk of the Town.
High Spirits. | Holiday Tasks.
Under One Roof. | The Burnt Million.
From Exile. | Sunny Stories.

By E. C. PRICE.
Valentina. | The Foreigners.
Mrs. Lancaster's Rival.

By CHARLES READE.
It is Never Too Late to Mend.
The Double Marriage.
Love Me Little, Love Me Long.
The Cloister and the Hearth.
The Course of True Love.
The Autobiography of a Thief.
Put Yourself in his Place.
A Terrible Temptation.
Singleheart and Doubleface.
Good Stories of Men and other Animals.
Hard Cash. | Wandering Heir.
Peg Woffington. | A Woman-Hater.
ChristieJohnstone. | A Simpleton.
Griffith Gaunt. | Readiana.
Foul Play. | The Jilt.

By Mrs. J. H. RIDDELL.
Her Mother's Darling.
Prince of Wales's Garden Party.
Weird Stories.

By F. W. ROBINSON.
Women are Strange.
The Hands of Justice.

By W. CLARK RUSSELL.
An Ocean Tragedy.

By JOHN SAUNDERS.
Guy Waterman. | Two Dreamers.
Bound to the Wheel.
The Lion in the Path.

Two-Shilling Novels—*continued.*

By WILKIE COLLINS.

Armadale.	A Rogue's Life.
After Dark.	My Miscellanies.
No Name.	Woman in White.
Antonina.	Basil.	The Moonstone.
Hide and Seek.	Man and Wife.
The Dead Secret.	Poor Miss Finch.
Queen of Hearts.	The Fallen Leaves.
Miss or Mrs?	Jezebel's Daughter
New Magdalen.	The Black Robe.
The Frozen Deep.	Heart and Science.
Law and the Lady.	"I Say No."
The Two Destinies.	The Evil Genius.
Haunted Hotel.	Little Novels.
Legacy of Cain.	

By M. J. COLQUHOUN.
Every Inch a Soldier.

By DUTTON COOK.
Leo. | Paul Foster's Daughter.

By C. EGBERT CRADDOCK.
Prophet of the Great Smoky Mountains.

By WILLIAM CYPLES.
Hearts of Gold.

By ALPHONSE DAUDET.
The Evangelist; or, Port Salvation.

By JAMES DE MILLE.
A Castle in Spain.

By J. LEITH DERWENT.
Our Lady of Tears. | Circe's Lovers.

By CHARLES DICKENS.

Sketches by Boz.	Oliver Twist.
Pickwick Papers.	Nicholas Nickleby.

By DICK DONOVAN.
The Man-Hunter. | Caught at Last!
Tracked and Taken.
Who Poisoned Hetty Duncan?
The Man from Manchester.
A Detective's Triumphs.

By CONAN DOYLE, &c.
Strange Secrets.

By Mrs. ANNIE EDWARDES.
A Point of Honour. | Archie Lovell.

By M. BETHAM-EDWARDS.
Felicia. | Kitty.

By EDWARD EGGLESTON.
Roxy.

By PERCY FITZGERALD.
Bella Donna. | Polly.
Never Forgotten. | Fatal Zero.
The Second Mrs. Tillotson.
Seventy-five Brooke Street.
The Lady of Brantome.

ALBANY DE FONBLANQUE.
Filthy Lucre.

By R. E. FRANCILLON.
Olympia. | Queen Cophetua.
One by One. | King or Knave?
A Real Queen. | Romances of Law.

By HAROLD FREDERIC.
Seth's Brother's Wife.
The Lawton Girl.

Two-Shilling Novels—*continued.*

By HAIN FRISWELL.
One of Two.

By EDWARD GARRETT.
The Capel Girls.

By CHARLES GIBBON.

Robin Gray.	In Honour Bound.
Fancy Free.	Flower of Forest.
For Lack of Gold.	Braes of Yarrow.
What will the	The Golden Shaft.
World Say?	Of High Degree.
In Love and War.	Mead and Stream.
For the King.	Loving a Dream.
In Pastures Green.	A Hard Knot.
Queen of Meadow.	Heart's Delight.
A Heart's Problem.	Blood-Money.
The Dead Heart.	

By WILLIAM GILBERT.
Dr. Austin's Guests. | James Duke.
The Wizard of the Mountain.

By HENRY GREVILLE.
A Noble Woman.

By JOHN HABBERTON.
Brueton's Bayou. | Country Luck.

By ANDREW HALLIDAY.
Every-Day Papers.

By Lady DUFFUS HARDY.
Paul Wynter's Sacrifice.

By THOMAS HARDY.
Under the Greenwood Tree.

By J. BERWICK HARWOOD.
The Tenth Earl.

By JULIAN HAWTHORNE.

Garth.	Sebastian Strome.
Ellice Quentin.	Dust.
Fortune's Fool.	Beatrix Randolph.
Miss Cadogna.	Love—or a Name.
David Poindexter's Disappearance.	
The Spectre of the Camera.	

By Sir ARTHUR HELPS.
Ivan de Biron.

By Mrs. CASHEL HOEY.
The Lover's Creed.

By Mrs. GEORGE HOOPER.
The House of Raby.

By TIGHE HOPKINS.
'Twixt Love and Duty.

By Mrs. ALFRED HUNT.
Thornicroft's Model. | Self Condemned.
That Other Person. | Leaden Casket.

By JEAN INGELOW.
Fated to be Free.

By HARRIETT JAY.
The Dark Colleen.
The Queen of Connaught.

By MARK KERSHAW.
Colonial Facts and Fictions.

By R. ASHE KING.
A Drawn Game. | Passion's Slave.
"The Wearing of the Green."

TWO-SHILLING NOVELS—*continued.*

By CHARLES READE.

It is Never Too Late to Mend.
Christie Johnstone.
Put Yourself in His Place.
The Double Marriage.
Love Me Little, Love Me Long.
The Cloister and the Hearth.
The Course of True Love.
Autobiography of a Thief.
A Terrible Temptation.
The Wandering Heir.
Singleheart and Doubleface.
Good Stories of Men and other Animals.

Hard Cash.	A Simpleton.
Peg Woffington.	Readiana.
Griffith Gaunt.	A Woman-Hater.
Foul Play.	The Jilt.

By Mrs. J. H. RIDDELL.

Weird Stories.	Fairy Water.

Her Mother's Darling.
Prince of Wales's Garden Party.
The Uninhabited House.
The Mystery in Palace Gardens.

By F. W. ROBINSON.

Women are Strange.
The Hands of Justice.

By JAMES RUNCIMAN.

Skippers and Shellbacks.
Grace Balmaign's Sweetheart.
Schools and Scholars.

By W. CLARK RUSSELL.

Round the Galley Fire.
On the Fo'k'sle Head.
In the Middle Watch.
A Voyage to the Cape.
A Book for the Hammock.
The Mystery of the "Ocean Star."
The Romance of Jenny Harlowe.
An Ocean Tragedy.

GEORGE AUGUSTUS SALA.

Gaslight and Daylight.

By JOHN SAUNDERS.

Guy Waterman.	Two Dreamers.

The Lion in the Path.

By KATHARINE SAUNDERS.

Joan Merryweather.	Heart Salvage.
The High Mills.	Sebastian.

Margaret and Elizabeth.

By GEORGE R. SIMS.

Rogues and Vagabonds.
The Ring o' Bells.
Mary Jane's Memoirs.
Mary Jane Married.

Tales of To-day.	Dramas of Life.

Tinkletop's Crime.

By ARTHUR SKETCHLEY.

A Match in the Dark.

By T. W. SPEIGHT.

The Mysteries of Heron Dyke.

The Golden Hoop.	By Devious Ways.

Hoodwinked, &c.

TWO-SHILLING NOVELS—*continued.*

By R. A. STERNDALE.

The Afghan Knife.

By R. LOUIS STEVENSON.

New Arabian Nights.	Prince Otto.

BY BERTHA THOMAS.

Cressida.	Proud Maisie.

The Violin-player.

By WALTER THORNBURY.

Tales for the Marines.
Old Stories Re-told.

T. ADOLPHUS TROLLOPE.

Diamond Cut Diamond.

By F. ELEANOR TROLLOPE.

Like Ships upon the Sea.

Anne Furness.	Mabel's Progress.

By ANTHONY TROLLOPE.

Frau Frohmann.	Kept in the Dark.
Marion Fay.	John Caldigate.

The Way We Live Now.
The American Senator.
Mr. Scarborough's Family.
The Land-Leaguers.
The Golden Lion of Granpere.

By J. T. TROWBRIDGE.

Farnell's Folly.

By IVAN TURGENIEFF, &c.

Stories from Foreign Novelists.

By MARK TWAIN.

Tom Sawyer.	A Tramp Abroad.

The Stolen White Elephant.
A Pleasure Trip on the Continent.
Huckleberry Finn.
Life on the Mississippi.
The Prince and the Pauper.

By C. C. FRASER-TYTLER.

Mistress Judith.

By SARAH TYTLER.

The Bride's Pass.	Noblesse Oblige.
Buried Diamonds.	Disappeared.
Saint Mungo's City.	Huguenot Family.
Lady Bell.	Blackhall Ghosts.

What She Came Through.
Beauty and the Beast.
Citoyenne Jaqueline.

By J. S. WINTER.

Cavalry Life.	Regimental Legends.

By H. F. WOOD.

The Passenger from Scotland Yard.
The Englishman of the Rue Cain.

By Lady WOOD.

Sabina.

CELIA PARKER WOOLLEY.

Rachel Armstrong; or, Love & Theology

By EDMUND YATES.

The Forlorn Hope.	Land at Last.

Castaway.

COLIN, SMALE AND CO. LIMITED, PRINTERS, GREAT SAFFRON HILL, E.C.